D1214428

RAYMOND CHANDLER SPEAKING

Raymond Chandler in 1958. *Photograph by Douglas Glass.*

RAYMOND CHANDLER SPEAKING

Edited by
Dorothy Gardiner and Kathrine Sorley Walker

Introduction by
Paul Skenazy

UNIVERSITY OF CALIFORNIA PRESS
Berkeley · Los Angeles · London

University of California Press
Berkeley and Los Angeles, California

University of California Press, Ltd.
London, England

First California Paperback Printing 1997

Library of Congress Cataloging-in-Publication Data

Chandler, Raymond, 1888–1959.
    Raymond Chandler speaking / edited by Dorothy Gardiner and
Kathrine Sorley Walker ; introduction by Paul Skenazy.
        p.   cm.
    Originally published: Boston : Houghton Mifflin Co., 1977. With
new introd.
    Includes bibliographical references and index.
    ISBN 0-520-20835-8 (alk. paper)
    1. Chandler, Raymond, 1888–1959—Interviews.   2. Authors,
American—20th century—Interviews.   3. Detective and mystery
stories—Authorship.   I. Gardiner, Dorothy, 1894–   .   II. Walker,
Kathrine Sorley.   III. Title
PS3505.H3224Z47   1997
813'.52—dc20   96-34571
[B]   CIP

Printed in the United States of America

1   2   3   4   5   6   7   8   9

CONTENTS

ILLUSTRATIONS

*Photographs courtesy of Department of Special Collections,
University Research Library, UCLA*

ACKNOWLEDGMENTS

THE EDITORS would like to thank not only those people who have been good enough to let them see and use letters from Raymond Chandler for publication in this book, but also those who lent letters which would have been included but for considerations of length. In a very few cases, the Editors' efforts to locate recipients of letters, copies of which were in Chandler's files, were unsuccessful. To these 'lost' correspondents, the Editors extend their regrets for reprinting the letters without formal permission and thanks for their use.

Introduction

BY

PAUL SKENAZY

IF YOU LOOK AT pictures of Raymond Chandler, like the ones you'll find in this volume, you see a rather staid man, foppish in youth, scholarly in maturity, a pipe invariably in mouth or hand—someone who resembles one's image of an accountant far more than a purveyor of crime and violence to the masses. Yet along with Dashiell Hammett, it was Chandler who transformed the hard-boiled detective story into a form flexible and resonant, and provided a new mythology for California's new urban coastal populations.

For Chandler was both an accountant *and* a purveyor of crime, a staid and bookish contemplative and a clinician of sin. He once said that if he ever wrote a nonfiction book, "it would probably turn out to be the autobiography of a split personality." These splits permeate Chandler's life and work, at once revealing and essential to his particular genius. He was a man of two continents, two centuries, and two languages. Born in Chicago, educated in England, trained in classical literature, and bred on an Edwardian literary sensibility, he came to America to stay in 1912. He was a successful businessman, drank himself out of a job, and then, in his forties, taught himself to write detective novels. He struggled all his life to write "serious" literature but now his claim to immortality rests on the ways he transformed tough-guy fiction into a chronicle of the quiet desperations of the city of Los Angeles. His critical taste remained rooted in sentimental traditions of fantasy and romance, yet his power as a novelist comes from the way he gave voice—plaintive and raucous voice—to failed lives of self-denial, poverty, and greed. And even as Chandler proclaimed himself an aesthetic snob, he helped to create a genre grounded in working-class longing and despair, and a hero—Phillip Marlowe—with fiercely democratic sympathies.

Chandler depended on that "split personality" of his as a touchstone: a way to remain an exile in his Southern California world. In his finest novels, like *The Big Sleep*; *Farewell, My Lovely*; and *The Long Goodbye*, he was able to mine his own ambiguous position for its cultural resonance. Although he lived in Southern California for almost fifty years, he remained an outsider, and articulated the needs of a generation of travellers like himself, anxious to discount their frustrated pasts, eager to remake themselves in this fresh and seemingly boundless California sunshine. He revealed a Los Angeles still inchoate, its new history still untranscribed, and created his legendary city as a mirror of some of his own anxieties and perceptions as a sojourner. The newcomers—primarily midwesterners—who populate his books share his own sense of a doubleness to their lives, their personalities nurtured by one set of historical and geographical conditions, confronted by new times and new circumstances. These were Chandler's citizens and subject, and in his novels the anxieties and discontinuities of their stories invariably emerge in terms of submerged secrets and suppressed acts of violence, resulting in blackmail, or revenge.

Chandler's own contradictory traits—his European heritage and class-consciousness absorbed in his attraction to the nascent California culture—took more sedate forms than they do for his characters. But one feels the discordances, the doubleness, in everything he wrote: in the mixtures of illusion and despair, hope and defeat, that provide plot for his dark tales; in his language, so lush yet slangy, the street jargon always burnished with a classical sheen; and most especially in the way he realigns the detective tradition with its forgotten antecedents, like the epic, quest, and medieval knight errant traditions. This grafting of old forms and new times is Chandler's grace as a novelist.

The "split personality" that distinguishes Chandler's fiction is also part of the intelligence one encounters in Chandler's essays, letters, and other casual writings. Despite the faint echoes in the novels of his own experiences, and the frequent moments one feels Chandler's prejudices bleeding into Phillip Marlowe's commentaries, Chandler's fictions are determinedly not autobiographical. It is in his letters that Chandler tells us what little we know of his attitudes to events in his life, and in his letters too that we find some of his richest commentary and most judicious self-assessments. Adopting the pose of Phillip Marlowe in his novels allows Chandler to give voice to a part of his sensibility as it limits other aspects; as he himself notes, "I suppose in my letters I more or less revealed those facets of my mind which had to be obscured or distorted in what I wrote for publication."

These multiple "facets" of Chandler's personality fill his correspondence. Never much of an extrovert, Chandler became more and more reclusive, particularly after he and his wife Cissy moved to La Jolla, California (near San Diego) in 1946. Cissy's failing health, and Chandler's habit of staying up nights to care for her, provided him with both the seclusion and time to compose lengthy and elaborate responses to his many regular correspondents. Letter writing seems to have provided Chandler with a perfect form for his personality: at once intimate yet distant, controllable while a depository for intuition, contemplative if also available for the occasional angry or frustrated rant. Unlike what Chandler himself often described as his slow-paced rhythms as a novelist, he dictated most of his letters and composed them in the heat, so it seems, of a particular mood or subject. His letters became his release from isolation. Although some of Chandler's correspondents were also people he saw socially, others were almost strangers whom he rarely, or never, encountered except on the page; as he himself realized late in his life, "all of my best friends I have never met." So the letters become, as his biographer Frank MacShane notes, "a writer's notebook, a record of Chandler's range and growth." They are full of fine observations —witty commentaries on the times; pointed, often pungent, remarks about other writers; and vivid renditions of events in his own life, from his travels, to film work, to feelings about his beloved cat Taki.

One finds these attributes in abundance in *Raymond Chandler Speaking*. This volume, originally published in 1962, was the first and for many years the only collection of Chandler's letters and occasional writings available. In the years it has been out of print, Frank MacShane's edition of Chandler's *Selected Letters* and the second volume of Chandler's works in the Library of America series, *Later Novels and Other Writings,* have been published. Yet even given these volumes, and despite its editorial shortcomings, *Raymond Chandler Speaking* remains the fullest compact, and inexpensive, collection of Chandler's self-commentary available, and it contains many pieces found nowhere else.

The bulk of the book consists of excerpts from Chandler's correspondence, supplemented with some self-contained commentaries from Chandler's notebooks and papers ("Casual Notes on the Mystery Novel," "Notes on English and American Style," a "1939 Plan of Work," and notations about some famous actual criminal cases), two essays which first appeared in the *Atlantic Monthly* in the 1940s ("Writers in Hollywood," and "Ten Per Cent of Your Life"), and two previously unpublished pieces of fiction: "A Couple of Writers," and the first chapters from *The Poodle Springs Story*, a Phillip Marlowe novel Chandler left unfinished at his death in 1959.

Neither work of fiction is particularly powerful in its own right, though both are valuable additions to the Chandler canon. Each stumbles over the representation of an intimate relationship between a man and a woman rather than focusing on the isolated figure of Phillip Marlowe, who dominates the great novels; they confirm our suspicion that it is only in the character of the loner that Chandler taps into his own imaginative strength and vision. The notebook excerpts and magazine articles are of more interest because they reveal another facet of Chandler's gifts: his abundant skills as a critic, formal theorist, and social analyst. There is a pointed series of remarks, for example, on the details of speech variations between American and English usage. The two *Atlantic Monthly* essays explore the difficulties of a professional writer's life: the problems of artistic integrity in the film industry, where individual artistry is engulfed by the conflicting plans of others; and the altered position of the writer in relation to his or her agent, which Chandler sees as moving from a relationship of trust based on artistic and personal commitments to one of salesmanship in which the art and artist are transformed into commodities. Perhaps most valuable of all are Chandler's notes on the mystery genre—a list of imperatives for the writer in which Chandler elaborates a set of rules or conditions essential to a quality mystery, and concludes with some pride that the mystery novel is "a form which has never really been licked, . . . [which] is still fluid, still too various for easy classification, still putting out shoots in all directions."

But it is the excerpts from Chandler's letters rather than the anthology of occasional writings that make this book so essential, and so readable. They range in size from a few sentences to sev-

eral pages, though most are brief, and are edited to provide suc-
cinct, and distinct, commentaries by Chandler on aspects of his
craft and world: his personal background; the mystery story as a
genre and its practitioners; writing, film, TV, and publishing; and
his own fiction. The mixture of ruthless pruning and careful selection to maintain a thematic approach allows the book's editors,
Dorothy Gardiner and Kathrine Sorley Walker, to display Chandler's intelligence and verbal gifts at their invigorating best. As
Chandler himself freely admits, even in his fiction his best work
is scenic and syntactic rather than found in plot construction or
more extended narrative sequences. These same skills make him
a superb correspondent, where the unbridled letter form displays
his sharp wit and clarity of phrase and sentence to advantage, and
provides latitude for an opinionated man like Chandler to let loose.
Again and again one finds acute remarks and pungent aphoristic
wisdom. The pages of this volume are filled with fine sentences
and telling observations, and reading through the pieces one is impressed by Chandler's sagacious, serious, thoughtful approach to
his artistic vocation, and to his surrounding artistic community.
The scattered comments accumulate and resonate with each
other, providing not only a transcript of Chandler's perceptions
but a kind of haphazard documentation of a time.

The careful selection and precise cuts and splices create a com-
pelling collection, but they also represent incompletely the ongo-
ing record of a life lived. Inevitably, one would like a larger sam-
pling of that "split personality" that is Chandler's unique position
as a writer and reader, citizen and exile. Gardiner and Walker's
thematic approach achieved their primary objective of creating a
book at once readable and focused. But letters are relational and
occasional as well as thematic, so we lose something of Chandler's personal intimacies with particular individuals, and some
of the feel of chronological shifts of mood and attention, that
other organizational structures might have provided. In addition,
Gardiner and Walker's patchwork method of construction re-
sulted in some inconsistent editorial principles at times: a letter
reprinted with the first and second half reversed in order; an ir-
regular use of ellipses to indicate excisions, sometimes leaving a
reader to conclude he or she is seeing a continuous document
when in actuality there are omissions or sections from different
parts of a letter that have been joined together by the editors.

The volume appeared in 1962, we must remember, just after Chandler's death. Though Chandler was well established by then as a novelist of gifts, he still struggled with literary judgments that distinguished between "popular" arts and artists, and "high" culture. Those distinctions have, properly, faded with the years, and Chandler's artistic stock has risen in value appreciably. But at the time, Gardiner and Walker were making a case for Chandler's critical acumen, for his virtues as a writer aware of the consequences of his artistic decisions, and for the incisiveness of his intellect as it confronted issues of form, politics, character, and language.

The free editorial privilege that Gardiner and Walker took in preparing *Raymond Chandler Speaking* for publication—a freedom few editors would take upon themselves these days, when issues of representation and selection are central critical, and cultural, questions—makes it impossible to turn to this book as the single, definitive source for Chandler's actual words. At the same time, it is our most accessible, and often our only, source for many of his most interesting comments on his work and his time. Many of Chandler's more caustic, or maudlin, or abusive comments are not available in *Raymond Chandler Speaking*. Some of Chandler's more defensive statements—as in a response to someone accusing him of anti-semitism—are ignored in favor of a view of Chandler as a by and large self-possessed, deeply thoughtful, quite knowledgeable and fair-minded critic of his own work, his Hollywood world, the world of publishing and the work of other mystery writers.

These critical limitations acknowledged, it is hard not to treasure this collection. For all of its editorial inconsistencies and its gestures to excise the more unappealing aspects of Chandler's personality, *Raymond Chandler Speaking* remains our most intimate picture of this complex, sometimes surly, frequently brooding man. If the "split personality" is muted, it emerges still, as if lurking in the ellipses—between the lines, in the literary posturing, among the acerbic comments on trends in the arts, alongside the generous homages to other writers, amid the self-scrutiny. We tend to want our artists with more of their warts showing these days than back in 1962. Whether this impulse to disparage artists comes from our desire to humanize or to belittle the artistry is never quite clear, but certainly represents a very different sense of the ties of life and work than reigned during Chandler's era, or than one sees in his self-assessments. *Raymond Chandler Speaking* offers an abundant, engrossing self-portrait. There are enough turns and contradictory assertions to complicate the judgment, and enough moments of startling insight to confirm one's feeling that Chandler was a writer of acute self-knowledge, and acutely painful self-doubt: at once able to claim that he managed to "recreate a worn-out medium," and that he "never wrote anything really worth" his wife Cissy's attention—"no book that I could dedicate to her." It is this texture of pride and shame, realization and uncertainty, that makes Chandler's letters what they are, a mosaic of a writer's mind contemplating its labor.

Paul Skenazy
1996

Foreword

BY

DOROTHY GARDINER

RAYMOND CHANDLER, who possessed an English classical education, an inquiring and critical mind, an extensive knowledge of languages and literature, and a talent close to genius for the pointed phrase and the *mot juste*, may well have been, as his admirers insist, this century's most brilliant writer of detective fiction; unquestionably he was one of its most prolific and original letter-writers.

'If a collection of letters is to mean anything, it should reveal all sides of a man's character, not only the sweetness and light.' So Chandler wrote to Hamish Hamilton, and so far as possible the editors of this book have been mindful of this dictum. Chandler's character, however, was a many-sided one; his letters reveal the man, but not the whole man. They tell nothing of his personal charm, to which even those who did not like him responded; they cannot reflect his shyness, which he sometimes hid under an abruptness of manner and an acidity of comment called malice by men who did not know him.

Chandler's many aversions do emerge from the letters, his dislike of agents, professional critics and plagiarists, to name a few; they never speak of his private generosities, known only to his close friends. Many of the letters are argumentative, for as he himself admitted, Chandler was a 'contentious fellow'; some are bitter, some are deeply touching. Sometimes they border on the mild obscenity used between close friends; frequently they are highly libellous—often hilariously so—in their comments on living persons, and these remarks the editors, to their regret, have had to delete.

What distinguishes Chandler from his co-workers in the field of blood and mayhem are his classical education, his knowledge of books and history as well as of life, and above all his ability to depict a character, a situation, a background, in a dozen words.

To some extent these same qualities are present in his letters. He uses the quick terse American English that fascinated him. He is forever talking of 'magic' in writing, which means, in the final analysis, the use of the right word in the right place.

Although the letters in this volume were written with no thought of publication, Raymond Chandler himself suggested that a collection might perhaps appear in book form. On May 16, 1957, he wrote from La Jolla, California, where he lived, to his London friend and publisher, Hamish Hamilton:

Dear Jamie,

. . . I have a faint—really quite faint—recollection that at one time you thought my letters might be worth publishing. I raise the subject now only because I have such an accumulation of them that I must destroy them unless my recollection was right. A friend of yours called me a 'flaming egotist'. For a long time I thought myself to be a rather modest man, but I am beginning to believe this friend was right, that all writers are bound to be egotists since they drain their hearts and souls to write at all, and therefore become introspective. I think I have lately become worse, because I have been praised too much, because I live a lonely life, and have no hope of anything else from now on.

As to the letters, some are analytical, some are a bit poetical, some sad, and a good many caustic or even funny . . . It would be quite a job to sort them out and select those which might be worth anyone's attention . . . I don't want to do it, if it is of no interest. You must over the years have received enough letters from me to get some idea whether the project is worth the time and expense . . .

To this Hamish Hamilton replied:

Dear Ray,

. . . Your recollection is perfectly correct, I well remember that, some years ago, when our correspondence was in full spate and we were exchanging several pages almost every week on life, literature, loves and hates, I asked whether you had ever considered publishing your letters and you replied 'Perish the thought' or words to that effect. All the same, in the hope that you might some day change your mind, and reluctant to destroy such pearls of correspondence, I kept them on the files and there must be hundreds of them still extant[1]—plentifully sprinkled, of course, with libel, but comparatively painless operations would soon fix that.

I am delighted to know that there are so many others and I am sure that a collection . . . would be absolutely fascinating. There is a great curiosity about you throughout the English-speaking world and I am sure that readers would welcome the opportunity of learning more about you than they can through your books.

If Chandler attempted to edit the letters himself he never said so—perhaps he found the task too difficult or too heart-breaking. Most of the letters in his own files, including all those to his wife, he later burned. But fortunately hundreds of other letters survive. They were saved by perceptive recipients who have generously permitted them to form the basis of this present volume.

Of the other material in this book, the short story *A Couple of Writers*, the beginning of the new Marlowe novel *The Poodle Springs Story*, the *Casual Notes on the Mystery Novel* and *Notes on Famous Crimes* were all found among Chandler's papers and are here published for the first time. *Writers in Hollywood* and *Ten Per Cent of Your Life* were first printed in *The Atlantic Monthly*, and are republished here as they have a direct bearing on a number of his letters.

---

[1] Many of Chandler's letters to Hamish Hamilton Ltd were lost in a fire there in 1948.

Raymond Chandler: Chronology
(Revised and Corrected)

1888 Born Raymond Thornton Chandler, July 23, Chicago, Illinois. Parents: Maurice Benjamin Chandler, born 1858 in Philadelphia, Pennsylvania, and Florence Dart Thornton, born 1860 in Waterford, Ireland.

1889–94 Father drinks, is often absent, and eventually leaves and provides no support.

1895 Brought to London by his mother after her divorce from his father.

1900 Moved to Dulwich. Entered Dulwich College as a day pupil.

1905 Left Dulwich College.

1905–11 In France and Germany as a student (1905–06). Became naturalized British subject (1907). Studied for Civil Service examination and, after passing it, went to Admiralty for six months (1907). Lived in Bloomsbury and worked as a journalist for the *Daily Express*, *The Westminster Gazette* and *The Academy* (1908-11).

1912 Returned to the U.S. (California). Studied bookkeeping.

1914 Outbreak of World War I.

1917–19 Enlisted with the Canadian Gordon Highlanders. Served in France with the First Division of the Canadian Expeditionary Force. In 1918 joined the Royal Flying Corps (R.A.F.). Demobilised in England in 1919.

1919 Returned to California with his mother, entered oil business.

1924 On the death of his mother, Chandler married (February 8) Pearl Cecily (Cissy) Pascal, *née* Pearl Eugenie Hurlburt. Pearl Cecily Hurlburt was born in 1870 in Perry, Ohio, and had been twice married when she met Chandler. Her second divorce went through in 1920.

1919– Chandler did various types of work in the oil business,
32   eventually becoming a vice-president of the Dabney Oil Syndicate (later South Basin Oil Company). In 1932 during the depression he lost his job for drinking and absenteeism.

1933 His first story, "Blackmailers Don't Shoot," was published in *Black Mask*.

1934 The stories "Finger Man" and "Smart-Aleck Kill" published in *Black Mask*.

1935 The stories "Nevada Gas," "Spanish Blood," and *"Killer in the Rain" published in *Black Mask*.

1936 The stories "Goldfish," "Guns at Cyrano's, *"The Man Who Liked Dogs" and *"The Curtain" published in *Black Mask*. "Pick-Up on Noon Street" (first title, "Noon Street Nemesis") published in *Detective Fiction Weekly*.

1937 The story *"Try the Girl" published in *Black Mask*. The story *"Mandarin's Jade" published in *Dime Detective Monthly*.

1938 The stories "Red Wind," "The King in Yellow," and *"Bay City Blues" published in *Dime Detective Monthly*.

1939 Chandler's first full-length novel, *The Big Sleep*, published by Alfred A. Knopf, U.S., and Hamish Hamilton, London.

* Chandler later used parts of these stories in his novels and, therefore, called them his 'cannibalized stories.'

The stories "Pearls Are a Nuisance," "Trouble Is My Business," and *"The Lady in the Lake" published in *Dime Detective Monthly*. The story "I'll Be Waiting" published in *Saturday Evening Post*. The fantastic story "The Bronze Door" published in the U.S. magazine *Unknown*.

1940 The novel *Farewell, My Lovely* published by Knopf and Hamish Hamilton.

1941 The story *"No Crime in the Mountains" published in *Detective Story Monthly*.

1942 The novel *The High Window* published by Knopf. *Farewell, My Lovely* used as basis for film *The Falcon Takes Over* (RKO).

1943 Chandler works for Paramount in Hollywood with director Billy Wilder on the screenplay of James M. Cain's *Double Indemnity*. *The High Window* published by Hamish Hamilton. The novel *The Lady in the Lake* published by Knopf.

1944 *Double Indemnity* released in April; receives Academy Award nomination. Worked on screenplay of *And Now Tomorrow* (shared credit with Frank Partos) and *The Unseen* (with Hager Wilde) for Paramount. *Murder, My Sweet*, second film version of *Farewell, My Lovely*, released by RKO. *The Lady in the Lake* published by Hamish Hamilton. Essay, "The Simple Art of Murder," published in *The Atlantic Monthly*.

1945 The article "Writers in Hollywood" published in *The Atlantic Monthly*. Original screenplay of *The Blue Dahlia* for Paramount. (The film is released in 1946; Chandler receives Academy Award nomination and Edgar award from Mystery Writers of America for the screenplay.) Worked for MGM on screenplay of *The Lady in the Lake;* left after disagreement with studio.

1946 *The Big Sleep* filmed by Warners. Worked on screenplay of

The Innocent Mrs. Duff for Paramount; ends his work before screenplay is completed. Moved from Los Angeles to La Jolla, California.

1947   *The High Window* filmed as *The Brasher Doubloon* by Twentieth Century Fox. Began writing original screenplay *Playback* for Universal. (Film is not produced)

1948   The article "Oscar Night in Hollywood" published in *The Atlantic Monthly*.

1949   The novel *The Little Sister* published by Houghton Mifflin and Hamish Hamilton.

1950   Collection of short stories and one essay, *The Simple Art of Murder*, published by Houghton Mifflin and Hamish Hamilton. Collection of short stories, *Trouble Is My Business*, published by Penguin Books. Worked with Alfred Hitchcock on screenplay adaptation of Patricia Highsmith's *Strangers on a Train* for Warners; eventually replaced by Czenzi Ormonde and they shared credit for screenplay when film released in 1951. The fantasy story "Professor Bingo's Snuff" published in *Park East* (U.S.) and *Go* (London).

1951   Chandler wrote the story "A Couple of Writers" (here published for the first time).

1952   The article "Ten Per Cent of Your Life" published in *The Atlantic Monthly*.

1953   The novel *The Long Goodbye* published by Hamish Hamilton.

1954   T*he Long Goodbye* published by Houghton Mifflin (novel wins Edgar award from the Mystery Writers of America in 1955).

Chandler's wife, Cissy, died (December 12).

1957 Chandler wrote the story "English Summer" (originally begun in the 1930s).

1958 The novel *Playback* published by Houghton Mifflin and Hamish Hamilton. Chandler wrote the story "The Pencil" published posthumously (1960) in the U.S. magazine *Manhunt*. Wrote the opening chapters of "The Poodle Springs Story" (novel unfinished at time of death), here published for the first time.

1959 Elected president of Mystery Writers of America. Chandler died in La Jolla, California, on March 26, 1959.

CHANDLER ON CHANDLER

Nov. 10, 1950
To: Hamish Hamilton[1]
    . . . I was born in Chicago, Illinois, so damned long ago that
I wish I had never told anybody when. Both my parents were
of Quaker descent. Neither was a practising Quaker. My mother
was born in Waterford, Ireland,[2] where there was a very famous
Quaker school and perhaps still is. My father came of a Pen-
sylvania farming family, probably one of the batch that settled
with William Penn. At the age of seven I had scarlet fever in a
hotel, and I understand this is a very rare accomplishment. I
remember principally the ice-cream and the pleasure of pulling
the loose skin off during convalescence . . .

Nov. 20, 1944
To: Charles W. Morton[3]
    . . . I had an uncle in Omaha who was a minor politician.
I've been there a time or two. As a very small boy I used to be
sent to spend part of the summer at Plattsmouth (Nebraska). I
remember the oak trees and the high wooden sidewalks beside
the dirt roads and the heat and the fireflies and the 'walking-
sticks' and a lot of strange insects and the gathering of wild
grapes in the fall to make wine and the dead cattle and once in
a while a dead man floating down the muddy river and the
dandy little three-hole privy behind the house. I remember the
rocking chairs on the edge of the sidewalk in a solid row outside
the hotel and the tobacco spit all over the place. And I remember
a trial run on a mail car with a machine my uncle invented to
take on mail without stopping, but somebody beat him out of
it and he never got a dime.
    After that I went to England and was raised on Latin and

[1] Managing Director of Hamish Hamilton Ltd, Chandler's London
  pubiisher.
[2] Chandler's mother, Florence Thornton, went to the U.S. to visit her
  sister Grace who was married in Omaha, Nebraska, and there met
  Maurice Chandler.
[3] Associate Editor, *The Atlantic Monthly*.

Greek, like yourself . . . I don't think education ever did me any great harm.

Aug. 24, 1945
Interview with Irving Wallace[1]
    . . . My father was a graduate of Penn, a civil engineer. Divorced when I was seven . . . Never saw my father again.

March 31, 1957
To: Leroy A. Wright[2]
    . . . My mother soon after returned to England to live with her mother and manage the house,[3] and of course I went with her.

Jan. 1, 1945
To: Charles W. Morton
    . . . I have a great many Irish relatives, some poor, some not poor, and all Protestants, and some of them Sinn Feiners, and some entirely pro-British. The head of the family,[4] if he is still living, is a very wealthy lawyer who hated the law, but felt obliged to carry on his father's firm. He had a housekeeper who came from a county family and did not regard my uncle as quite a gentleman because he was a solicitor. She used to say: There are only four careers for a gentleman, the Army, the Navy, the Church and the Bar. A barrister was a gentleman but not a solicitor . . .
    An amazing people, the Anglo-Irish. They never mixed with Catholics socially . . . I grew up with a terrible contempt for Catholics, and I have trouble with it even now . . . My uncle's

---

[1] Author and freelance writer.

[2] Chandler's attorney: partner of Glenn & Wright, San Diego, Calif.

[3] Chandler's grandmother lived in Norwood, London, with her daughter, Ethel.

[4] Ernest Thornton.

snob housekeeper wouldn't have a Catholic servant in the house, although they were probably much better than the trash she did have.

July 15, 1954
To: Hamish Hamilton

. . . What a strange sense of values we had. What godawful snobs! My stupid and arrogant grandmother referred to one of the nicest families we knew as 'very *respectable* people' because there were two sons, five golden-haired but unmarriageable daughters and no servant. They were driven to the utter humiliation of opening their own front door.

Nov. 11, 1957
To: Wesley Hartley[1]

. . . I was educated at Dulwich College, an English Public School,[2] not quite on a level with Eton and Harrow from a social point of view but very good educationally. In my time they had two 'sides', a Modern Side intended mostly for boys who expected to go into some sort of business, and a Classical Side for those who took Latin and Greek and expected to go to Oxford and Cambridge. I went up the Modern Side to the top and then switched down to the lowest form in the senior school on the Classical Side. I went up that to the Sixth, the top form. I left the school at seventeen—the usual leaving age then was before one's twentieth birthday . . . After this I had six months each in Paris and Germany. In Paris at school and in Germany with a private tutor. I could speak German well enough then to be taken for a German but not now, alas. French one never speaks well enough to satisfy a Frenchman. *Il sait se faire comprendre* is about as far as they will go.

[1] High School teacher of American literature and English, La Canada, California.
[2] Chandler's Irish uncle helped with his school expenses.

Note by Chandler in
The Twentieth Century Authors' Supplement

At school I displayed no marked literary ability. My first poem was composed at the age of nineteen, on a Sunday, in the bathroom, and was published in *Chambers' Journal.* I am fortunate in not possessing a copy. I had, to be frank, the qualifications to become a pretty good second-rate poet, but that means nothing because I have the type of mind that can become a pretty good second-rate anything, and without much effort.

March 31, 1957
To: Leroy A. Wright

. . . When I was eighteen years old, my mother and my rich but dominating Irish uncle decided that I should take a Civil Service examination . . . I wanted to be a writer, but I knew my Irish uncle would not stand for that, so I thought perhaps that the easy hours in the Civil Service might let me do that on the side. I passed third in a group of about six hundred. I went to the Admiralty, but I found the atmosphere so stultifying that after six months I resigned. This was a bombshell; perhaps no one had ever done it before. My Irish uncle was livid with rage. So I holed up in Bloomsbury, lived on next to nothing, and wrote for a highbrow weekly review[1] and also for *The Westminster Gazette,*[2] perhaps the best evening paper the world ever saw. But at the best I made only a very bare living.

April, 1949
To: Hamish Hamilton

. . . J. A. Spender was the first editor who ever showed me any kindness. He was editing *The Westminster Gazette* in the days when I worked for him. I got an introduction to him from a wonderful old boy named Roland Ponsonby Blennerhasset, a barrister with a House of Lords practice, a wealthy Irish landowner (he owned some fabulous number of acres in Kerry), a

[1] *The Academy.*
[2] Chandler also wrote for *The Spectator.*

member, as I understood from my uncle in Waterford, of one of these very ancient untitled families that often make earls and marquesses appear quite parvenu. Spender bought a lot of stuff from me, verses, sketches, and unsigned things such as paragraphs lifted from foreign publications. He got me into the National Liberal Club for the run of the reading-room. I was seconded by his political cartoonist, a famous man in those days, but I have forgotten his name. I never met him in the flesh.

I got about three guineas a week out of all these, but it wasn't enough. I also worked for a man named Cowper[1] who succeeded Lord Alfred Douglas in ownership of *The Academy*, and did a lot of book reviewing for him, and some essays which I still have, they are of an intolerable preciousness of style, but already quite nasty in tone. I seldom got the best books to review, and in fact the only one of any importance I got my hands on was *The Broad Highway* (Jeffrey Farnol) for whose author, then unknown, I am glad to say I predicted an enormous popularity. I reviewed Eleanor Glyn and how. Like all young nincompoops I found it very easy to be clever and snotty, very hard to praise without being ingenuous.

Dec. 11, 1950
To: Hamish Hamilton
. . . I wrote quite a lot of verses for *The Westminster Gazette* also, most of which now seem to me as deplorable, but not all, and a good many sketches, mostly of a satirical nature—the sort of thing Saki did so infinitely better. As a matter of fact, I had only the most limited personal contact with Spender. I would send the stuff in, and they would either send it back or send me proof. I never corrected the proof, I simply took it as a convenient form of acceptance. I appeared regularly on a certain day each week at their cashier's office and received payment in gold and silver, being required to affix a penny stamp in a large book and sign my name across it by way of receipt. What a strange world it seems now!

I suppose I have told you of the time I wrote to Sir George Newnes and offered to buy a piece of his trashy but successful

[1] Cecil Cowper, J.P., Editor of *The Academy*, 1910-1916.

weekly magazine *Tit-Bits*? I was received most courteously by a
secretary, definitely public school, who regretted that the publication was not in need of capital, but said that my approach
had at least the merit of originality. By the same device I did
actually make a connection with *The Academy* . . . (Cowper)
was not disposed to sell an interest in his magazine, but pointed
to a large shelf of books in his office and said they were review
copies and would I care to take a few home to review. I wonder
why he did not have me thrown down his murky stairs; perhaps
because there was no one in the office who could do it since his
entire editorial staff seemed to consist of one placid middle-aged
lady and a mousy little man named Vizetelly, who was (I believe)
the brother of another and more famous Vizetelly—the one
who ran into trouble in New York in connection with an
obscenity complaint over the American publication of the translation of *Madame Bovary*.

I met there also a tall, bearded, and sad-eyed man called
Richard Middleton, of whom I think you may have heard.
Shortly afterwards he committed suicide in Antwerp, a suicide of
despair, I should say. The incident made a great impression on
me, because Middleton struck me as having far more talent than
I was ever likely to possess; and if he couldn't make a go of it,
it wasn't very likely that I could. Of course in those days as
now there were popular and successful writers, and there were
clever young men who made a decent living as free lances for
the numerous literary weeklies and in the more literary departments of the daily papers. But most of the people who did this
work either had private incomes or jobs, especially in the civil
service. And I was distinctly not a clever young man. Nor was
I at all a happy young man. I had very little money, although
there was a great deal of it in my family. I had grown up in
England and all my relatives were either English or Colonial.
And yet I was not English. I had no feeling of identity with the
United States, and yet I resented the kind of ignorant and snob-
bish criticism of Americans that was current at that time.

During my time in Paris I had run across a good many
Americans, and most of them seemed to have a lot of bounce
and liveliness and to be thoroughly enjoying themselves in
situations where the average Englishman of the same class
would be stuffy or completely bored. But I wasn't one of them.

I didn't even speak their language. I was, in effect, a man without a country . . . All in all, perhaps I ought to have stayed in Paris, although I never really liked the French. But you didn't exactly have to like the French to be at home in Paris. And you could always like some of them. On the other hand, I did like the Germans very much, that is the South Germans. But there wasn't much sense in living in Germany, since it was an open secret, openly discussed, that we would be at war with them any time now . . .

March 31, 1957
To: Leroy A. Wright
. . . America seemed to call me in some mysterious way. So, when I was 23, I managed to get a loan of £500 from my irate uncle (every penny of it was repaid with six per cent interest) . . .

Nov. 10, 1950
To: Hamish Hamilton
. . . I served in the first Division of the Canadian Expeditionary Force in what used to be called the Great War,[1] and was later attached to the R.A.F. but had not completed flight training when the Armistice came . . . I arrived in California in 1919 with a beautiful wardrobe, a public school accent, and had a pretty hard time trying to make a living. Once I worked on an apricot ranch ten hours a day, twenty cents an hour. Another time I worked for a sporting goods house, stringing tennis rackets for $12.50 a week, 54 hours a week. I taught myself book-keeping[2] and from there on my rise was as rapid as the growth of a sequoia. I detested business life, but in spite of that I finally became an officer or director of half a dozen independent oil corporations.

[1] Chandler enlisted with the Canadian Gordon Highlanders in 1914 and was sent to Victoria, B.C., for training. He joined the Canadian Army because they paid a dependent's allowance which he could send his mother. He served in France and became a platoon commander. In 1918 he joined the Royal Flying Corps (later the R.A.F.). He was demobilized in England; his mother returned with him to California.

[2] Chandler actually did a three-year book-keeping course in six weeks.

May 5, 1957
To: Helga Greene[1]

. . . They were small companies, but very rich. I had the best office staff in Los Angeles and I paid them higher salaries than they could have got anywhere else and they knew it. My office door was never closed, everyone called me by my Christian name, and there was never any dissension, because I made it my business to see that there was no cause for it . . . I had a talent for picking out the capabilities of people. There was one man, I remember, who had a genius for filing. Others were good at routine jobs but had no initiative. There were secretaries who could remember everything and secretaries who were wonderful at dictation and typing but whose minds were really elsewhere. . . . Business is very tough and I hate it. But whatever you set out to do, you have to do as well as you know how . . .

Nov. 10, 1950
To: Hamish Hamilton

. . . The depression finished that. Wandering up and down the Pacific Coast in an automobile, I began to read pulp magazines, because they were cheap enough to throw away and because I never had at any time any taste for the kind of thing which is known as women's magazines. This was in the great days of the *Black Mask* (if I may call them great days) and it struck me that some of the writing was pretty forceful and honest, even though it had its crude aspect. I decided that this might be a good way to try to learn to write fiction and get paid a small amount of money at the same time.

I spent five months over an 18,000 word novelette[2] and sold it for $180. After that I never looked back, although I had a good many uneasy periods looking forward. I wrote *The Big Sleep* in three months . . .[3]

I went to Hollywood in 1943 to work with Billy Wilder on *Double Indemnity*. I was under contract to Paramount after

[1] Chandler's literary agent.
[2] *Blackmailers Don't Shoot.*
[3] *The Big Sleep* was published by Knopf and Hamish Hamilton in 1939.

Raymond Chandler in his younger days.

that and did several pictures for them. By the end of 1946 I had had enough. I moved to La Jolla.

I have been married since 1924[1] and have no children. I am supposed to be a hardboiled writer, but that means nothing. It is merely a method of projection. Personally I am sensitive and even diffident. At times I am extremely caustic and pugnacious; at other times very sentimental. I am not a good mixer because I am very easily bored, and the average never seems good enough, in people or in anything else. I am a spasmodic worker with no regular hours, which is to say I only write when I feel like it. I am always surprised at how very easy it seems at the time, and at how very tired one feels afterwards . . .

Oct. 2, 1946
To: Dale Warren[2]

. . . I (we) have moved to La Jolla permanently, or as permanently as anything can be nowadays. We live close to the sounding sea—just across the street and down a low cliff—but the Pacific is usually very sedate. We have a much better home than an out-of-work pulp writer has any right to expect.

March 18, 1949
To: Alex Barris, Toronto[3]

. . . La Jolla is built on a point north of San Diego, and is never either hot or cold. So we get two seasons of tourists, one in winter, one in summer. Ten years ago the town was very quiet, exclusive, expensive and almost as dull as a Victoria[4] afternoon in February. Now it is just expensive. Our living room has a picture window which looks south across the bay to Point Loma, the most westerly part of San Diego, and at night there is a long lighted coastline almost in our laps. A radio writer came down here to see me once and he sat down in front of this

---

[1] The year his mother died.
[2] Editor, Houghton Mifflin Co.
[3] Correspondent of *New Liberty Magazine*.
[4] Victoria, B.C.

window and cried because it was so beautiful. But we live here, and the hell with it.

My wife desires no publicity, is pretty drastic about it. She doesn't paint or write. She does play a Steinway grand when she gets time. About half to two-thirds of the time we are between cooks, and she does not have time. She is a New Yorker and connected with the family to which Clarence Day's mother belonged.

Feb. 5, 1951
To: Edgar Carter [1]

. . . *Picture Post* is for people who move their lips when they read. Surely they can get anything they want to know about me from my English publisher, Hamish Hamilton Ltd. The questions you quote from them would seem to me to indicate the intellectual level of the editorial department of *Picture Post*.

Yes, I am exactly like the characters in my books. I am very tough and have been known to break a Vienna roll with my bare hands. I am very handsome, having a powerful physique, and I change my shirt regularly every Monday morning. When resting between assignments I live in a French Provincial chateau on Mulholland Drive. It is a fairly small place of forty-eight rooms and fifty-nine baths. I dine off gold plate and prefer to be waited on by naked dancing girls. But of course there are times when I have to grow a beard and hole up in a Main Street flophouse, and there are other times when I am, although not by request, entertained in the drunk tank in the city jail.

I have friends from all walks of life. I have fourteen telephones on my desk, including direct lines to New York, London, Paris, Rome, and Santa Rosa. My filing case opens out into a very convenient portable bar, and the bartender, who lives in the bottom drawer, is a midget. I am a heavy smoker and according to my mood I smoke tobacco, marijuana, corn silk and dried leaves. I do a great deal of research, especially in the apartments of tall blondes. I get my material in various ways, but my favourite procedure consists of going through the desks of other writers after hours. I am thirty-eight years old and have been

[1] Then of H. N. Swanson Inc., Chandler's Hollywood agent.

for the last twenty years. I do not regard myself as a dead shot, but I am a pretty dangerous man with a wet towel. But all in all I think my favourite weapon is a twenty dollar bill.

Oct. 5, 1951
To: Hamish-Hamilton

. . . I do hope to have a book in 1952, I hope very hard. But dammit I have a great deal of trouble getting on with it . . . I am worn down by worry over my wife . . . We have a big house, rather, hard to take care of, and the help situation is damn near hopeless. Cissy can do very very little, she has lost a lot of ground in the last two years. She is a superb cook and we are both pretty much over-fastidious, but we can't help it. I have thought that the sensible thing might be to get a small house and do for ourselves, but I am afraid she is no longer capable even of that. When I get into work I am already tired and dis-spirited. I wake in the night with dreadful thoughts. Cissy has a constant cough which can only be kept down by drugs and the drugs destroy her vitality.

April, 1951
To: Mrs Juanita Messick[1]

We are going to cut out the afternoon tea for a while; it is one more chore in a day already overloaded with them so far as I'm concerned. It looks to me as if until my wife gets better I'm going to have to do most of the cooking.

I'm a pretty good short order cook. I can cook steak, chops and vegetables better than the restaurants can . . . but it's a grind and there's no doubt about that. I get up at 8 o'clock in the morning. It takes me until 10 o'clock to get the two break-fasts and tidy. That gives me until one o'clock to try to do a little writing. Then I have to go uptown and market, which doesn't matter because I was never any good at working in the after-noon, even as a schoolboy I was always dead in the afternoon.

[1] Then Chandler's secretary.

Then I come back and the minute I'm inside the house, there's this damn tea . . .

By 5 o'clock I have to get busy in the kitchen. Then after dinner there are the dishes. I think I might leave the dinner dishes—stick 'em down in the dishwasher, something of that sort. But it's almost as much trouble to do that and tidy up and wash off the stove and sink and drainboard as to do the whole job.

July 31, 1952

To: Roger Machell[1]

. . . We are thinking of taking a boat trip from the Pacific Coast to London and staying there a week or two and then coming back the same way. My wife and I are both very tired for many reasons. She is weakened by a long siege of bronchitis, and I think perhaps a trip like that would do more good than anything else that could be devised. There will be no round of gaiety in London, because she simply could not face it.

Nov. 5, 1952

To: Hamish Hamilton

. . . We loved London and we had a lovely time there. What little inconveniences we happened to have suffered were all due to our own inexperience and probably would not happen again. . . . There are things I regret, such as losing several days over my vaccination, such as not going to any of the picture galleries, such as only seeing one rather poor play. I spent too much time talking about myself, which I don't enjoy, and too little time listening to other people talk about themselves, which I do enjoy. I missed seeing something of the English countryside. And childish as it may sound, I missed very much not having hired a Rolls Royce and a driver for a day. But all in all, there was a hell of a lot I did not miss and all of it good.

[1] A director of Hamish Hamilton Ltd.

Nov. 13, 1952
To: Dale Warren
  . . . It was nice meeting you. I can't say I fell in love with New York but I didn't see the best side of it . . . I developed a certain amount of subconscious reluctance to have anything to do with New York taxi-drivers. Those that don't whine or bluster want to make a travelogue out of a ten-block ride.

Jan. 6, 1953
To: H. F. Hose[1]
  . . . I must say I like London very much, in spite of the climate, the monotony of the food, the cold rooms. It seemed to me that everybody did an awful lot of drinking, but you can stand more of it in that climate than you can in Southern California. There is a fundamental decency about the English people and a sort of effortless sense of good manners which I find very attractive. English people themselves seem to think their manners have deteriorated, but they are still far better than they are anywhere else in the world. I am speaking of averages, of course. Americans can be very polite too, but you do not in casual contact, and especially in big cities, find that effortless courtesy which seems to be normal behaviour in England.

March 15, 1953
To: Roger Machell
  . . . This is going to be awful because I'm balling the jack myself and on a Corona yet. On Sunday nobody works but Chandler and he breaks his heart seven days a week and without no music . . . Thank you for sending me the stuff from *John o' London's*, and the piece from the Westminster Bank. In most ways I liked that better. Every interview makes a different man and that is one reason I don't like them . . . The physical description of Chandler is unrecognizable by anyone who knows him. He calls me small. Attired for the street I am an inch short of six feet. My nose is not sharp but blunt, the result of trying

  [1] Mr Hose had been Chandler's form-master at Dulwich College.

to tackle a man as he was kicking the ball. For an English nose it would hardly even be called prominent. Wispy hair like steel wool? Nuts. It is limp. Walks with a forward-leaning lope, huh? Chandler cantered gaily into the cocktail lounge, rapidly consumed three double gimlets and fell flat on his kisser, his steel wool hair curling gracefully against the pattern of the carpet . . .

Of course I'm not really complaining. Interviews are always like this. Sometimes I think the only really good ones are done with trained interviewees, gents who have learned a particular pose in which to display themselves and use it without much variation. They give a performance.

Sept. 16, 1953
To: H. F. Hose

. . . I have lost weight lately and I tire easily. I do a little work, then business letters, and after that no energy. No doubt you know the feeling. After sixty a man should not worry about trifles but I do . . . The best doctor I know has told me that I shall probably die of exhaustion, as there is nothing else to kill me. No deterioration. I don't remember as well as I did. I have to make notes and lists. Sometimes quite familiar names slip off the edge and hang out of sight, then pop back grinning . . .

(*Chandler's wife died on December* 12, 1954. *The difference of nearly eighteen years between them was never of any significance to Chandler.*)

Jan. 1955
To: Leonard Russell[1]

. . . I have received much sympathy and many letters, but yours is somehow unique in that it speaks of the beauty that is lost rather than condoling with the comparatively useless life that continues on. She was everything you say, and more. She was the beat of my heart for thirty years. She was the music heard faintly at the edge of sound. It was my great and now

[1] Assistant Editor of the *Sunday Times*, London.

useless regret that I never wrote anything really worth her attention, no book that I could dedicate to her. I planned it. I thought of it but I never wrote it. Perhaps I couldn't have written it. Perhaps by now she realises that I tried, and that I regarded the sacrifice of several years of a rather insignificant literary career as a small price to pay, if I could make her smile a few times more.

Jan. 5, 1955
To: Hamish Hamilton
   . . . Please don't send me any more books, as they will only have to go into storage. I have sold the house and I will be out of here about March 15th or before. I'll let you know as soon as I know myself about when I shall be in London. I gather from your letter that you would like me to stay with you at your house for a little while. But if I may say so without sounding ungrateful, I should rather be on my own. I'd like to be at a hotel until you can help me find a service flat. I don't want to be a burden or a nuisance to anyone. I am pretty badly broken up, and for me it may last a long time, as my emotions are not superficial.
   You probably realized when we were in London that Cissy was in rather frail health. When we got back she looked and felt better than she had in a couple of years, but it didn't last. She got weaker and weaker and more and more tired. She had an obscure and rather rare ailment, I am told, called fibrosis of the lungs. It's a slow hardening of the lung tissue, starting at the bottom of the lungs and progressing upwards . . . As far back as 1948 her X-rays showed the condition as existing, but it was quite a long time before I realized that it could have only one ending. I don't think that she herself ever quite gave up hope, or if so during the last weeks, she didn't let anyone else know that she had given up hope . . .
   She was in an oxygen tent all the time, but she kept pulling it away so that she could hold my hand. She was quite vague in her mind about some things, but almost too desperately clear about others. Then she would turn her head away and when I was no longer in her line of vision, she seemed to forget all about me.

A little after noon on December 12th, which was a Sunday, the nurse called up and said she was very low. When I got there they had taken the oxygen tent away and she was lying with her eyes half open . . . The doctor had his stethoscope over her heart and was listening. After a while he stepped back and nodded. I closed her eyes and kissed her and went away.

Of course in a sense I had said goodbye to her long ago. In fact many times during the past two years in the middle of the night I had realized that it was only a question of time until I lost her. But that is not the same thing as having it happen. But I was glad that she had died. To think of this proud, fearless bird caged in a room in some rotten sanitarium for the rest of her days was such an unbearable thought that I could hardly face it at all.

I am sleeping in her room. I thought I couldn't face that, and then I thought that if the room were empty it would just be haunted, and every time I went past the door I would have the horrors, and that the only thing was for me to come in here and fill it up with my junk and make it look like the kind of mess I'm used to living in. It was the right decision.

For thirty years, ten months and four days, she was the light of my life, my whole ambition. Anything else I did was just the fire for her to warm her hands at.

March 19, 1957
To: Helga Greene

. . . I wasn't faithful to my wife out of principle but because she was completely adorable, and the urge to stray which afflicts many men at a certain age, because they think they have been missing a lot of beautiful girls, never touched me. I already had perfection. When she was younger she used to have sudden and very short-lived tempers, in which she would throw pillows at me. I just laughed. I liked her spirit. She was a terrific fighter. If an awkward or unpleasant scene faced her she would march right in, and never hesitate a minute to think it over. And she always won, not because she deliberately put on the charm at the tactical moment, but because she was irresistible without even knowing or caring about it. So she had to die by

Pearl Cecily Chandler — 'Cissy.'

half-inches. I suppose everything has to be paid for in some manner.

Feb. 7, 1955
To: Roger Machell
    . . . I sit up half the night playing records when I have the blues and can't get drunk enough to feel sleepy. My nights are pretty awful. And they don't get any better. I've been alone since Saturday morning except for Mabel the Marble, my Pennsylvania Dutch cook and housekeeper. She has a lot of fine qualities but she is not much company. Perhaps when I get away from this house and all its memories I can settle down to do some writing. And then again I may just be homesick, and to be homesick for a home you haven't got is rather poignant.
    Tomorrow is or would have been our thirty-first wedding anniversary. I'm going to fill the house with red roses and have a friend in to drink champagne, which we always did. A useless and probably foolish gesture because my lost love is utterly lost and I have no belief in any after life. But just the same I shall do it. All us tough guys are hopeless sentimentalists at heart.

In February 1955 Chandler made what one of his friends later termed 'the most inefficient effort at suicide on record'. Afterwards he never hesitated to discuss the incident, which was reported all over the world, in highly garbled versions, by newspapers and radio. The official police report of the affair was made available for this book on the condition that the names of the police officers involved were held in confidence and the report used with restraint and understanding—because, the police said, 'Ray was one of the best'.
    The report runs: 'Chandler dramatized his wife's death pretty severely, and his active imagination had something to do with the motivation . . . Sergeant xxx, patrol division, La Jolla, in a report on the gunshot suicide attempt of February 22, 1955, said that on the 5th of February, just prior to the shooting, he had gone to the Chandler residence and 'talked him out' of threats to commit suicide. This suicide threat of February 5 was the

*third the police had received.' On the afternoon of February 22
Chandler's sister-in-law[1] called the La Jolla police station to report that he was making more threats to kill himself. 'The officer
in charge, well aware of the situation, talked to Ray on the phone
stalling him until police officers could arrive.'*

*At 3.50 p.m. the patrolman who arrived was talking to
Chandler's sister-in-law 'when he heard two shots from the bathroom'. He ran to the bathroom and found Chandler sitting on
the shower floor, the gun in his lap. He describes Chandler at
the time as being under the influence of alcohol . . . He took the
gun away from Chandler, who was dressed in robe, pajamas and
bedroom slippers. He said the two—only two—bullets from the
gun went into the ceiling or the tile of the shower stall, and the
suicide was aborted because they were fired upward, missing any
supposed target.*

*'Chandler was despondent over the recent death of Mrs
Chandler, and a recent wedding anniversary date had not helped
his mental feelings. He was sent to the psychiatric ward of the
County Hospital, and was later transferred by negotiation of
friends to a private sanitarium.'*

March 5, 1955
To: Roger Machell

. . . I couldn't for the life of me tell you whether I really intended to go through with it or whether my subconscious was
putting on a cheap dramatic performance. The first shot went
off without my intending it to. I had never fired the gun and the
trigger pull was so light that I barely touched it to get my hand
in position when off she went and the bullet ricocheted around
the tile walls of the shower bath and went up through the ceiling.
It could just as easily have ricocheted into my stomach. The
charge seemed to me to be very weak. This was borne out when
the second shot (the business) didn't fire at all. The cartridges
were about five years old and in this climate I guess the charge
had decomposed. At that point I blacked out. The police officer
who came in then told me later I was sitting on the floor of the
shower trying to get the gun into my mouth, and then when he

[1] Mrs Lavinia Brown of Los Angeles.

asked me to give him the gun I just laughed and handed it to him.

I haven't the slightest recollection of this. And I don't know whether or not it is an emotional defect that I have absolutely no sense of guilt nor any embarrassment at meeting people in La Jolla who all knew what had happened. It was on radio here, on the wire services, in papers all over the country, and I had piles of letters from all over the place.

In England, I believe, and in some other places attempted suicide, or what looks like it, is a crime. In California it is not, but you have to go through the observation ward at the County Hospital. I talked myself out of it the next noon but on condition I went to a private sanitarium . . . I had more trouble talking myself out of that. I stuck it for six days and then announced that I was going to discharge myself. Upheaval. This simply wasn't done. All right, I said, tell me the law that keeps me here. There wasn't any and the head guy knew it.

So I came home and since then nothing has mattered to me about the whole business except that they shot me so full of dope to keep me tractable that I still have a little hangover from it. Isn't it amazing that people should sit around depressed and bored and miserable in these places, worried about their jobs and their families, longing to go home, subjected every other day to electrical shock treatments (they didn't dare try that on me) and in between insulin shock, worrying about the cost of it all and the feeling of being a prisoner, and yet not have the guts to get up and walk out? I suppose it is part of what's the matter with them. If they had more guts, they wouldn't be there in the first place. But that's hardly an answer. If I had had more guts I shouldn't have let despair and grief get me down so far that I did what I did. But when I found myself dealing with . . . a lot of psychiatric claptrap and with a non-existent authority that tried to make me think it had power, I didn't find that it took any special amount of daring to tell them all what I was going to do and to do it. And in the end strangely enough they almost seemed to like it. The head nurse kissed me and said I was the politest, the most considerate and cooperative, and the most resilient patient they had ever had there, and that God help any doctor who tried to make me do anything I wasn't convinced I ought to do.

Early March, 1955
To: William Campbell Gault[1]

. . . Yesterday I finished the rather agonising business of getting the furniture out of the house and closing it up for the new buyer. When I walked through the empty rooms checking the windows and so on I felt a little like the last man on a dead world. But it will pass. On Wednesday I leave for Old Chatham, New York, stay with my best friend [Ralph Barrow] and on April 12 I sail on the *Mauretania*. I expect to be back about the end of October and to find a house in La Jolla—much smaller, of course—because it is an easy place to live in and everybody knows me here.

April 24, 1955, Connaught Hotel, London
To: Hardwick Moseley[2]

. . . I am here at least until May 8, after which I may have to sleep in Green Park. I am not happy and I am terribly hoarse from laryngitis. The racket here is just too intense also. You go to luncheon with eight people and next day five of them invite you to a dinner party. So dine, drink and drab is about all you do. I love this hotel, but I do not love being stared at and being pointed out to people and I do not love newspaper interviews.

June 3, 1955
To: Neil Morgan[3]

. . . I don't think you would recognize me if you saw me now, I have become so damned refined that at times I loathe myself. I still don't sleep well and often get up at 4 or 5 in the morning.

I've lately been indulging in a form of polite pornography. You should understand that the basic motif behind this is an attempt to spoof the upper middle-class sort of talk. There can

---

[1] Author of novels and short stories.
[2] A director of Houghton Mifflin Co.
[3] Columnist on *San Diego Evening Tribune*.

be no greater mistake than to think that we and the English people speak the same language . . .

It has been a wonderful spring, the squares flaming with the most gorgeous tulips three and even four feet high. Kew Gardens is a paradise of green and color, rhododendrons, azaleas, amaryllis, flowering trees of every kind. It catches you by the throat after the hard dusty green of California. The shops are beautifully dressed and full of all kinds of wonderful things. The traffic control system here is superb. The one thing they lack is tender meat. They simply haven't got the storage to age it.

But the women! If they ever had buck teeth I don't see them now. I've seen glamour girls at parties that would stun Hollywood. And they are so damned honest they won't even let you pay their taxi fares.

Oct. 14, 1955, Chatham, New York
To: Michael Gilbert[1]

. . . The voyage was hell. Still practising to be a non-drinker (and it's going to take a damn sight more practising than I have time for) I sat alone at a table in the corner and refused to have anything to do with the other passengers, which did not seem to cause them any grief.

Feb. 20, 1956, London
To: Neil Morgan

. . . One of these days I intend to write you a long and detailed letter describing my flutterings over Europe and North Africa, and you will find it as boring as most postcards (I hope not). I am having a delightful time here soaking my feet in boiling water to restore the circulation and lying in bed under four blankets, an eiderdown and an electric pad . . . My health has been bad, and every doctor finds something else the matter with me. But all that is really the matter with me is that I have no home, and no one to care for in a home, if I had one.

[1] Chandler's London solicitor.

June 5, 1956, New York Hospital
To: Neil Morgan

. . . What was the matter with me—and has been for a long time—was a total mental, physical and emotional exhaustion masked by my drinking enough whisky to keep me on my feet, and then a severe malnutrition . . . It has never been difficult for me to stop drinking, but what have you got left? They taught me here that what you have left is a scientific high-protein diet which in a mere matters of days has you eating about three times as much as you thought you could ever get down, and then looking around for more . . . On the fifth day I woke up and a miracle had been passed. I felt happy, absolutely happy, for the first time since my wife died. All the rest had been play-acting. This was genuine and the mood has not changed . . . My love to you both, and don't give me up. I need friends.

June 14, 1956, La Jolla
To: H. N. Swanson[1]

. . . I'm back in circulation again. I got in Tuesday morning on the midnight (N.Y.) plane, pretty damn bushed. The English winter, especially that awful cold spell in January, did me a lot of no good. For some reason I couldn't work in London—too damn much social life, I guess, too many lovely ladies . . . But I had to go back . . . I didn't feel I could stand it to live in La Jolla so soon after my wife's death. The place was haunted for me. But I am more hardened now. I think I'll make it.

Aug. 23, 1956
To: Dorothy Gardiner

. . . I've been away for several weeks in one of the hottest damn places in California, to wit, Pasadena, the home of quiet peace and sweaty undershirts. God knows it's hot enough here right now, which shouldn't happen to a La Jollan, but our climate has been gradually changing and I believe that for the next million years we are in for a tropical spell, to be followed no

---

[1] Chandler's Hollywood agents.

doubt by an ice age, but I don't expect to be around quite that long.

March 28, 1957
To: Edgar Carter

. . . In Arizona I learned to like driving again. For years I hated it. But my English friend made me drive Arizona from north to south, from east to west, from the Mexican border to the mountains (Flagstaff has the best trout I ever tasted). And I became a very fast driver. In Arizona you hardly ever see a highway patrol car. I learned that the two absolute essentials are perfect tires and absolute concentration. Four hours of this is all I can take at my age, but I enjoyed it.

Sept. 27, 1957
To: Edgar Carter

. . . Life here bores me and I wish I could go back to England, but the tax accountant says I must stay out until after next April 5th . . . Since my two best girl friends are in London, this is very tough.

Dec. 2, 1957
To: Hamish Hamilton

. . . I am coming back to London towards the end of January as an intending resident. That requires a visa and if you enter on that basis you can bring or send your household goods and books . . . I suppose my main purpose in coming to London and staying there, apart from my love for it—except perhaps in January to March—is to try to write plays. You have so many active theatres and they will usually give a play a chance even if the critics don't get hysterical with delight.

It will be jolly to see you and Yvonne and Roger again. Also the nice chap who is head of the warehouse, and sink me for an oyster, I can't remember his name. I'm bad at remembering

names . . . I tried to hire a Burmese elephant to remember for
me, but I decided that his trumpeting would annoy my neigh-
bors and that his backside would splinter the furniture.

Oct. 5, 1958
To: Hardwick Moseley

. . . I go to Palm Springs for a couple of weeks in November,
December and January. I am very fond of Palm Springs. This
time I should go there for my health because I am a good
swimmer and diver and once used to do fancy diving from the
high board, but I haven't the spring in my legs to try the high
board (and there isn't one there). But I can still have a lot of
fun on the low board. It will build me a lot.

Feb. 7, 1959
To: The Mystery Writers of America[1]

. . . I am sure you realize that I take this honor as a token of
a long career, and that I do not take it very personally. I feel
very humble about this, but I suppose there must be reasons why
I have been chosen, even if these reasons are obscure to me.
After all, most of my life has been spent in trying to make
something out of the mystery story—perhaps a little more
than it was intended to be—but I am not at all sure that I have
succeeded . . .

I feel that as titular head of an incomparable organization, I
should make some effort to make our mutual endeavor seem
as important as it really is. How to go about this requires assistance of other brains than mine. Mine, such as they are, are
always at your disposal; but mine alone are not enough . . .

This is an honor I never expected or deserved, but since it
has been given to me I should like in as far as it is in my power
to express my great obligation to the Mystery Writers of
America and to wish that I could do more for them in a practical
way than is now possible.

[1] Chandler had been elected President of the M.W.A.

Chandler, who was ill when he wrote this, died in La Jolla on March 26, 1959. The Times (London), in its obituary notice, said of him: 'His name will certainly go down among the dozen or so mystery writers who were also innovators and stylists; who, working the common vein of crime fiction, mined the gold of literature.'

CHANDLER ON
THE MYSTERY NOVEL

Chandler on the Mystery Novel

Apr. 9, 1939
To: George Harmon Coxe[1]

Thanks for your letter and I much appreciate your remarks about the detective story business in general. I suppose if you are good enough there is a bare living in it—very bare. However, I'm used to that . . . Knopf seems to think that if anybody comes along who can write as well as Hammett,[2] he should have Hammett's success. Knopf being a publisher should know his business, but my feeling is that somebody might come along who wrote a great deal better than Hammett and still not have anything like Hammett's success. But of course these things are quite unpredictable.

June 27, 1940
To: George Harmon Coxe

What the war has done to the writer as writer is bad enough. What it has done to the book business I guess we shall both find out rather soon.

I still cling to the opinion that in times like these a good strong detective story is a godsend. On your recommendation and yours alone I read Agatha Christie's *And Then There Were None*,[3] and after reading it I wrote an analysis of it, because it was blurbed as the perfect crime story . . . As entertainment I liked the first half and the opening, in particular. The second half got pallid . . . The fundamental conception of the book in particular annoyed me. Here is a judge, a jurist, a man with a touch of sadism but withal a passion for exact justice, and this man condemns to death and murders a group of people on nothing but hearsay evidence. In no case did he have a shred of actual proof that any one of them had actually committed a murder. In every case it was merely someone's opinion, or a possible, even probable, inference from circumstances. Some of

[1] Author of crime fiction.
[2] Dashiell Hammett, died 1961.
[3] English title *Ten Little Niggers*.

these people admit their crimes, but this is all *after* the murders were planned, the judgment entered, the sentence pronounced.

But I'm very glad I read the book because it finally and for all time settled a question in my mind that had at least some lingering doubt attached to it. Whether it is possible to write a strictly honest mystery of the classic type. It isn't. To get the complication you fake the clues, the timing, the play of coincidence, assume certainties where only 50 per cent chances exist at most. To get the surprise murderer you fake the character, which hits me hardest of all, because I have a sense of character.

Jan. 26, 1944
To: James Sandoe[1]

. . . You are certainly not without company in your wish that 'something could be done about the disadvantages of the red-light segregation of detective stories in the reviews'. Once in a long while a detective story writer is treated as a writer, but very seldom. However, I think there are a few very good reasons why this is so. For example (a) most detective stories are very badly written; (b) their principal sale is to lending libraries which depend on a commercial reading service and pay no attention to reviews; (c) I believe the detective story is marketed wrong. It is absurd to expect people to pay any more for it than they would for a movie; (d) the detective or mystery story as an art form has been so thoroughly explored that the real problem for a writer now is to avoid writing a mystery story while appearing to do so. However none of these reasons, valid or invalid as they may be, changes the essential irritation to the writer, which is the knowledge that however well and expertly he writes a mystery story it will be treated in one paragraph, while a column and a half of respectful attention will be given to any fourth-rate, ill-constructed, mock-serious account of the life of a bunch of cotton pickers in the deep south. The French are the only people I know of who think about writing as writing. The Anglo-Saxons think first of the subject matter and second, if at all, of the quality.

[1] Mystery novel critic for *New York Herald-Tribune*. Assistant Professor in Humanities and Bibliography, University of Colorado.

July 17, 1944
To: Charles W. Morton

Sanders, my agent in New York, wrote to me some time ago saying that you might be interested in having me do a short article on the modern detective story for the *Atlantic*. Naturally I was both flattered and interested . . .

The last time I had an opportunity I tried to do a rough draft of such an article, only to discover that I hadn't the least idea how to go about it. The trouble seemed to be partly that I hadn't read enough detective stories to be able to indulge in the usual casual display of erudition, and partly that I really don't seem to take the mystery element in the detective story as seriously as I should. The detective story as I know and like it is a not too successful attempt to combine the attributes of two disparate types of minds: the mind which can produce a coolly thought-out puzzle can't, as a rule, develop the fire and dash necessary for vivid writing.

Dec. 16, 1944
To: James Sandoe

. . . I didn't check, but I had a vague impression here and there I had been ever so gently toned down.[1] I know they had to cut, because the thing was too long, and is overlength as it is. I had a very snazzy beginning which they cut out, because it didn't really have anything to do with detective stories. It was simply a general expression of contempt for what is known as significant writing . . . I have enough material left over for another one. But I think most critical writing is drivel and half of it is dishonest . . . and there is no point in my adding to it. It is a short cut to oblivion, anyway. Thinking in terms of ideas destroys the power to think in terms of emotions and sensations.

Oct. 13, 1945
To: Charles W. Morton

. . . As to talking about Hammett in the past tense, I hope he

[1] *The Simple Art of Murder*, published in *The Atlantic Monthly*, Dec. 1944.

is not to be so spoken of. As far as I know he is alive and well, but he has gone so long without writing—unless you count a couple of screenplay jobs—that I wonder. He was one of the many guys who couldn't take Hollywood without trying to push God out of the high seat. I recall an incident reported to me when Hammett was occupying a suite at the Beverly-Wilshire Hotel. A party wished to make him a proposition and called late of a morning, was admitted by Hammett's house boy to a living room, and after a very long wait an inner door opened and the great man appeared in it, clad in an expensive lounging robe with a scarf draped tastefully around his neck. He stood in silence as the man expounded. At the end he said politely: 'No'. He turned and withdrew, the door closed, the house boy ushered the gent out, and the silence fell . . .

If you ever saw Hammett, you will realise the dignity and pathos of this little scene. He is a very distinguished-looking guy, and I imagine he could say 'no' without perceptible trace of a Brooklyn accent. I liked him very much. It was a great pity that he stopped writing. I've never known why. I suppose he may have come to the end of his resources in a certain style and have lacked the intellectual depth to compensate for that by trying something else. But I'm not sure . . .

Nov. 9, 1945
To: Erle Stanley Gardner[1]

. . . A few weeks ago I went up to Big Bear Lake to get over a case of complete exhaustion such as you will never know, you dynamo. The only thing I could read was the Perry Mason stories. There were a whole flock of them I hadn't read—I don't know why. Perhaps my tastes have changed, perhaps my constant legal battles over contracts have made me enamoured of the law. Anyhow I read one a night and loved them. It was interesting also to see how as time went they became so much smoother and more adept.

---

[1] Author of crime fiction; writes also as 'A. A. Fair'.

Jan. 29, 1946

To: Erle Stanley Gardner

... I now address the Court, by permission, on the subject of one Gardner, an alleged writer of mysteries. The reading public is intellectually adolescent at best, and it is obvious that what is called 'significant literature' will only be sold to this public by exactly the same methods as are used to sell it toothpaste, cathartics and automobiles. It is equally obvious that since this public has been taught to read by brute force it will, in between its bouts with the latest 'significant' bestseller, want to read books that are fun and excitement. So, like all half-educated publics in all ages, it turns with relief to the man who tells a story and nothing else. To say that what this man writes is not literature is just like saying that a book can't be any good if it makes you want to read it.

When a book, any sort of book, reaches a certain intensity of artistic performance it becomes literature. That intensity may be a matter of style, situation, character, emotional tone, or idea, or half a dozen other things. It may also be a perfection of control over the movement of a story similar to the control a great pitcher has over the ball. That is to me what you have more than anything else and more than anyone else . . . Every page throws the hook for the next. I call this a kind of genius . . . Perry Mason is the perfect detective because he has the intellectual approach of the juridical mind and at the same time the restless quality of the adventurer who won't stay put.

So let's not have any more of that phooey about 'as literature my stuff still stinks'. Who says so—William Dean Howells?

Dec. 9, 1946

To: Howard Haycraft[1]

... Like most anthologies . . . it leaves out some things which the reader thinks must inevitably have been included: for example, Somerset Maugham's article originally published in the *Saturday Evening Post*[2] and Perelman's wonderful parody of the

[1] Critic and editor of crime fiction. He had edited an anthology *The Art of the Mystery Story*.

[2] *Give Me a Murder*, by Somerset Maugham, *Saturday Evening Post*, Dec. 28, 1940.

hard boiled mystery . . .[1] Taste is a strange thing. Unlike me, you have what is known as a catholic taste, but you must not take a polemic piece of writing like my own article from the *Atlantic*[2] too literally. I could have written a piece of propaganda in favor of the English detective story just as easily. All polemic writing is over-stated. The instant you admit that both sides in a controversy may be right, you have thrown away your whole argument . . .

Sept. 4, 1948
To: Cleve F. Adams[3]

. . . I did not invent the hard boiled murder story and I have never made any secret of my opinion that Hammett deserves most or all of the credit. Everybody imitates in the beginning. What Stevenson called playing the 'sedulous ape'. I personally think that a deliberate attempt to lift a writer's personal tricks, his stock in trade, his mannerisms, his approach to his material, can be carried too far—to the point where it is a kind of plagiarism and a nasty kind because the law gives no protection. The law recognizes no plagiarism except that of basic plots . . .

Since Hammett has not written for publication since 1932 I have been picked out by some people as a leading representative of the school. This is very likely due to the fact that *The Maltese Falcon* did not start the high budget mystery picture trend, although it ought to have. *Double Indemnity* and *Murder, My Sweet* did, and I was associated with both of them. The result is that everybody who used to be accused of writing like Hammett may now be accused of trying to write like Chandler.

Oct. 17, 1948
To: James Sandoe

. . . *The Franchise Affair*[4] is a real discovery and I'm immensely

[1] *Farewell my Lovely Appetizer*, included in *The Most of S. J. Perelman*.
[2] *The Simple Art of Murder*.
[3] Author of crime fiction.
[4] By Josephine Tey.

grateful. I thoroughly enjoyed it and should like to know Miss Tey better. And why is it that women do books like this so much better than men? Are they more patient and observant?

There is no top-drawer critical writing about the murder or mystery novel, factually based or otherwise. Neither in this country nor in England has there been any critical recognition that far more art goes into these books at their best than into any number of fat volumes of goosed history or social-significance rubbish. The psychological foundation for the immense popularity with all sorts of people of the novel about murder or crime or mystery hasn't been scratched . . . And if you have to have significance . . . it is just possible that the tensions in a novel of murder are the simplest and yet most complete pattern of the tensions on which we live in this generation.

March 11, 1949
To: Bernice Baumgarten[1]

. . . Every now and then I get a shock by seeing myself through other eyes. In the current number of *Partisan Review*, a man writing about *Our Mutual Friend* says: 'It is possible that the question of true-to-life did not arise, and that Dickens' contemporaries accepted his dark vision of London and England as readily as we today accept Raymond Chandler's California with its brutal and neurotic crew of killers and private eyes . . .' etc. Another writer in this avant garde magazine[2] referred to me as a 'Cato of the Cruelties'. Apart from the obvious compliment of being noticed at all by the rarefied intellectuals who write for these publications—and I should understand them well, because I was one of them for years—I cannot grasp what they do with their sense of humor. Or let me put it in a better way: Why is it that Americans—of all people the quickest to reverse their moods —do not see the strong element of burlesque in my kind of writing . . .

The mystery writer's material is melodrama, which is an exaggeration of violence and fear beyond what one normally

[1] Then of Brandt & Brandt (Chandler's literary agent in New York).
[2] *A Cato of the Cruelties*, by R. W. Flint, *Partisan Review*, May-June, 1947.

experiences in life. (I say normally: no writer ever approximated the life of the Nazi concentration camps.) The means he uses are realistic in the sense that such things happen to people like these and in places like these; but this realism is superficial; the potential of emotion is overcharged, the compression of time and event is a violation of probability, and although such things happen, they do not happen so fast and in such a tight frame of logic to so closely knit a group of people.

Apr. 14, 1959
To: James Sandoe

Have read *The Moving Target* by John Ross Macdonald and am a good deal impressed by it, in a peculiar way. In fact I could use it as the springboard for a sermon on How Not to be a Sophisticated Writer . . . What strikes me about the book (and I guess I should not be writing about it if I didn't feel that the author had something) is first an effect that is rather repellent. There is nothing to hitch to; here is a man who wants the public for the mystery story in its primitive violence and also wants it to be clear that he, individually, is a highly literate and sophisticated character. A car is 'acned with rust', not spotted. Scribblings on toilet walls are 'graffiti'; one refers to 'podex osculation' (medical latin, too, ain't we hell?). 'The seconds piled up precariously like a tower of poker chips', etc. The simile that does not quite come off because it doesn't understand what the purpose of the simile is.

The scenes are well handled, there is a lot of experience of some kind behind this writing, and I should not be surprised to find the name was a pseudonym for a novelist of some performance in another field. The thing that interests me is whether this pretentiousness in the phrasing and choice of words makes for better writing. It does not. You could only justify it if the story itself were devised on the same level of sophistication, and you wouldn't sell a thousand copies, if it was. When you say 'spotted with rust' (or pitted, and I'd almost but not quite go for 'pimpled') you convey at once a simple visual image. But when you say 'acned with rust' the attention of the reader is instantly jerked away from the thing described to the pose of the writer. This is of course a very simple example of the stylistic misuse of language, and I think that certain writers are under a compulsion to write in recherche phrases as a compensation for a lack of some kind of natural animal emotion. They feel nothing, they are literary eunuchs, and therefore they fall back on an oblique terminology to prove their distinction. It is the sort of mind that keeps the avant garde magazines alive, and it is quite interesting to see an attempt to apply it to the purpose of this kind of story.

Apr. 16, 1949
To: Alex Barris[1]

. . . Best mystery writer? Can't answer, too many types. By sales Gardner and Christie. Can't read Christie, Gardner close personal friend. Carter Dickson I can't read but others love him. Best character and suspense writer for consistent but not large production, Elisabeth Holding. Best plodding detail man, Freeman Wills Crofts. Best Latin and Greek quoter, Dorothy Sayers. Writer with best natural charm, Philip Macdonald. Best scary writer: none, they don't scare me. But Dorothy Hughes does it to most. Most intriguing character I can think of offhand, the M.C. in Margaret Millar's *Wall of Eyes* (M.C. meaning Master of Ceremonies). Best idea man: Cornell Woolrich (William Irish), but you have to read him fast and not analyze too much; he's too feverish.

This is a lot of nonsense. You have to agree on definitions and standards. You even have to maintain a mood. You have to decide whether you will judge by overall output or a single book which happened to be a natural.

Apr. 21, 1949
To: Bernice Baumgarten

. . . Dorothy Sayers tried to make the jump from the mystery to the novel of manners and take the mystery along with her. She tried to move over, with all her baggage, from the people

[1] Alex Barris had sent Chandler a questionnaire.

who can plot but can't write to the people who can write and, all too often, can't plot. She didn't really make it, because the novel of manners she aimed at was in itself too slight a thing to be important. It was just the substitution of one popular trivial kind of writing for another. I am not satisfied that the thing can't be done nor that sometime, somewhere, perhaps not now or by me, a novel cannot be written which, ostensibly a mystery and keeping the spice of mystery, will actually be a novel of character and atmosphere with an over-tone of violence and fear.

May 14, 1949
To: James Sandoe
    . . . In spite of several mentions by you I have only just discovered Michael Innes. I think he is quite wonderful and am about to buy up all the books of his that are still in print. Even if the plot were rotten, it would still be a pleasure to come into contact with a whole literate mind, full of sly humor and soft chuckles. What the typical mystery addict makes of him, God knows. Very little, I imagine, but he suits me fine, and makes all the words-of-one-syllable boys sound like so many lame-brain-dead-end-kids.

May 20, 1949
To: James Sandoe
    . . . Your problem of nomenclature is a stiff one. I agree that there should be some agreed use of terms, but all three of the English terms are silly to me. *'Tec* is that sort of halfwitted English slang (like ripping, posh, wizard, grisly) which lacks imagination and is therefore inane. *Thriller* and *shocker* both imply a derogative attitude which is beside the point, even if it is justified at the moment.
    Casting my untidy mind over the field as I see it, I can only say what the various phrases seem to mean to me. *Novel* (or tale) *of detection* implies that the thing is mainly about physical and sensory facts, their discovery, organization, elucidation,

making a pattern of them. This sort of yarn derives its interest from a process, a technique (watching the man at work), uses character as best it can, emotion as little as possible. Most of the genre is fraudulent in some manner, but in so far as it is not it is the classic form and entitled to the use of the word detection.

Mystery is an unfortunate term, really. It is the best generic term because it includes most and excludes least, but the trouble is we need it also for a more specific purpose: to indicate that type of story in which the search is not for a specific criminal, but for a raison d'être, a meaning in character and relationship, what the hell went on, rather than who done it. The story can be violent or calm, brutal or elegant, but the emphasis is always on people, not on facts, and there is always something to be discovered before the thing makes sense, in which it differs entirely from the:

Novel of Suspense. In this there is mystery, perhaps, and a detective, perhaps, but these are part of the external pressure. In this story someone is always in a jam and the story is told from that person's point of view. There is a bastard form in which the detective is in a jam, but I don't favor it . . .

The *Inverted Detection Tale* is, as you say, a detailed and carefully executed crime followed by an even more detailed elucidation and discovery . . .

The *Fluttery Female*, or *Will He Strangle Her on the Stairs*, type of rubbish is a bastard variant of the suspense story . . .

The *Chase.* I suppose this is really a sub-type, but it has such vitality when well done, especially on film, that it seems to deserve a drawer to itself. The materials of its effect seem very close to the spy novel told from the spy's point of view. The suspense rests on the fact that the hero or heroine has no weapons but flight and secrecy. Simply to be caught is to lose, therefore the incidents of the case are the whole story . . .

The *Psycho-thriller* is a phoney. It's on the wane, I think, and is almost always a bore. It has no sound basis (neither has psychiatry itself as a rule) and when it holds you, that owes almost nothing to the form itself.

The *Novel of Murder* does not seem to me to belong here at all. *An American Tragedy,*[1] for example, has no more to do with

---

[1] By Theodore Dreiser.

mystery or detection than *The Lost Week-End*.[1] Murder in a story does not bring it into the detective or mystery category
    Want any more?

June 16, 1949
To: James Sandoe
    . . . Reading at random last night in *The Art of the Mystery Story*[2] I was struck with the low quality of mystery criticism. The whole discussion is on a plane of diminished values and there is constant haste to deprecate the mystery story as literature.

    The sort of semi-literate educated people one meets nowadays . . . are always saying to me, more or less, 'You write so well I should think you would do a serious novel.' You would probably insult them by remarking that the artistic gap between a really good mystery and the best serious novel of the last ten years is hardly measurable compared with the gap between the serious novel and any representative piece of Attic literature from the Fourth Century B.C.

    You cannot have art without a public taste and you cannot have a public taste without a sense of style and quality throughout the whole structure. Curiously enough this sense of style seems to have very little to do with refinement or even humanity. It can exist in a savage and dirty age, but it cannot exist in the Coca-Cola age . . . the age of the Book-of-the-Month and the Hearst Press. You cannot have it in an age whose dominant note is an efficient vulgarity, a completely unscrupulous scramble for the dollar, an age when the typical middle-class family (in California at any rate) seems to exist to support a large, gaudy and expensive automobile which as a piece of engineering is outmoded junk.

Oct. 14, 1949
To: James Sandoe
    Your remarks about Peter Cheyney amused me, especially as

---

[1] By Charles Jackson.
[2] Edited by Howard Haycraft.

I had just received a batch of five of his books from the Penguin people in England. One of them, *Dark Duet*, seems to me damn good . . . Am now reading Marquand's *So Little Time*. As I recall or seem to recall it was rather deprecated when it came out, but it seems to me full of good sharp wit and liveliness and altogether a much more satisfying job than *Point of No Return*.

But I always like the wrong books anyhow. And the wrong pictures. And the wrong people. And I have a bad habit of starting a book and reading just enough to make sure that I want to read it, and then putting it to one side while I break the ice on a couple more. In that way when I feel dull and depressed, which is too often, I know I have something to read late at night, and not that horrid blank feeling of not having anybody to talk or listen to.

As for mysteries, that's hopeless. There don't seem to be any worth the trouble. It would be an excellent thing right now if someone would come along with a good cool analytical mystery, the hell with suspense and witty dialogue, and let us look at the fundamentals for fresh. The whole form has lost its way, the emphasis has gone to inessential matters.

Dec. 13, 1949
To: Hamish Hamilton
. . . This man Austin Freeman is a wonderful performer. He has no equal in his genre and he is also a much better writer than you might think, if you were superficially inclined, because in spite of the immense leisure of his writing he accomplishes an even suspense which is quite unexpected. The apparatus of his writing makes for dullness, but he is not dull. There is even a gaslight charm about his Victorian love affairs, and those wonderful walks across London which the long-legged Dr Thorndyke takes like a stroll around a garden, accompanied by his cheerful and brainless Watson, Dr Jervis, whom no man in his senses would hire for any legal or medico-legal operation more exacting than counting the toes of a corpse.

Freeman has so many distinctions as a technician that one is apt to forget that within his literary tradition he is a damn good writer. He invented the inverted detective story. He proved the possibility of forging fingerprints and of detecting the forgeries long before the police thought of such a thing. His knowledge is vast and very real. The great scene would have been a court-room battle between Thorndyke and Spilsbury, and for my money Thorndyke would have won hands down.

Oct. 13, 1950

To: Hamish Hamilton

. . . Does anybody in England publish Elisabeth Sanxay Holding? For my money she's the top suspense writer of them all. She doesn't pour it on and make you feel irritated. Her characters are wonderful; and she has a sort of inner calm which I find very attractive. I recommend for your attention, if you have not read them, *Net of Cobwebs*, *The Innocent Mrs Duff*, *The Blank Wall*.

Dec. 7, 1950

To: James Sandoe

. . . I have just been reading a book called *The Beast Must Die* by Nicholas Blake, the pseudonym of Cecil Day Lewis. Once again I am struck, you might even say shattered, by the devasta-ting effect on the story of the entrance of the detective, Nigel Strangeways, an amateur with wife tagging along—this wife is one of the world's three greatest female explorers, which puts her in the same distinguished and to me utterly silly class as the artist wife of Ngaio Marsh's Roderick Alleyn. Up to that point the story is damn good and extremely well written, but the amateur detective just won't do. He wouldn't even do when his brother was a duke and he had a title and was a classical scholar of considerable attainments, and he won't do as Nigel Strange-ways any better, or as well. The private eye is admittedly an ex-aggeration—a fantasy. But at least he's an exaggeration of the possible.

Apr. 16, 1951
To: Bernice Baumgarten

... It would seem to me that Eric Ambler has fallen between two stools and that he has succumbed to a danger which afflicts all intellectuals who attempt to deal with thriller material. I know I have to fight it all the time. It is no easy trick to keep your characters and your story operating on a level which is understandable to the semi-literate public and at the same time give them some intellectual and artistic overtones which that public does not seek or demand or, in in effect, recognize, but which somehow subconsciously it accepts and likes. My theory has always been that the public will accept style, provided you do not call it style either in words or by, as it were, standing off and admiring it.

There seems to me to be a vast difference between writing down to the public (something which always flops in the end) and doing what you want to do in a form which the public has learned to accept. It's not so much that Ambler let himself get too intellectual as that he let it become apparent that he was being intellectual.

Jan. 16, 1952
To: James Sandoe

The Handbook for Poisoners[1] is on its way back to you ... Most of Bond's stories I have seen before. I enjoyed the introduction very much, especially the clinical description of the effects of the viper bite on the curator of the Chicago Zoo. But there is certainly an awful lot of poisons Mr Bond has left out when you consider the amount of research and reading he must have done.

I wish that Bond had gone into some detail about antidotes in his discussion of poisons and brought out such interesting little facts, for example (if, as I hope, they are facts): that there are only two real antidotes in the whole field of poisons, atropine and muscarin, which are mutual antidotes; that morphia circulates through the stomach, and some cases of morphia poisoning can be cured by constant stomach washing; that arsenic is stored

[1] By Raymond Bond.

in the liver and circulates through from there to the heart and sometimes kills by affecting the heart muscles; and that cyanide poisoning, supposed to be so quick and so irrevocable, might in some cases be overcome by artificial respiration if applied quickly enough and kept up long enough, since the poison itself oxidizes rather quickly. Oh well, you can't have everything in seventy-two pages . . .

Oct. 1955
To: Hillary Waugh[1]

. . . Over here[2] I am not regarded as a mystery writer but as an American novelist of some importance. I won't say how important, because the percentage varies.

A thriller writer in England, if he is good enough, is just as good as anyone else. There is none of that snobbism which makes a fourth-rate serious novelist, without style or any real talent, superior by definition to a mystery writer who might have helped recreate a whole literature. People—well-bred English people— come to me in this rather exclusive hotel and introduce themselves and thank me for the pleasure my books have given them. I don't think somehow we shall ever reach that status in America. Certainly not in my time. I'm afraid our instinct for classification is too strong. I'm afraid our fundamental intellectual ignorance is too great. If it isn't a small best-seller or a book club selection, the hell with it.

. . . I agree that too many mysteries are mediocre, but too many books of every kind are mediocre by any exacting standards. But let us never accept the point of view that mysteries are written by hacks. The poorest of us shed our blood over every chapter. The best of us start from scratch with every new book. Hacks are people who do with facility something which they know is not worth doing but which they do for the money. No mystery writer I have ever met ever thought what he was doing was not worth doing; he only wished he could do it better.

I happen to have been one of the lucky ones, and, believe me, it takes luck . . .

[1] Author of crime fiction.
[2] London.

CASUAL NOTES ON
THE MYSTERY NOVEL
(Written in 1949)

(1) The mystery novel must be credibly motivated both as to the original situation and the denouement. It must consist of the plausible actions of plausible people in plausible circumstances, it being remembered that plausibility is largely a matter of style. This rules out most trick endings and the so-called 'closed circle' stories in which the least likely character is forcibly made over into the criminal without convincing anyone. It also rules out such elaborate mise-en-scènes as Christie's *Murder in the Calais Coach*,[1] in which the whole set-up for the crime reveals such a fluky set of events that nobody could ever really believe them. Here as everywhere of course plausibility is a matter of effect, not of fact, and one writer will succeed with a pattern which in the hands of a lesser artist would just seem foolish.

(2) The mystery story must be technically sound about methods of murder and detection. No fantastic poisons or improper effects such as death from improper doses, etc. No silencers on revolvers (they won't work because chamber and barrel are not continuous), no snakes climbing bellropes. If the detective is a trained policeman, he must act like one and have the mental and physical equipment to go with the job. If he is a private investigator or amateur he must at least know enough of police routine not to make a fool of himself. The mystery story must take into account the cultural stage of its readers; things that were acceptable in Sherlock Holmes are not acceptable in Sayers or Christie or Carter Dickson.

(3) It must be realistic as to character, setting and atmosphere. It must be about real people in a real world. There is of course an element of fantasy in the mystery story. It outrages probability by telescoping time and space. Hence the more exaggerated the basic premise the more literal and exact must be the proceedings that flow from it. Very few mystery writers have any talent for character work, but that does not mean it is superfluous. Those who say the problem overrides everything are

[1] English title *Murder in the Orient Express*.

merely trying to cover up their own inability to create character and atmosphere. Character can be created in various ways: by the subjective method of entering into the character's thoughts and emotions; by the objective or dramatic method as on the stage, that is, by the appearance, behavior, speech and actions of the character; and by the case history method in what is now known as the documentary style. This last is particularly applicable to the kind of detective novel which tries to be as factual and un-emotional as an official report. But whatever the method character must be created, if any kind of distinction is to be achieved.

(4) The mystery novel must have a sound story value apart from the mystery element. The idea is revolutionary to some of the classicists and most distasteful to all second-rate performers. Nevertheless it is sound. All really good mysteries are reread, some of them many times. Obviously this would not happen if the puzzle were the only motive for the reader's interest. The mysteries that survive over the years invariably have the qualities of good fiction. The mystery story must have color, lift, and a reasonable amount of dash. It takes an enormous amount of technical adroitness to compensate for a dull style, although the trick has been turned occasionally, especially in England.

(5) The mystery novel must have enough essential simplicity of structure to be explained easily when the time comes. The ideal denouement is the one in which everything is made clear in a brief flash of action. Ideas as good as this are always rare, and a writer who can achieve this once is to be congratulated. The explanation need not be short (except on the screen) and often cannot be short. The important thing is that it should be interesting in itself, something the reader is anxious to hear, not a new story with a new or unrecognizable set of characters dragged in to justify a leaky plot. It must not be merely a long-winded assembling of minute circumstances that the reader could not possibly be expected to remember. There is nothing more difficult to manage than an explanation. If you say enough to assuage the stupid reader you will have said enough to in-furiate the intelligent one, but this merely points up one of the essential dilemmas of the mystery writer, that the mystery novel has to appeal to a cross section of the entire reading public and

cannot possibly appeal to all of these by the same devices. Not since the early days of the three-decker novel has any one type of fiction been read by so many different sorts of people. Semi-literates don't read Flaubert and intellectuals don't as a rule read the current fat slab of goosed history masquerading as an historical novel. But everyone reads mysteries from time to time —or almost everyone—and a surprising number of people read almost nothing else. The handling of the explanation vis-à-vis this variously educated public is an almost insoluble problem. Possibly, except for the dyed in the wool aficionado who will stand anything, the best solution is the Hollywood rule: 'No exposition except under heat, and break it up at that.' (This means that an explanation must always be an accompaniment to some kind of action, and that it must be given in short doses rather than all at once.)

(6) The mystery must elude a reasonably intelligent reader. This, and the problem of honesty, are the two most baffling elements in mystery writing. Some of the best detective stories ever written do not elude an intelligent reader to the end (those of Austin Freeman, for instance). But it is one thing to guess the murderer and quite another to be able to justify the guess by reasoning. Since readers are of many minds some will guess a cleverly-hidden solution and some will be fooled by the most transparent plot. (Could *any* modern reader be fooled by *The Red-Headed League*?[1] Could any modern police routine miss *The Purloined Letter*?[2]) But it is not necessary or even desirable to fool to the hilt the real aficionado of mystery fiction. A half-guessed mystery is more intriguing than one in which the reader is entirely at sea. It ministers to the reader's self esteem to have penetrated some of the fog. The essential is that there be a little fog left at the end for the author to blow away.

(7) The solution, once revealed, must seem to have been in-evitable. At least half of all the mystery novels published violate this law. Their solutions are not only not inevitable, they are very obviously trumped-up because the writer had realized that his original murderer had become too apparent.

[1] By Sir A. Conan Doyle.
[2] By Edgar Allan Poe.

(8) The mystery novel must not try to do everything at once. If it is a puzzle story operating in a cool mental climate, it cannot also be a story of violent adventure or passionate romance. An atmosphere of terror destroys logical thinking. If the story is about the intricate psychological pressures that drive people to commit murder, it cannot also contain the dispassionate analysis of the trained investigator. The detective cannot be hero and menace at the same time; the murderer cannot be a tormented victim of circumstances and also a heavy villain.

(9) The mystery novel must punish the criminal in one way or another, not necessarily by operation of the law courts. Contrary to popular belief, this has nothing to do with morality. It is part of the logic of the form. Without this the story is like an unresolved chord in music. It leaves a sense of irritation.

(10) The mystery novel must be reasonably honest with the reader. This is always said, but the full implications are seldom realized. What is honesty in this connection? It is not enough that the facts be stated. They must be fairly stated, and they must be the sort of facts that can be reasoned from. Not only must important or any clues not be concealed from the reader, but they must not be distorted by false emphasis. Unimportant facts must not be presented in such a way as to make them portentous. Inferences from the facts are the detective's stock in trade, but he should disclose enough of his thinking to keep the reader's mind thinking along with him. It is the basic theory of all mystery writing that at some stage of the proceedings the reader could, given the necessary acuteness, have closed the book and revealed the essence of the denouement. But this implies more than mere possession of the facts; it implies that the ordinary lay reader could honestly be expected to draw the right conclusions from these facts. The reader cannot be charged with special and rare knowledge nor with an abnormal memory for insignificant details. For if such were necessary, the reader did not in fact have the materials for the solution, he merely had the unopened packages they came in.

The submerging of the big clue in a puddle of talk about nothing is a permissible trick when the movement of the story has created enough tension to put the reader on guard. If the reader has to know as much as Dr Thorndyke to solve a mystery, obviously he cannot solve it. If the premise of *Trent's Last Case*[1] is plausible, then logic and realism have no meaning. If the actual time when a murder was committed is conditioned by the murdered person having been a hemophilic, then the reader cannot be expected to deal with the matter intelligently until he knows of the hemophilia; when he does (the story I refer to is Sayers' *Have His Carcase*) the mystery disappears because the alibis no longer apply to the necessary times.

Obviously it is much more than a trick, acceptable or otherwise, for the detective to turn out to be the criminal, since the detective by tradition and definition is the seeker after the truth. There is always an implied guarantee to the reader that the detective is on the level, and this rule should of course be extended to include any first person narrator or any character from whose point of view the story is told. The suppression of facts by the narrator as such or by the author when pretending to show the facts as seen by a particular character is a flagrant dishonesty. (For two reasons I have always been quite unmoved to indignation by *The Murder of Roger Ackroyd*'s[2] violation of this rule. (1) The dishonesty is rather cleverly explained and (2) the whole arrangement of the story and of its dramatis personae make it clear that the narrator is the only possible murderer, so that to an intelligent reader the challenge of this story is not 'Who committed the murder?' but 'Watch me closely and catch me out if you can'.)

It seems evident by this time that the whole question of dishonesty is a matter of intention and emphasis. The reader expects to be fooled, but not by a trifle. He expects to misinterpret some clue but not because he failed to master chemistry, geology, biology, pathology, metallurgy and half a dozen other sciences at the same time. He expects to forget some detail that later turns out to be important, but not if the price of remembering it is to remember a thousand trivialities which have no importance whatsoever. And if, as in some of Austin Freeman's stories, the matter of exact proof turns on scientific knowledge, the reader expects that the detection of the criminal may be achieved

---

[1] By E. C. Bentley.
[2] By Agatha Christie.

by an ordinary attentive brain, even though the specialist is needed to drive the guilt home.

There are, of course, subtle dishonesties which are intrinsic in the form itself. Mary Roberts Rinehart, I think it was, once remarked that the point of the mystery story was that it was two stories in one: the story of what happened and the story of what appeared to have happened. Since a concealment of the truth is implied, there must be some means of effecting that concealment. It is all a question of degree. Some tricks are offensive because they are blatant and because, once they are shown up, there is nothing left. Some are pleasing because they are insidious and subtle, like a caught glance the meaning of which one does not quite know although one is suspicious that it is not flattering. All first person narration, for example, could be accused of a subtle dishonesty because of its appearance of candor and its ability to suppress the detective's ratiocination while giving a clear account of his words and acts and many of his emotional reactions. There must come a time when the detective has made up his mind and has not given the reader this bit of news, a point as it were (and many old hands recognize it without much difficulty) when the detective suddenly stops thinking out loud and ever so gently closes the door of his mind in the reader's face. Back in the days when the audience was still innocent and had to be hit in the face with a stale flounder in order to realize that something was fishy, the detective used to do this by saying, for example: 'Well, there are the facts. If you give them your careful attention, I am sure your thoughts will be rich in possible explanations of these strange events.' Nowadays it is done with less parade, but the effect of a closing door is just as unmistakable.

It ought to be added to close this subject that the question of fair play in a mystery story is purely professional and artistic and has no moral significance at all. The point is whether the reader was misled within the rules of fair play or whether he was hit below the belt. There is no possibility of perfection. Complete frankness would destroy the mystery. The better the writer the farther he will go with the truth, the more subtly he will disguise that which cannot be told. And not only is this game of skill without moral laws, but it is constantly changing the laws by which it does act. It has to; the reader is growing wiser by the minute. It may be that in Sherlock Holmes' day if the butler skulked outside the library window with a shawl over his head, he became a suspect. Today that course of action would instantly eliminate him from all suspicion. For not only does the contemporary reader refuse to follow any such will o' the wisp as a matter of course, but he is constantly alert to the writer's effort to make him look at the wrong things and not look at the right ones. Anything passed over lightly becomes suspicious, any character not mentioned as a suspect *is* a suspect, and anything which causes the detective to chew the ends of his mustache and look grave is by the alert reader suitably dismissed as of no importance. It often seems to this particular writer that the only reasonably honest and effective method of fooling the reader that remains is to make the reader exercize his mind about the wrong problem, to make him, as it were, solve a mystery (since he is almost sure to solve something) which will land him in a bypath because it is only tangential to the central problem. And even this takes a bit of cheating here and there.

Addenda

(1) The perfect mystery cannot be written. Something must always be sacrificed. You can have only one paramount value. This is my complaint against the deductive story. Its paramount value is something which does not exist: a problem which will stand up against the kind of analysis that a good lawyer gives to a legal problem. It is not that such stories are not intriguing, but that they have no way of compensating for their soft spots.

(2) It has been said that 'nobody cares about the corpse'. This is nonsense, it is throwing away a valuable element. It is like saying that the murder of your aunt means no more to you than the murder of an unknown man in a city you never visited.

(3) A mystery serial seldom makes a good mystery novel. The curtains depend for their effect on your not having the next chapter. When the chapters are put together the moments of false suspense are merely annoying.

(4) Love interest nearly always weakens a mystery because it introduces a type of suspense that is antagonistic to the detective's struggle to solve the problem. It stacks the cards, and, in nine cases out of ten, it eliminates at least two useful suspects. The only effective kind of love interest is that which creates a personal hazard for the detective—but which, at the same time, you instinctively feel to be a mere episode. A really good detective never gets married.

(5) It is the paradox of the mystery novel that while its structure will seldom if ever stand up under the close scrutiny of an analytical mind, it is precisely to that type of mind that it makes its greatest appeal. There is of course the blood-lust type of reader just as there is the worrier-about-the-character type of reader and the vicarious-sex-experience type of reader. But all of these put together would probably be a smallish minority compared with the alert kind of people who love the mystery story precisely because of its imperfections.

It is, that is to say, a form which has never really been licked, and those who have prophesied its decline and fall have been wrong for that exact reason. Since its form has never been perfected, it has never become fixed. The academicians have never got their dead hands on it. It is still fluid, still too various for easy classification, still putting out shoots in all directions. Nobody knows exactly what makes it tick and there is no one quality you can attribute to it that is not found to be missing in some successful example. It has produced more bad art than any type of fiction except the love story and probably more good art than any form which is so widely accepted and liked.

(6) Show me a man or woman who cannot stand mysteries and I will show you a fool, a clever fool—perhaps—but a fool just the same.

CHANDLER ON THE CRAFT
OF WRITING

Chandler on the Craft of Writing

May 5, 1939
To: Erle Stanley Gardner

. . . When we were talking about the old *Action Detective* magazine, I forgot to tell you that I learned to write a novelette on one of yours about a man named Rex Kane, who was an alter ego of Ed Jenkins and got mixed up with some flowery dame in a hilltop house in Hollywood who was running an anti-blackmail organization. You wouldn't remember. It's probably in your file No. 54276-84 . . .

I made an extremely detailed synopsis of your story and from that rewrote it and then compared what I had with yours, and then went back and rewrote it some more, and so on. In the end I was a bit sore because I couldn't try to sell it. It looked pretty good. Incidentally I found out that the trickiest part of your technique was the ability to put over situations which verged on the implausible but which in the reading seemed quite real. I hope you understand that I mean this as a compliment. I have never come even near to doing it myself. Dumas had this quality in a very strong degree. Also Dickens. It's probably the fundamental of all rapid work, because naturally rapid work has a large element of improvisation, and to make an improvised scene seem inevitable is quite a trick. At least I think so.

And here I am at 2.30 a.m. writing about technique, in spite of a strong conviction that the moment a man begins to talk about technique that's proof that he is fresh out of ideas.

Jan. 15, 1945
To: Charles W. Morton

. . . I do not write for you for money or for prestige, but for love, the strange lingering love of a world wherein men may think in cool subtleties and talk in the language of almost forgotten cultures. I like that world and I would on occasion sacrifice my sleep and my rest and quite a bit of money to enter it gracefully. Do you think I want money? And as for prestige, what is it? What greater prestige can a man like me (not too

greatly gifted, but very understanding) have than to have taken
a cheap, shoddy, and utterly lost kind of writing, and have made
of it something that intellectuals claw each other about?

Dec. 27, 1946
To: Mrs Robert J. Hogan[1]

... My experience with trying to help people to write has been
limited but extremely intensive. I have done everything from
giving would-be writers money to live on to plotting and re-
writing their stories for them, and so far I have found it to be
all waste. The people whom God or nature intended to be
writers find their own answers, and those who have to ask are impossible to help. They are merely people who want to be writers.

Jan. 5, 1947
To: Charles W. Morton

... Have just finished reading *Command Decision*.[2] I found it
absolutely (or almost) unputdownable and at the same time as
complete a waste of time in a sense as one of Gardner's Perry
Mason stories which I also find unputdownable. *B.F.'s Daughter*[3]
is the same, but has a little more penetration into character.
Books like this start me pondering without getting very far on
just what literature is turning into. What bothers me about this
book, *Command Decision*, and others like it is that it has everything in the way of skill and perception and wit and honesty a
good novel ought to have. It has a subject, something I never
had yet; it has a sharp immediate sense of life, as it is right now.
I'd be hard put to it to say just what it does *not* have, but that thing,
whatever it is, is more important than what it does have ...

Is it that these books are written very quickly, in a kind of
heat? No answer; so was a lot of literature that has lasted a long
time. The time of composition has nothing to do with it; some
minds distil much faster than others. Is it that the writers of

---

[1] Editor of a magazine for writers, Lake Mohawk, New Jersey.
[2] By William W. Haines.
[3] By J. P. Marquand (English title *Polly Fulton*).

these books are using completely borrowed techniques and consequently do not convey the feeling that they have created, but rather that they have reported? Close but still not quite the answer. Undoubtedly we are getting a lot of adept reportage which masquerades as fiction and will go on getting it, but essentially I believe that what is lacking is an emotional quality. Even when they deal with death, and they often do, they are not tragic. I suppose that is to be expected. An age which is incapable of poetry is incapable of any kind of literature except the cleverness of a decadence. The boys can say anything, their scenes are almost tiresomely neat, they have all the facts and all the answers, but they are little men who have forgotten how to pray. As the world grows smaller, so the minds of men grow smaller, more compact, and more empty. These are the machine-minders of literature.

March 7, 1947
To: Mrs Robert J. Hogan
    . . . One of my peculiarities and difficulties as a writer is that I won't discard anything. I can't overlook the fact that I had a reason, a feeling, for starting to write it, and I'll be damned if I won't lick it.
    Another of my oddities (and this one I believe in absolutely) is that you never quite know where your story is until you have written the first draft of it. So I always regard the first draft as raw material. What seems to be alive in it is what belongs in the story. A good story cannot be devised; it has to be distilled. In the long run, however little you talk or even think about it, the most durable thing in writing is style, and style is the most valuable investment a writer can make with his time. It pays off slowly, your agent will sneer at it, your publisher will misunderstand it, and it will take people you have never heard of to convince them by slow degrees that the writer who puts his individual mark on the way he writes will always pay off. He can't do it by trying, because the kind of style I am thinking about is a projection of personality and you have to have a personality before you can project it. But granted that you have one, you can only project it on paper by thinking of something else.

This is ironical in a way: it is the reason, I suppose, why in a generation of 'made' writers I still say you can't make a writer. Preoccupation with style will not produce it. No amount of editing and polishing will have any appreciable effect on the flavour of how a man writes. It is the product of the quality of his emotion and perception; it is the ability to transfer these to paper which makes him a writer . . .

Aug. 10, 1947
To: James Sandoe

The *Partisan Review* arrived. It is rather a good magazine of the sort. It has no Cyril Connolly or Orwell, and certainly it is far below the old *Dial* for which I had a rather exacerbated devotion during the early twenties. These clever-clever people are a useful catharsis to the more practical minded writer who, whether he be commercial or not, has usually lived long enough not to take any set of opinions too seriously.

As a very young man, when Shaw's beard was still red, I heard him lecture in London on Art for Art's Sake, which seems to have meant something then. It did not please Shaw of course; few things did unless he thought of them first. But art for propaganda's sake is even worse. And a critical magazine whose primary object is not to think intelligently but to think in such a form as to exploit a set of political ideas of whatever color always ends up by being critical only in the colloquial sense and intelligent only in the sense of a constant and rather labored effort to find different meanings for things than other people have found. So after a while these magazines all perish; they never achieve life, but only a distaste for other people's views of it. They have the intolerance of the very young and the anaemia of closed rooms and too much midnight smoking . . .

Oct. 28, 1947
To: Charles W. Morton

. . . I had an idea for some time back that I should like to do an article on *The Moral Status of the Writer*. It seems to me that in all this yapping about writers selling themselves to Hollywood or some transient propaganda idea instead of writing sincerely from the heart about what they see around them, the people making these complaints overlook the point that no writer ever in any age got a blank check. He always had to accept some conditions imposed from without, respect certain taboos, try to please certain people. It might have been the Church, or a rich patron, or a generally accepted standard of elegance, or the commercial wisdom of a publisher or editor, or perhaps even a set of political theories. If he did not accept them, he revolted against them. In either case they conditioned his writing . . . Oh, the hell with it. Ideas are poison. The more you reason the less you create.

Jan. 18, 1948
To: Edward Weeks[1]

. . . Would you convey my compliments to the purist who reads your proofs and tell him or her that I write in a sort of broken-down patois which is something like the way a Swiss waiter talks, and that when I split an infinitive, God damn it, I split it so it will stay split, and when I interrupt the velvety smoothness of my more or less literate syntax with a few sudden words of bar-room vernacular, that is done with the eyes wide open and the mind relaxed but attentive. The method may not be perfect, but it is all I have. I think your proof-reader is kindly attempting to steady me on my feet, but much as I appreciate the solicitude, I am really able to steer a fairly clear course, provided I get both sidewalks and the street between.

May 7, 1948
To: Frederick Lewis Allen[2]

. . . It would be invidious for me to remark (even if I knew what I was talking about) that Eric Bentley is probably the best dramatic critic in the U.S. . . . The rest of the boys are just think-piece writers whose subject happens to be plays. They are interested in exploiting their own personal brand of verbal glitter.

[1] Editor, *The Atlantic Monthly*.
[2] Then Editor, *Harper's Magazine*.

They are witty and readable and sometimes cute, but they tell you next to nothing about the dramatic art and the relationship of the play in question to that art.

It is not enough for a critic to be right, since he will occasionally be wrong. It is not enough for him to give colorable reasons. He must create a reasonable world into which his reader may enter blindfold and feel his way to the chair by the fire without barking his shins on the unexpected dust mop. The barbed phrase, the sedulously rare word, the highbrow affectation of style—these are amusing but useless. They place nothing and reveal not the temper of the times. The great critics, of whom there are piteously few, build a home for the truth.

It is wrong to be harsh with the New York critics, unless one admits in the same breath that it is a condition of their existence that they should write entertainingly about something which is rarely worth writing about at all. This leads or forces them to develop a technique of pseudo-subtlety and abstruseness which permits them to deal with trivial things as though they were momentous. This is the basis of all successful advertising copy writing. Criticism is impossible in a world where the important thing is not to be right, but to write a column about a play—any damn play at all—which column, however insignificant the ostensible subject, never lets down on the significance of the references to the subject . . . Good critical writing is measured by the perception and evaluation of the subject; bad critical writing by the necessity of maintaining the professional standing of the critic.

Dec. 6, 1948
To: Lenore Glen Offord[1]

. . . Writers as a class I have found to be oversensitive and spiritually under-nourished. I hate that little glint back of the eye which waits for the praise of the last book or story. Some of my friends (which doesn't mean much, I have so few) are to me unreadable. I do not talk about their books to them. I do not read their bloody books. I see no earthly reason why they should have written them. This makes social intercourse rather edgy. And that's one thing I like about Hollywood. The writer is there

[1] Mystery novel critic of *San Francisco Chronicle*.

A dinner of *Black Mask* writers in the late
twenties or early thirties — the only time
Chandler (second from left, standing) met
Dashiell Hammett (extreme right, standing).

revealed in his ultimate corruption. He asks no praise, because his praise comes to him in the form of a salary check. In Hollywood the average writer is not young, not honest, not brave, and a bit overdressed. But he is darn good company, which book writers as a rule are not. He is better than what he writes. Most book writers are not as good.

March 18, 1949
To: Alex Barris

. . . What do I do with myself from day to day? I write when I can and I don't write when I can't; always in the morning or the early part of the day. You get very gaudy ideas at night but they don't stand up. I found this out long ago. It ought to be pretty obvious to you that I do my own typing. When we came down here to live I got a dictaphone outfit and dictated script into that, but I never use it for fiction. Almost all dictating writers suffer from logorrhea. When you have to use your energy to put those words down, you are more apt to make them count.

I'm always seeing little pieces by writers about how they don't ever wait for inspiration; they just sit down at their little desks every morning at eight, rain or shine, hangover and broken arm and all, and bang out their little stint. However blank their minds or dull their wits, no nonsense about inspiration from them. I offer them my admiration and take care to avoid their books.

Me, I wait for inspiration, although I don't necessarily call it by that name. I believe that all writing that has any life in it is done with the solar plexus. It is hard work in the sense that it may leave you tired, even exhausted. In the sense of conscious effort it is not work at all. The important thing is that there should be a space of time, say four hours a day at least, when a professional writer doesn't do anything else but write. He doesn't have to write, and if he doesn't feel like it he shouldn't try. He can look out of the window or stand on his head or writhe on the floor, but he is not to do any other positive thing, not read, write letters, glance at magazines, or write checks. Either write or nothing. It's the same principle as keeping order in a school. If you make the pupils behave, they will learn something just to keep from being bored. I find it works. Two very simple rules. A. You don't have to write. B. You can't do anything else. The rest comes of itself.

I had to learn American just like a foreign language. To learn it I had to study and analyze it. As a result, when I use slang, colloquialisms, snide talk or any kind of off-beat language I do it deliberately. The literary use of slang is a study in itself. I've found that there are only two kinds that are any good: slang that has established itself in the language, and slang that you make up yourself. Everything else is apt to be passé before it gets into print . . .

FROM CHANDLER'S WORKING NOTEBOOK

Notes on English and American Style

The merits of American style are less numerous than its defects and annoyances, but they are more powerful.

It is a fluid language, like Shakespearian English, and easily takes in new words, new meanings for old words, and borrows at will and at ease from the usages of other languages, for example, the German free compounding of words and the use of noun or adjective as verb. Its overtones and undertones are not stylized into a social conventional kind of subtlety which is in effect a class language.

It is more alive to clichés. Its impact is emotional and sensational rather than intellectual. It expresses things experienced rather than ideas.

It is a mass language only in the same sense that its baseball slang is born of baseball players. That is, it is a language which is being moulded by writers to do delicate things and yet be within the grasp of superficially educated people. It is not a natural growth, much as its proletarian writers would like to think so. But compared with it at its best English has reached the Alexandrian stage of formalism and decay.

It has disadvantages
It overworks its catchphrases until they become not merely

meaningless playtalk, like English catchphrases, but sickening, like overworked popular songs.

Its slang, at its best superb, is invented by writers and palmed off on simple hoodlums and ballplayers and often has a phoney sound, even when fresh.

The language has no awareness of the continuing stream of culture. This may or may not be due to the collapse of classical education and it may or may not happen also in English. It is certainly due to a lack of the historical sense and to shoddy education, because American is an ill-at-ease language, without manner or self-control.

It has too great a fondness for the *faux naif*, by which I mean the use of a style such as might be spoken by a very limited sort of mind. In the hands of a genius like Hemingway this may be effective ... When not used by a genius it is as flat as a Rotarian speech.

The last-noted item is very probably the result of the submerged but still very homespun revolt against English cultural superiority. 'We're just as good as they are, even if we don't talk grammar.' This attitude is based on complete ignorance of the English people as a mass. Very few of them talk good grammar. Those that do probably speak more correctly than the same type of American, but the homespun Englishman uses as much bad grammar as the American, some of it being as old as Piers Plowman, but still bad grammar. But you don't hear English professional men making elementary mistakes in the use of their own language. You do hear that constantly in America ...

Since political power still dominates culture, American will dominate English for a long time to come. And American cannot as yet vitalize itself—it just isn't good enough. America is a land of mass production which has only just reached the concept of quality. Why then can it produce great writing, or at any rate writing as great as this age is likely to produce? The answer is, all the best American writing has been done by men who are, or at some time were, cosmopolitans. They found here a certain freedom of expression, a certain richness of vocabulary, a certain wideness of interest. But they had to have European taste to use the material.

Final note—out of order. The tone quality of English speech is usually overlooked. This is infinitely variable. The American voice is flat, toneless and tiresome. The English tone quality makes a thinner vocabulary and a more formalized use of language capable of infinite meanings. Its tones are of course read into written speech by association. This makes good English a class language and that is its fatal defect. The English writer is a gentleman first and a writer second.

Apr. 22, 1949

To: Hamish Hamilton

. . . Connolly's account of the silken barbarity of Eton[1] is wonderful, of course, and the way these fellows thought and wrote and talked, at an age when Americans can hardly spell their own names, is also most impressive. Nevertheless, there is something about the literary life that repels me, all this desperate building of castles on cobwebs, the long-drawn acrimonious struggle to make something important which we all know will be gone forever in a few years, the miasma of failure which is to me almost as offensive as the cheap gaudiness of popular success.

I believe the really good people would be reasonably successful in any circumstance; that to be very poor and very beautiful is most probably a moral failure much more than an artistic success. Shakespeare would have done well in any generation because he would have refused to die in a corner; he would have taken the false gods and made them over; he would have taken the current formulae and forced them into something lesser men thought them incapable of. Alive today he would undoubtedly have written and directed motion pictures, plays and God knows what. Instead of saying 'This medium is not good', he would have used it and made it good. If some people called some of his work cheap (which some of it is), he wouldn't have cared a rap, because he would know that without some vulgarity there is no complete man. He would have hated refinement, as such, because it is always a withdrawal, a shrinking, and he was much too tough to shrink from anything.

[1] *Enemies of Promise.*

May 2, 1949
To: Charles W. Morton

... I've always enjoyed reading Marquand and have always felt while doing so that he came as close to being an artist as any writer could who wasn't one. But somehow his successful, oh-so-successful souffles always make me think of little lost books like *Gatsby*[1] and *Miss Lonelyhearts*[2]—books which are not perfect, evasive of the problem often, side-stepping scenes which should have been written (and which Marquand would have written at twice the necessary length) but somehow passing along, crystallized, complete, and as such things go nowadays eternal, a little pure art—great art or not I wouldn't know, but there is such a strange difference between the real stuff and a whole shelf full of Pulhams and Forsytes and Charlie Grays.

Not that I class myself with any of these people. I really don't class myself at all, nor greatly care about it. I'm still an amateur, still, psychologically speaking, perfectly capable of chucking writing altogether and taking up the study of law or comparative philology. The writer faces a peculiar moral problem in these days (probably always faced it in some form). In an age which really has only one yardstick, money, he is supposed, if he is any good, to make a vow of poverty. If he makes any money he is automatically a corruptionist.

July 22, 1949
To: Carl Brandt[3]

... If I were to write what is called a straight novel, it might or might not be a success, but it would not succeed on the strength of anything I had written before. But this dilemma has always existed. The intelligent part of a writer's public wants a change of pace, they want him to try new themes and new places, but the public that buys a book in quantity wants the same standard brand of merchandise they have been getting. It has seemed to

---

[1] *The Great Gatsby* by F. Scott Fitzgerald.
[2] By Nathanael West.
[3] Chandler's literary agent in New York.

me for a long time now that in straight novels the public is more and more drawn to the theme, the idea, the line of thought, the sociological or political attitude, and less and less to the quality of the writing as writing. For instance, if you were to consider Orwell's *1984* purely as a piece of fiction you could not rate it very high. It has no magic, the scenes are only passably well handled, the characters have very little personality; in short it is no better written, artistically speaking, than a good solid English detective story. But the political thought is something else again and where he writes as a critic and interpreter of ideas rather than of people or emotions he is wonderful.

Dec. 4, 1949
To: Hamish Hamilton

    . . . Of course Maugham is right, as he always is. It is more *difficult* to write plays, harder work, I have no doubt, although I have never tried to write one . . . But it does *not*, in my opinion, take the same quality of talent. It may take a more exacting use of the talent, a more beautiful job of cabinet work, a fine or more apt ear for the current jargon of a certain kind of people, but it is much more superficial all round. Take any good, but not great, play and put it in fiction form and you have a very slight matter. No richness, no vistas, no overtones, no feeling of the country beyond the hill. It is all clear and literal and immediate. The novelist, if he is any good, gives you a thousand things that he never actually says.

    Incidentally, if I knew Maugham, which I fear I never shall, I should ask him for an inscribed copy of *Ashenden.* I've never asked a writer for an inscribed copy and as a matter of fact I attach very little value to such things. (I wouldn't mind having the prompt copy of *Hamlet.*) And I suppose it declares my own limitations of taste to pick *Ashenden.* But I'm a bit of a connoisseur of melodramatic effects, and *Ashenden* is far ahead of any other spy story ever written . . . A classic in any manner appeals to me more than the large canvas. *Carmen* as Mérimée wrote it, *Hérodias, Un Coeur Simple, The Captain's Doll, The Spoils of Poynton, Madame Bovary, The Wings of a Dove* and so forth and so on (*A Christmas Holiday*, by God, too)[1] these are all perfect. Long or short, violent or still, they do something that never will be done as well again. The list, thank God, is long and in many languages . . .

Dec. 28, 1949

To: James Sandoe

Thanks very much for *The 39 Steps* . . . I liked the dedication in which Buchan said 'the romance where the incidents defy the probabilities, and march just inside the borders of the possible'. That's a pretty good formula for the thriller of any kind . . .

I liked *Tunnel from Calais*[2] very much. It's not much as a spy story but there's a lot of vivid writing in it and that feeling you so often get in English books and so seldom in ours that the country with all its small details is a part of their lives and that they love it. We are so rootless here. I've lived half my life in California and made what use of it I could, but I could leave it forever without a pang.

The spy story strikes me as a field which needs cultivating. The level of performance is not high. The mystery and 'tec are on the wane and the science fiction is a flash in the pan, I believe. The genuine novel of suspense is always solid if you can find one. But here in the spy story is a formula which has hardly been scratched. What I complain of in most of these yarns is that they simply do not succeed in creating or using any scary motivation. *Ashenden* and to some lesser extent *Handbook for Spies*[3] read as though there were always something vague and sinister just behind the curtain. In most of the others you are just afraid of the man with the gun.

[1] *Hérodias*, and *Un Coeur Simple*, contained in *Trois Contes* (Gustave Flaubert); *The Captain's Doll* (D. H. Lawrence); *The Spoils of Poynton* (Henry James); *Madame Bovary* (Gustave Flaubert); *The Wings of a Dove* (Henry James); *A Christmas Holiday* (W. Somerset Maugham).
[2] By A. D. Divine.
[3] By Alexander Foote.

Jan. 5, 1950

To : Hamish Hamilton

Ashenden with very handsome dedication received safely . . .
Of course I'll write to the old boy . . . I have a feeling that fundamentally he is a pretty sad man, pretty lonely. His description of
his seventieth birthday is pretty grim. I should guess that all in
all he has had a lonely life, that his declared attitude of not
caring much emotionally about people is a defence mechanism,
that he lacks the kind of surface warmth that attracts people and
at the same time is such a wise man that he knows that however
superficial and accidental most friendships are, life is a pretty
gloomy affair without them . . . I get my feeling from his writing
and that is all. In a conventional sense he probably has many
friends. But I don't think they build much of a fire against the
darkness for him. He's a lonely old eagle.

I don't suppose any writer was ever more completely the professional. He has an accurate and fearless appraisal of his own
gifts, the greatest of which is not literary at all, but is rather that
neat and inexorable perception of character and motive which
belongs to the great judge or the great diplomat . . . He can convey the setting for emotion but very little the emotion itself. His
plots are cool and deadly and his timing is absolutely flawless.
. . . He never makes you catch your breath or lose your head,
because he never loses his. I doubt that he ever wrote a line
which seemed fresh from creation, and many lesser writers have.
But he will outlast them all with ease, because he is without folly
or silliness. He would have made a great Roman.

May 26, 1950

To : Dale Warren

. . . When I open a book and see writing like 'her appearance
was indeed shocking', 'I felt the first stab of remorse', 'rich full-
blooded beauty' etc. I get the impression that I am reading a
dead language . . . As a matter of fact this book, being an
English South African novel, is rather an interesting specimen.
It demonstrates how the Colonial always speaks the cultural
language of his grandmother and explains, to me at any rate,

why no intelligent introvert could possibly live in a British colony without going crazy.

I have to thank you for DeVoto's last book, *The World of Fiction*. This I did read, every word of it, and enjoyed it very much. This is vintage DeVoto, vivid, courageous, uncompromising, thoroughly readable, and almost completely superficial. It says nearly nothing (not *quite* nothing) that stays with you forty-eight hours after you have closed the book, and yet every moment of your actual reading holds your attention. What I like about DeVoto is that he doesn't give a damn for anyone and doesn't hesitate to say so. What I don't like about him, what makes him a bit superficial to me, is that all his attitudes arise from resentments. His ideas about the art of fiction probably would not exist if someone else had not first had ideas which DeVoto didn't like.

May 18, 1950
To: Hamish Hamilton

I have to thank you for Eric Partridge's *Here There and Everywhere*. Partridge is interesting but makes me uneasy. These scholars of the vernacular, cant, slang, etc. cover an awful lot of ground and one wonders how accurately they do it, if one happens to have any special knowledge of a small part of their field and find their report on that shading a little off the exact. Take 'chiv'. This does not mean a razor. Chiv, or more commonly shiv, means a knife, a stabbing or cutting weapon, perhaps (but I don't think so) including a razor, but that is not the meaning. 'Flop' means to go to bed and perhaps includes the idea of sleep, but doesn't mean sleep. Flophouse is a cheap transient hotel where a lot of men sleep in large rooms. I also question the translation of 'gay-cat' as 'look-out man or finder'. A gaycat is a young punk who runs with an older tramp and there is always a connotation of homosexuality. Again, he could be a 'look-out' (outside man) or a 'finder' (finger or finger man), but that is a derived or occasional meaning and not exact. 'Piped' does not mean 'found' but saw or spotted (with the eyes). Flivvers are not 'cheap cars'; they are Fords and only Fords, at least in my part of the country. Of course when this piece was written, 1926, there were no other cars as cheap. The nearest was a Chevrolet, always 'chevvy'. (A couple of flivvers and a chevvy.) Page 107, 1.18, 'case dough'. This means the same as nest egg really, not money for a trial which would be only one of many, many uses. It is the theoretically untouchable reserve for emergencies—that and nothing more. ('I'm down to case dough' means 'I've spent all my spare money and have nothing left but a get-away stake', etc.)

In his analysis of 'queer' Partridge is no doubt historically correct and all that, but it has only two meanings in modern American slang: counterfeit and sexually abnormal. He uses or quotes 'beak' several times as meaning judge. In England, yes, but not in America . . . Also, Walla Walla is *not* a penitentiary for women. It is the Washington state penitentiary, just like Sing Sing or San Quentin . . . And doesn't he overlook some of the most commonly used words of soldier-slang? E.g. 'bomb-proofer', 'cushy job', 'bivvy', and above all 'napoo', 'strafe', long a, for bombardment (the morning strafe), 'street cars' or 'tram cars' for heavy long range shells, 'whizzbangs' for rapid small shells, and the inimitable American 'goldbrick' which is as superior to English 'lead-swinger' as 'milk run' (from the last war) is to 'piece of cake'.

What always gets me about these scholarly excursions into the language of the underworld, so to speak, is how they smell of the dictionary. The so-called experts in this line have their ear to the library, very seldom to the ground. They do not realize what a large proportion of these cant terms (using cant a bit too broadly) is of literary origin, how many of them crooks and cops use *after* writers have invented them. It is very difficult for the literary man to distinguish between a genuine crook term and an invented one. How do you tell a man to go away in hard language? Scram, beat it, take off, take the air, on your way, dangle, hit the road, and so forth. All good enough. But give me the classic expression actually used by Spike O'Donnell (of the O'Donnell brothers of Chicago, the only small outfit to tell the Capone mob to go to hell and live). What he said was: 'Be missing.' The restraint of it is deadly.

Throughout his play *The Iceman Cometh*, O'Neill used 'the big sleep' as a synonym for death. He used it, so far as one can judge from the context, as a matter of course, apparently in the belief that it was an accepted underworld expression. If so, I'd like to see whence it comes, because I invented the expression. It is quite possible that I reinvented it, but I never saw it in print before I used it, and until I get the evidence I shall continue to believe that O'Neill took it from me, directly or indirectly, and thought I was using a standard term.

Those who investigate cant, underworld or sports jargon etc. at the source are always surprised by how little of the picturesque lingo is used by the very people who are supposed to use nothing else . . . Some invented slang, not all, becomes current among the people it is invented for. If you are sensitive to this sort of thing, I believe you could often, not always, distinguish between the colored-up lingo that writers produce, and the hard simplicity of the terms that originate in the circle where they are actually used. I don't think any writer could think up an expression like 'mainliner' for a narcotic addict who shoots the stuff into a vein. It's too exact, too *pure*.

My apologies to Mr Partridge, but if he enters the field he must expect to get mixed up with people like me. And for a parting shot, 'yegg' is not a 'tough itinerant bank robber' at all. A yegg is a safe-cracker, a box man. He wouldn't go near a bank, because he couldn't open a bank safe, even if it didn't have a time lock. He could only open a rather cheap and vulnerable safe. Opening a good safe (without a time lock) requires expensive and heavy tools, the finest drills either to drill out the lock or to get in the nitro if he is a peterman, a tremendously powerful jemmy if he is a can-opener (only works on poor safes), but used *after* drilling to prise out the lock on good safes sometimes, or gas tanks and torches, if he is going to cut the steel with acetylene, which is a very slow job on high grade steel. The most this yegg would have would be a sledge hammer and a few cold chisels, with which he might open the safe in a country grocery store.

Oct. 9, 1950
To: Charles W. Morton
Quite a lapse in our once interesting correspondence, don't you think. You are most correct in saying that I owe you a letter. For quite a long time I have owed practically everybody

a letter. Why? Apparently it is what the years do to you. The horse which once had to be driven with a tight rein now has to be flicked with a whip in order to make him do much more than amble . . . As your energies shrink, you become rather niggardly in spending them. Normally a man should do his day's work, whatever it is, and then write a couple of letters to keep in touch with people he likes and doesn't see in person. But I find that when I have done what passes for a day's work, I am sucked dry . . .

My compliments to Mr Weeks on belonging to that very small minority of critics who did not find it necessary to put Hemingway in his place over his last book.[1] I have been reading the book. Candidly, it's not the best thing he's done, but it's still a hell of a sight better than anything his detractors could do . . . You would think some of them might have asked themselves just what he was trying to do. Obviously he was not trying to write a masterpiece; but in a character, not too unlike his own, trying to sum up the attitude of a man who is finished and knows it, and is bitter and angry about it. Apparently he had been very sick and he was not sure that he was going to get well, and he put down on paper in a rather cursory way how that made him feel to the things in life he had most valued. I suppose these primping second-guessers who call themselves critics think he shouldn't have written the book at all. Most men wouldn't have. Feeling the way that he felt, they wouldn't have had the guts to write anything. I'm damn sure I wouldn't. That's the difference between a champ and a knife thrower. The champ may have lost his stuff temporarily or permanently, he can't be sure. But when he can no longer throw the high hard one, he throws his heart instead. He throws something. He doesn't just walk off the mound and weep.

Late 1950
To: Carl Brandt

. . . From now on I am going to write what I want to write as I want to write it. Some of it may flop. There are always going to be people who will say I have lost the pace I had once, that

[1] *Across the River and into the Trees.*

I take too long to say things now, and don't care enough about tight active plots. But I am not writing for those people now. I am writing for the people who understand about writing as an art and are able to separate what a man does with words and ideas from what he thinks about Truman or the United Nations . . .

Feb. 5, 1951
To: Hamish Hamilton
     . . . I am not much interested in stories about Martians or 3000 A.D. I have the sort of feeling about fantastic stories that H. G. Wells had: you inject a miracle into a perfectly ordinary setting and then watch the consequences, which are usually bad. The trouble with fantastic fiction as a general rule is the same trouble that afflicts Hungarian playwrights—no third act. The idea and the situation resulting from the idea are fine; but what happens then? How do you turn the corner? . . . If a man should wake up in the morning and find that he was nine inches high, I wouldn't be interested in how he got that way but in what he was going to do about it . . .

July 2, 1951
To: H. R. Harwood[1]
     I could not advise any man either to become a writer or not to become one. Contrary to popular belief, it is a very arduous profession and only a small fraction of those who attempt it ever succeed in making any kind of a decent income. The decline of the pulp magazine makes it more difficult for beginners even than it used to be, and it was never anything but difficult. I gather, however, that your special circumstances are such that this writing trade is physically within your means, and I am hoping that you do not have to make a living out of writing for at least a long time to come, since the chances that you will are very, very slight.
     You say you are arranging 'for immediate schooling in the fundamental principles of the narrative technique that any

     [1] O'Reilly Veterans' Hospital, Springfield, Missouri.

beginner should have'. Let me warn you out of such experience as
I have that any writer who cannot teach himself cannot be taught
by others, and apart from the extension courses of reputable
universities I take a very dim view of writing instruction in
general, above all the sort that is advertised in the so-called
writers' magazines. They will teach you nothing that you cannot
find out by studying and analyzing the published work of other
writers. Analyze and imitate; no other school is necessary. I
admit that criticism from others is helpful and sometimes even
necessary but when you have to pay for it, it is usually suspect.

As to methods of plotting and plot outlines, I am afraid I cannot help you at all, since I have never plotted anything on paper.
I do my plotting in my head as I go along, and usually I do it
wrong and have to do it all over again. I know there are writers
who plot their stories in great detail before they begin to write
them, but I am not one of that group. With me plots are not
made; they grow. And if they refuse to grow, you throw the
stuff away and start over again. Perhaps you will get more helpful advice from one who works from a blueprint. I hope so.

Sept. 19, 1951
To: Hamish Hamilton
     . . . A writer who hates the actual writing is as impossible as a
lawyer who hates the law or a doctor who hates medicine. Plotting may be a bore even if you are good at it. At least it is something that has to be done so that you can get on with the real
business. But a writer who hates the actual writing, who gets no
joy out of the creation of magic by words, to me is simply not a
writer at all.

The actual writing is what you live for. The rest is something
you have to get through in order to arrive at the point. How can
you hate the actual writing? What is there to hate about it? You
might as well say that a man likes to chop wood or clean house
and hates the sunshine or the night breeze or the nodding of
flowers or the dew on the grass and the song of birds. How can
you hate the magic which makes a paragraph or a sentence or a
line of dialogue or a description something in the nature of a
new creation?

April, 1954
To: The Editor, *The Third Degree*[1]
   As a writer of twenty years professional experience I have met all kinds of people. Those who know most about writing are those who can't write. The less attention you pay to them the better. They are on the outside looking in and what they see is no good to the man inside; it is in a different category of mind. So I have made three rules of writing for myself that are absolutes: Never take advice. Never show or discuss work in progress. Never answer a critic.

Sept. 22, 1954
To: Hamish Hamilton
   . . . As to writing my memoirs, Jamie, and you are not the only one who has suggested it to me nor is this the first time you have suggested it, I can only say that I don't think I could face it. It seems to me there are people who can write their memoirs with a reasonable amount of honesty, and there are people who simply cannot take themselves seriously enough. I think I might be the first to admit that the sort of reticence which prevents a man from exploiting his own personality is really an inverted sort of egotism.
   . . . If you want to know what I should really like to write, it would be fantastic stories, and I don't mean science fiction. But they wouldn't make a thin worn dime. That would be just a wonderful way to become a Neglected Author. God, what a fascinating document could be put together about these same Neglected Authors and also the one-book writers: fellows like Edward Anderson who long ago wrote a book called *Thieves Like Us*, one of the best crook stories ever written . . . Then there was James Ross who wrote a novel called *They Don't Dance Much*, a sleazy, corrupt but completely believable story of a North Carolina town. I've never heard that he wrote anything else . . . And there was Aaron Klopstein. Who ever heard of him? He committed suicide at the age of 33 in Greenwich Village by shooting himself with an Amazonian blow gun, having published two novels entitled *Once More the Cicatrice* and *The Sea*

[1] Magazine of the Mystery Writers of America Inc.

Gull Has No Friends, two volumes of poetry, one book of short stories and a book of critical essays entitled *Shakespeare in Baby Talk*.

Feb. 27, 1957
To: Edward Weeks

Herewith I am sending you three poems or verses[1] or whatever they are, not in any great hope of your wanting to publish them, but because my secretary insists. I never thought of myself seriously as a poet. A long time ago in London I did write a good deal of verse that was published in various magazines, but I haven't even kept any of it. Which shows, I hope, that I have in these things a certain modesty.

You must know very well that writers do all sorts of things— at least I do—which are not intended to make money, but to satisfy one's realization that one exists on several levels of thought. Also I have been trying to learn the English language which is superficially like ours but very, very different in its implications. Ours, when not too professional, is creative, imaginative, free and even rather wild. Something like the English of Elizabeth's time. English is almost a mandarin language, but it is beginning to loosen up and I think I might possibly do something with it, since I am beginning to feel that I have done about all I can do with the mystery story. A writer gets awfully tired of his tricks, or I hope he does—certainly I do . . .

May 25, 1957
To: Helga Greene

. . . To accept a mediocre form and make something like literature out of it is in itself rather an accomplishment. They tell me—I don't say this on my own information—that hundreds of writers today are making some sort of living from the mystery story because I made it respectable and even dignified. But, hell, what else can you do when you write? You do the best you can

[1] One of these, *Requiem*, was accepted by *The Atlantic Monthly* but never published.

in any medium. I was lucky, and it seems that my luck inspired others. Steinbeck and I agreed that we should like the writer who is to be remembered and honoured after we were gone to be some unknown, perhaps far better than either of us, who did not have the luck—or perhaps the drive. Any decent writer who thinks of himself occasionally as an artist would far rather be forgotten so that someone better might be remembered. We are not always nice people, but essentially we have an ideal that transcends ourselves . . . There are, of course, cheap and venal writers, but a real writer always at the bottom of his heart, when he runs across something good, makes a silent prayer that 'this guy may be better than I am'. Any man who can write a page of living prose adds something to our life, and the man who can, as I can, is surely the last to resent someone who can do it even better. An artist cannot deny art, nor would he want to. A lover cannot deny love. If you believe in an ideal, you don't own it— it owns you, and you certainly don't want to freeze it at your own level for mercenary reasons.

A COUPLE OF WRITERS

Feb. 3, 1951

To: Carl Brandt

Herewith a story, *A Couple of Writers*, with which I amused myself quite a lot although realizing it had no commercial value whatever—to our mutual regret, no doubt. Reading it over last night I thought it was a pretty fancy piece of writing all the same. So there . . .

A Couple of Writers

No matter how drunk he had been the night before Hank Bruton always got up very early and walked around the house in his bare feet, waiting for the coffee to brew. He would shut the door of Marion's room, extending a finger against the closing edge to brake it as it met the frame, and releasing the knob with great delicacy so as not to make a sound. It seemed rather strange to him that he was able to do this and that his hands were perfectly steady when the muscles of his legs and thighs twitched so badly, and he kept grinding his teeth, and he had that nasty feeling at the pit of his stomach. It seemed never to affect his hands at all, an idiosyncrasy which was curious and convenient, and after that the hell with it.

While the coffee was brewing and the house silent and no sound outside among the trees except occasionally the call of some distant bird and the still more distant sound of the river, he would go and stand by the screen door and look out at Phoebus, the big red tomcat sitting on the porch watching the door. Phoebus knew it wasn't time to eat and that Hank would not let him in, and he probably knew why: if he got in he would start yelling, and he could yell like a train conductor and Marion's morning sleep would be ruined. Not that Hank Bruton gave a damn about her morning sleep. He just liked the early morning to himself, quiet, no voices—especially not Marion's voice.

He looked down at the cat and Phoebus yawned and let out a sour note, not too loud, just enough to show nobody was fooling him.

'Shut up,' Henry said.

Phoebus sat down and stuck one hind leg high in the air and went about cleaning his fur. In the middle of this he paused with his leg straight up and stared at Hank in a deliberately insulting manner.

'Old stuff,' Hank said. 'Cats have been doing that for ten thousand years.'

Just the same it was effective. Maybe you had to be absolutely shameless to be a good comedian. That was a thought. Maybe he ought to make a note of it. No use. Somebody else would already have done that if Hank Bruton thought of it. He took the Cory off the asbestos mat and waited for it to sizzle. Then he poured a cup and added a little cold water and drank it down. He put cream and sugar in the next cup and sipped it slowly. The nervous feeling in his stomach got better, but his leg muscles were still giving him hell.

He turned the flame under the asbestos mat very low and put the coffee pot back on it. He left the house by the front door and walked barefoot down off the wooden porch and stepped sideways on to the dew-wet grass. It was an old house of no distinction but it had a lot of grass around it which needed cutting and a lot of not very large pine trees around that, except on the side that sloped down to the river. Not much of a house and the hell and gone from everywhere but for thirty-five dollars a month it was a find. They better hang on to it. If they were ever going to get anywhere it had better be here.

Over the tops of the pines he could see the half circle of low hills with a mist halfway up their slopes. The sun would soon take care of that. The air was cold but it was a mild kind of cold, not penetrating. It was a good enough place to live, Hank thought. Plenty good enough for a couple of would-be writers who, as far as talent was concerned, were strictly from hunger. A man ought to be able to live there without getting drunk every night. Probably a man could. But probably a man wouldn't be there in the first place. On the way down to the river he tried to remember what had happened last night that was unusual. He couldn't, but he had a vague sort of feeling that there had been some sort of crisis. Probably he might have said something about Marion's second act, but he couldn't remember what it was. It would not have been complimentary. But what was the use of being dishonest about her damn play? Tinkering with it didn't make it any better. Telling her it was good when it wasn't didn't move her ahead one square. Writers have to look themselves straight in the eye and if what they see there is nothing, that is the word you use.

He stopped and rubbed the pit of his stomach. He could see the steel grey water between the trees now and he loved to see it that way. He shivered a little knowing how cold it was going to be and also knowing that was what he liked about it. It murdered you for a few seconds but it didn't kill you, and afterwards you felt wonderful, although not for long enough.

He reached the bank and put down the towel and pair of sneakers he was carrying and stripped his shirt off. It was lonely down there. The small sound the water made was the loneliest sound in his world. As always, he wished he had a dog to frisk around his legs and yap and go in swimming with him, but you couldn't have a dog with Phoebus, who was too old and too tough to tolerate a dog. Either he would clean up on the dog or the dog would catch him off balance and break his back. Anyhow it would take an unusual kind of dog to go into that icy water. Hank would have to throw him in. And the dog would be scared and get in trouble with the current and Hank would have to pull him out. There were times when it was all he could do to get out himself.

He took his pants off and hit the water flat, pointed upstream. A furious giant hand took hold of his chest and squeezed the air out of him. Another giant hand dragged his legs the wrong way and he was swimming downstream instead of up with no breath and trying to yell but not able to make a sound. He threshed furiously and got turned around and after a moment he was breaking even with the current and then by putting all he had into the swimming, he was gaining a little. He reached the bank, although he couldn't quite make the spot from which he had gone in. He hadn't for a year now. That would be the whiskey. Well, it wasn't too great a price to pay. And if some morning he didn't make it at all but got sucked under and knocked out against a stone and drowned——

'Look,' he said out loud still panting a little, 'we don't start the day like this. We positively don't.'

He walked carefully along the rough bank and got his towel

and rubbed his skin violently and it began to feel warm and rested and lax. The worms in the muscles were gone. The solar plexus was as calm as a custard.

He put his clothes on and the sneakers and started back up the hill. On the way he began to whistle a theme from some symphonic movement. Then he tried to remember which it was and when he remembered he thought about the composer, the kind of life he had, the struggles, the misery, and now he was dead and rotten, like so many men Hank Bruton had known in the army.

Just like a lousy writer, he thought. Never the thing itself, always the cheap emotion that goes with it.

2

Phoebus was still out on the back porch, but he was yelling his head off now, and that meant that Marion was up. She was in the kitchen, dressed in street clothes with a tan colored smock over them.

Hank said: 'Why didn't you wait until I got back? I'd have brought your coffee up to you.'

She didn't answer him directly or look at him directly. She looked off in one corner as if she saw a cobweb there. 'Have a good swim?' she asked absently.

'Perfect. But she's sure a cold little old river.'

'Fine,' Marion said. 'Wonderful. Perfect. Amazing recovery. Even if after awhile it gets pretty damn monotonous. Feed the damn cat, will you?'

'Well, for Pete's sake,' Hank said. 'How did poor old Phoebus get to be a damn cat? I thought he was top man around here. On account of he doesn't get soused.'

' "He said with a winning smile," ' Marion sneered.

Hank looked at her thoughtfully. She had short black hair that lay close to her head. Her blue eyes were a much darker blue than Hank's. She had a small neat mouth which he had called provocative before he came to think of it as petulant. She was a very trim, very well-built girl, rather on the fragile side. The fragility of a mountain goat, Hank thought. 'I'm the Dorothy Parker type—without the wit,' she had told Hank when they first met. He had thought that rather charming. Neither of them quite realized it was true.

Hank opened the screen door and Phoebus came in tearing the atmosphere to shreds with his jungle howls. Hank opened a can of cat food and heaped a saucer and put it down in front of the sink. Without a word Marion set her coffee cup down and took the saucer and removed half of the cat food. She opened the screen door and put the saucer down outside. Phoebus hit the saucer as though he were a forty yard forward pass. Marion let the screen door bang shut.

'Okay,' Hank said. 'I'll remember next time.'

'You can feed him anyway you like next time,' Marion said. 'I won't be here.'

'I see,' Hank said slowly. 'Was I that bad?'

'No worse than usual,' she answered. 'And thanks for not saying "again". The last time I left——' she broke off and her voice caught a little. Hank started to move towards her, but she straightened up at once. 'You can fix yourself some breakfast. I have to finish packing. I did most of it in the night.'

'We ought to talk about this,' Hank said quietly.

She turned in the doorway. 'Oh sure.' Her voice was as hard as a boot heel now. 'We can spend a fascinating ten minutes at that, if you hurry.' She went out. Her steps rustled on the stairs going up.

' "She said, turning in the doorway," ' Hank mused, looking after her.

He turned abruptly and went out of the house. Phoebus was nosing around the edge of the saucer for the food he had pushed off. Hank bent down and helped him gather up the loose food. He scratched Phoebus' iron old head. Phoebus stopped eating and waited rigidly for Hank to take his hand away. When that happened he went back to his food.

Hank jerked open the folding doors of the garage and looked the Ford over for flats. The tires were worn, but still held air. The car was pretty dusty. I'm a writer, Hank thought. I don't have time for menial jobs. He went around the front end of the car into the dark corner where there was a pile of sacks. Under the sacks was a demijohn half full of corn whiskey. Hank eased the fat cork from the neck and hoisted the heavy jug on the outside of his arm in approved style. He stood holding it, poised like a weightlifter. Then he drank deeply and lowered the demijohn and corked it and put it back under the sacks.

I don't need it a damn bit, he told himself and almost believed it. But it'll be a satisfaction to her to smell it on me. Marion's a girl that likes to be right.

He was standing in the middle of the living room when she came down stairs. She had a cigarette in her mouth. She looked very cool. She even looked competent, but the living room furniture didn't agree with that diagnosis. They stood and looked at each other, while Hank filled a pipe and lit it.

'Had a swig from the jug?' Marion asked him mildly. He nodded and lit his pipe. Their eyes met again across the stretch of quiet air. Marion sat down slowly on the arm of a wicker settee. It creaked a little. Outside the house there was a sudden flutter of bird song, then an angry chirping which would be Phoebus taking a morning stroll near a nest.

'Car's all right,' Hank said. 'You want to catch that ten five?'

'Ten eleven,' Marion corrected him. 'Yes. I want to catch that. There's no sense in saying I'm sorry. I'm not sorry. The farther I get from this place the better I'll like it. Every mile will be a good mile.'

Hank looked at her blank-eyed. 'I don't want any of this junk,' Marion said, looking around at the second-hand out of date furniture which they had just barely been able to pay for. 'I don't want anything in this house. Except my clothes. My clothes and out.' Her eyes went to the work table in the corner, a massive rough wood thing with legs from two by fours and a burlap cover tacked over the undressed planks that made its top. She looked at the old Underwood and the loose blank paper and the pencils and the cream-colored box lettered in red that contained what had been accomplished of Hank's novel.

'Most especially, I don't want that,' Marion said pointing to the table. 'You hang on to that. When you get the book finished they can put a picture of that elegant specimen of Neanderthal Chippendale on the dust cover, instead of your photograph. Because by that time you won't take a very good photograph. Unless they could photograph your breath. They'd have a real rich presence if they could do that.' She passed a hand quickly across her forehead. 'I'm talking like a damn writer again,' she muttered and made a gesture which might have been despairing if it had not been so self-conscious.

'I could stop drinking whiskey,' Hank said slowly, through a puff of smoke.

She looked at him with a taut smile. 'Oh sure. And then what? You're not a man. You're just a physically perfect specimen of an alcoholic eunuch. You're a zombie in top condition. You're a dead man with an absolutely normal blood pressure.'

'You ought to write that down,' Hank said.

'Don't worry. I will,' Her eyes were hard and shiny now. There didn't seem to be any blue in them at all. 'And don't worry about me for God's sake. I'll get a job. Advertising, newspaper, what the hell. I can always get a job. I might even write that play I thought I could write here in these beautiful woods, with the beautiful quiet all around me, disturbed by nothing louder than the steady gurgle of a whiskey bottle.'

'It stinks,' Hank said.

Her eyes flared at him. 'What?'

'The dialogue. Also, it's too long,' Hank said. 'And the actors don't talk to the audience nowadays. They talk to each other.'

'I'm talking to you,' Marion said.

'Not really,' Hank said. 'Not really.'

She shrugged it off. Hank wasn't sure she even knew what he was saying to her, that she understood he was telling her indirectly, as so many times before, that literary set pieces don't make plays any more. Not the kind that are produced.

'Nobody could write a play here,' Marion said. 'Not even Eugene O'Neill. Not even Tennessee Williams. Not even Sardou. Just name somebody who could write a play here. Anybody at all. Just name him and I'll call you a liar.'

Hank glanced at his strap watch. 'You didn't marry me to write a play,' he said mildly. 'Any more than I married you to write a novel. And you did a nice bit of elbow bending yourself then, remember? There was that night when you passed out and I had to undress you and put you to bed.'

'Had to?'

'All right,' Hank said. 'Wanted to.'

'I thought you were quite a fellow then, didn't I?' The romantic memory, if that was what it was, made no more impression on her than a footstep makes on the floor. 'You had wit and imagination and a sort of buccaneering gaiety. But I didn't have to watch you drift into a stupor and lie awake in the night listening to you snoring the house down.' Her voice got a little breathless. 'And the worst of it—or almost the worst——'

'We're writers, we have to qualify everything,' Hank murmured to his pipe.

'——you're not even irritable in the morning. You don't wake up with a glassy eye and a head like a barrel. You just smile and go right on from where you left off. Which marks you as the everlasting natural born sot, born to the fumes of alcohol, living in them as the salamander lives in fire.'

'I think maybe you ought to write the novel and I ought to write the play,' Hank said.

Her voice sharpened towards hysteria. 'Don't you know what happens to men like you? Some fine day they fly into little pieces as though a shell had hit them. For years and years there's practically no sign of deterioration at all. They get drunk every night and every morning they start to get drunk again. They feel wonderful. It doesn't do a thing to them. And then comes that day when everything happens all at once that ought with a normal person to happen slowly, over the months and years, reasonable steps in reasonable time. One minute you're looking at a healthy man and then next you're looking at a shrivelled up horror that reeks of whiskey. Do you expect me to wait for that?'

He shrugged slightly, but didn't answer. What she said didn't seem to mean anything to him, hardly even to be said to him. It was like a monotone in the dark, on the other side of trees spoken by an invisible stranger he would never see. He looked at his strap watch again and she ground out her cigarette and stood up.

'I'll get the car around,' Hank said and went out of the room. She had said her piece, that was the main thing. She had lain awake in the night and figured it all out and put it into words and rehearsed it and tested it against the silence and now she had said it to him and the scene was achieved. He thought maybe it could have been done a little better just as it could have been shorter, but what the hell, they were just a couple of writers.

3

He hit the jug again before he backed the Ford out. When he brought it around to the front of the house Marion was standing at an outside corner of the porch looking out over the trees.

The sun was on the flanks of the hills and the mist was gone. But it was still a little cold at that altitude. Marion had a small unbecoming hat on her dark hair and her lips were clamped tight over a cigarette like a pair of pliers holding the end of a bolt. Hank went into the house without speaking to her. Upstairs were the two suitcases and the overnight bag and the hat box and the small green trunk with the rounded brass corners. He carried all that downstairs and stowed it in the back of the car. Marion was already in the seat.

Hank got in beside her and started up and they went down the gravelly drive to the dirt road that wound along beside the river for six miles and then dropped away down the side of the mountain to the little town through which the railroad went. Marion stared at the river and said:

'You like to fight that river, don't you? Is it dangerous?'

'Not if you've got a sound heart.'

'Why don't you fight something worthwhile?'

'Oh God,' Hank said.

Marion looked at him sharply, then looked straight in front through the dusty windshield.

'In a year I'll have forgotten you ever existed,' she said. 'It's a little sad. But how much of a woman's life does a man like you expect to drain away?'

She choked. He reached out and patted her shoulder. 'Take it easy,' he said. 'You'll put it all in a book some day.'

'I don't even know where to go,' she sobbed.

He patted her shoulder again and said nothing this time. Neither of them spoke until they reached the railroad station. Hank carried the stuff over and set it down beside the tracks. He wanted to check the trunk, but Marion said she would do it herself.

'Well, I'll sit in the car until you pull out,' Hank said. He squeezed her arm and she turned and walked away from him. He sat in the car for quite a long time before the train came. He began to want a drink. He thought Marion would look at him and at least wave when she got on the train. But she didn't. He needn't have waited. He might have been home and hit the jug long ago. It was an empty gesture, waiting. Worse than that, it didn't even have any style. He watched the train out of sight without moving a muscle. And that also was useless and without style.

4

When he got back to the house the sun was hot and the faint breeze that stirred across the grass was warm too. The trees whispered in it, talking to him, telling him it was a lovely day. He went slowly into the house and stood waiting for the silence to crowd down on him. But the house seemed no emptier than before. A fly buzzed and a bird rattled in a tree. He looked out of the window to see what kind of bird it was. He was a writer and he ought to know, but he didn't see the bird and he didn't give a damn anyway.

'If only I had a dog,' he said out loud, and waited for the mournful echo. He went over to the solid work table and took the cover off the box and read the top page of his script, without taking it out of the box.

'Pastiche,' he said drearily. 'Everything I write sounds like something a real writer threw away.'

He left the house to put the car back in the garage for no reason except that the whiskey jug was there. He carried the demijohn of corn into the house and set it on the work table. He got a glass and put that beside the jug. Then he sat down and stared at the jug. It was available and perhaps for that reason he didn't have to have it just then. He felt empty but not the kind of emptiness that a drink can fill.

I'm not even in love with her, he thought. Nor she with me. There's no tragedy, no real sorrow, just a flat emptiness. The emptiness of a writer who can't think of anything to write, and that's a pretty awful painful emptiness, but for some reason it never even approaches tragedy. Jesus, we're the most useless people in the world. There must be a hell of a lot of us too, all lonely, all empty, all poor, all gritted with small mean worries that have no dignity. All trying like men caught in a bog to get some firm ground under our feet and knowing all the time it doesn't make a damn bit of difference whether we do or not. We ought to have a convention somewhere, some place like Aspen, Colorado, some place where the air is very clear and sharp and stimulating, and we can bounce our little derived intelligences against one another's hard little minds. Maybe for just a little while we'd feel as if we really had talent. All the world's would-be writers, the guys and girls that have education and will and desire and hope and nothing else. They know all there is to know about how it's done, except they can't do it. They've studied hard and imitated the hell out of everybody that ever rang the bell.

What a fine warm bunch of nothing we would be, he thought. We'd hone each other razor sharp. The air would crackle with the snapping of our dreams. But the trouble is, it couldn't last. Then the convention is over and we have to go back home and sit in front of this damn piece of metal that puts the words down on the paper. Yeah, we sit there waiting—like a guy waiting in the death house.

He hoisted the demijohn and forgetting about the glass drank from the neck with the usual weight-lifting technique. It was warm and sour, but it didn't do much good this time. He just went on thinking about being a writer with no talent. After quite a while he took the demijohn back to the garage and tucked it up under the pile of sacks. Phoebus came around the corner with a large dirty looking grasshopper in his mouth. He was making a discontented sound. Hank bent down and pulled Phoebus's jaws open and let the grasshopper go, minus one leg, but still full of wanderlust. Phoebus looked up at Hank and pretended to be hungry. So Hank let him into the kitchen.

'Sit down anywhere,' Hank told the cat. 'The house is yours.' He offered Phoebus some food, but he knew Phoebus didn't want it and he didn't. So he went and sat at the work table and put a sheet of paper in the typewriter. After a while Phoebus got up on the table beside him and looked out of the window.

'Fellow doesn't work the day his wife leaves him, does he, Phoebus? He takes the day off.'

Phoebus yawned. Hank scratched his head close to one ear and Phoebus purred grindingly. Hank walked his fingers down Phoebus's spine and Phoebus reared up against his hand with surprising power.

'You're a real tough old bastard of a cat, aren't you, Phoebus? I ought to write a story about you.'

The afternoon passed slowly. Finally it was leaning towards the dusk and the emptiness was still there. Phoebus had been fed and had gone to sleep on the settee. Hank sat on the porch and watched some gnats dance in a shaft of late sunlight. Just before the mosquitoes would come out he heard the car coming. It was pretty rough. It sounded like old Simpson's Chevvy. Then he saw it along the dirt road in the distance and he was right. He could tell by the broken windwing. He was hardly even surprised when it turned into the driveway and curved ungracefully around to the steps. Old Simpson sat motionless with his knotty hands on the wheel and his watery eyes straight ahead. His jaws moved and he spat. He said nothing. He didn't even turn his head when Marion got out of the Chevvy.

'I paid Mr Simpson,' Marion said.

Hank lifted her things out of the car with no help from old Simpson. When they were all out old Simpson let in the clutch and departed, having said no word and looked at neither of them.

'What's he sore about?' Hank asked.

'He's not sore. He just doesn't like us. I'm sorry I wasted the money, Hank.' Her face looked beaten. 'I guess you're not surprised I came back?'

'I wasn't sure.' He shook his head vaguely. She began to cry untidily and he put his arm around her shoulders.

'I couldn't think of one goddam place I wanted to go,' she blubbered. 'It all seemed so pointless.' She jerked her hat off and loosened her hair. 'So completely utterly without any meaning at all. No high spots, no low spots, just a lot of stale emotion.'

Hank nodded and watched her wipe her eyes and work a stiff little embarrassed smile on to her face.

'Hemingway would have known where to go,' she said.

'Sure. He could have gone to Africa and shot a lion.'

'Or to Pamplona and shot a bull.'

'Or to Venice and shot a blank,' Hank said, and they both grinned. He picked up two of the suitcases and started up the steps.

'Where's Phoebus?' she called after him.

'On my work table,' Hank said. 'He's writing a story. Just a quickie—for the rent money.'

She ran up the steps and pulled his arm away from the door. He put the suitcases down with a sigh and faced her. He wanted to be kind but he knew that nothing they had said in the past or would say now or in the future really meant anything. It was all echoes.

'Hank,' she said desperately. 'I feel awful. What's going to happen to us?'

'Nothing much,' Hank said. 'Why should it? We can last six months yet.'

'I don't mean money. Your novel—my play. What's going to happen to them, Hank?'

Something turned over in his stomach because he knew the answer and Marion knew the answer and there was absolutely no sense in pretending it was an unsolved problem. The problem was never how to get something you knew you couldn't have. It was how to stop behaving as if it was just around the corner waiting for you to find it, hiding behind a bush or under a pile of dead leaves, but there, actual, real. It wasn't there and it never would be. So why did you go on pretending it was?

'My novel stinks,' he said quietly. 'So does your play.'

She hit him across the face with all her strength and ran into the house. She almost fell getting up the stairs. In a moment if he listened carefully he would hear the sobs. He didn't want to, so he went down off the porch and around to the garage and hefted the jug from under the pile of sacks. He took a long deep drink and lowered the jug carefully and corked it and put it back under the sacks.

He closed the garage doors and put the wooden pin in place. It was full twilight now and the spaces under the trees were deep and black.

'I wish I had a dog,' he said to the night. 'Why do I keep wishing that? I guess I need something to admire me.'

Inside the house he listened but he didn't hear any sobbing. He went halfway up the stairs and saw the light go on, so he knew she was all right. When he stood in the doorway of the room she was unpacking the overnight bag. She was whistling very softly between her teeth.

'Had yourself a drink, didn't you?' she said without looking up.

'Just one. I was drinking a toast. Salute to a Broken Heart.'

She straightened up sharply and stared at him under the fluffed out dark hair. 'That's nice,' she said coldly. 'Your heart —or mine?'

'Neither,' Hank said. 'It's just a title I happened to think of.'

'Title for what—a story?'

'The novel I'm not going to write,' Hank said.

'You're drunk,' Marion said.

'I didn't have any lunch.'

'I'm sorry I slapped you, Hank.'

'That's all right,' Hank said. 'I'd have done it myself if I had thought of it.'

He turned on his heel and started down the stairs, walking delicately, step by step, not touching the handrail, then across the hall and out of the door, letting the screen close softly, then down the steps, one by one carefully and firmly and then around the corner of the house, his shoes mushing on the gravel, on his endless predestined journey back to the jug under the pile of sacks.

CHANDLER ON THE FILM WORLD
AND TELEVISION

Chandler on the Film World and Television

In 1943 *Chandler went to work as a script-writer for Paramount Pictures in Hollywood. His first screenplay was* Double Indemnity *by James M. Cain, directed by Billy Wilder.*

Sept. 21, 1944
To: Charles W. Morton
... The article I should like to do, if I can get the time, is a piece about writers in Hollywood. There are some devastating things to be said on this subject. It is high time someone said them ...

Jan. 15, 1945
To: Charles W. Morton
Hollywood is such a mine of material one hardly knows where to start writing about it. It's worth a whole book—but some aspects would need research and the rewards might be rather slim.

I am back at the grind at Paramount ... In less than two weeks I wrote an original story of 90 pages. All dictated and never looked at it until finished.[1] It was an experiment and for one subject from early childhood to plot-constipation, it was rather a revelation. Some of the stuff is good, some very much not. But I don't see why the method could not be adapted to novel writing, at least by me. Improvise the story as well as you can, in as much detail or as little as the mood seems to suggest, write dialogue or leave it out, but cover the movement, the characters, and bring the thing to life. I begin to realise the great number of stories that are lost by us rather meticulous boys simply because we permit our minds to freeze on the faults rather than let them work for a while without the critical overseer sniping at everything that is not perfect. I can see where a special vice might also come out of this kind of writing; in fact two: the strange delusion that something on paper has a meaning because it is written. (My revered Henry James went to

[1] Chandler's original screenplay, *The Blue Dahlia*.

pieces a bit when he began to dictate.) Also, the tendency to worship production for its own sake.

March 5, 1945
To: Charles W. Morton
   . . . I have been working pretty hard, went to the studio January 2nd and have a picture about ready to begin shooting. I don't like this in some ways, I do like it in others. Possibly— I'm not sure—the rejuvenation of the motion picture, if and when it comes, will have to be through some such process of writing directly for the screen and almost under the camera. What you lose in finish you gain in movement; and movement is what the motion picture has been steadily losing for a long time. It has become a contrivance for photographing plays from odd angles; its true business is to photograph dramatic movement from the simplest possible angles—those of the two eyes. . . . Moving the camera has become a substitute for moving the action, and this is recession. It is imposing on the director the impossible task of creating an illusion of movement where no movement exists.
   . . . I'm still hoping to do that article for you, sometime in April. . . .

Writers in Hollywood [1]

(Published in *The Atlantic Monthly*, November, 1945)

1

   Hollywood is easy to hate, easy to sneer at, easy to lampoon. Some of the best lampooning has been done by people who have never been through a studio gate, some of the best sneering by egocentric geniuses who departed huffily—not forgetting to collect their last pay check—leaving behind them nothing but the exquisite aroma of their personalities and a botched job for the tired hacks to clean up.

[1] The article alluded to in the foregoing letters to Charles W. Morton.

Even as far away as New York, where Hollywood assumes all really intelligent people live (since they obviously do not live in Hollywood), the disease of exaggeration can be caught. The motion picture critic of one of the less dazzled intellectual weeklies, commenting recently on a certain screen-play, remarked that it showed 'how dull a couple of run-of-the-mill $3000-a-week writers can be'. I hope this critic will not be startled to learn that 50 per cent of the screenwriters of Hollywood made less than $10,000 last year, and that he could count on his fingers the number that made a steady income anywhere near the figure he so contemptuously mentioned. I don't know whether they could be called run-of-the-mill writers or not. To me the phrase suggests something a little easier to get hold of.

I hold no brief for Hollywood. I have worked there a little over two years, which is far from enough to make me an authority, but more than enough to make me feel pretty thoroughly bored. That should not be so. An industry with such vast resources and such magic techniques should not become dull so soon. An art which is capable of making all but the very best plays look trivial and contrived, all but the very best novels verbose and imitative, should not so quickly become wearisome to those who attempt to practise it with something else in mind than the cash drawer. The making of a picture ought surely to be a rather fascinating adventure. It is not; it is an endless contention of tawdry egos, some of them powerful, almost all of them vociferous, and almost none of them capable of anything much more creative than credit-stealing and self-promotion.

Hollywood is a showman's paradise. Showmen make nothing; they exploit what someone else has made. But the showmen of Hollywood control the making—and thereby degrade it. For the basic art of motion pictures is the screenplay; it is fundamental, without it there is nothing . . . But in Hollywood the screenplay is written by a salaried writer under the supervision of a producer—that is to say, by an employee without power or decision over the uses of his own craft, without ownership of it, and, however extravagantly paid, almost without honor for it . . .

I am not interested in why the Hollywood system exists or persists, nor in learning out of what bitter struggles for prestige it arose, nor in how much money it succeeds in making out of bad pictures. I am interested only in the fact that as a result of it there is no such thing as an art of the screenplay, and there never will be as long as the system lasts, for it is the essence of this system that it seeks to exploit a talent without permitting it the right to be a talent. It cannot be done; you can only destroy the talent, which is exactly what happens—when there is any to destroy.

Granted that there isn't much. Some chatty publisher (probably Bennett Cerf) remarked once that there are writers in Hollywood making two thousand dollars a week who haven't had an idea in ten years. He exaggerated—backwards: there are writers in Hollywood making two thousand a week who never had an idea in their lives, who have never written a photographable scene, who could not make two cents a word in the pulp market if their lives depended on it. Hollywood is full of such writers, although there are few at such high salaries. They are, to put it bluntly, a pretty dreary lot of hacks, and most of them know it, and they take their kicks and their salaries and try to be reasonably grateful to an industry which permits them to live much more opulently than they could live anywhere else.

And I have no doubt that most of them would like to be much better writers than they are, would like to have force and integrity and imagination—enough of these to earn a decent living at some art of literature that has the dignity of a free profession. It will not happen to them, and there is not much reason why it should. If it ever could have happened, it will not happen now. For even the best of them (with a few rare exceptions) devote their entire time to work which has no more possibility of distinction than a Pekinese has of becoming a Great Dane: to asinine musicals about technicolor legs and the yowling of night-club singers; to 'psychological' dramas with wooden plots, stock characters, and that persistent note of fuzzy earnestness which suggests the conversation of schoolgirls in puberty; to sprightly and sophisticated comedies (we hope) in which the gags are as stale as the attitudes, in which there is always a drink in every hand, a butler in every doorway, and a telephone on the edge of every bathtub; to historical epics in which the male actors look like female impersonators, and the lovely feminine star looks just a little too starry-eyed for a babe who has spent half her life swapping husbands; and last but not least, to those pictures of deep social import in which everybody is thoughtful and grown-up and sincere and the more difficult problems of life are wordily resolved into a unanimous vote of confidence in the inviolability of the Constitution, the sanctity of the home, and the paramount importance of the streamlined kitchen.

And these, dear readers, are the million-dollar babies—the cream of the crop. Most of the boys and girls who write for the screen never get anywhere near this far. They devote their sparkling lines and their structural finesse to horse operas, cheap gun-in-the-kidney melodramas, horror items about mad scientists and cliff hangers concerned with screaming blondes and circular saws. The writers of this tripe are licked before they start. Even in a purely technical sense their work is doomed for lack of the time to do it properly. The challenge of screenwriting is to say much in little and then take half of that little out and still preserve an effect of leisure and natural movement. Such a technique requires experiment and elimination. The cheap pictures simply cannot afford it.

2

Let me not imply that there are no writers of authentic ability in Hollywood. There are not many, but there are not many anywhere. The creative gift is a scarce commodity, and patience and imitation have always done most of its work. There is no reason to expect from the anonymous toilers of the screen a quality which we are very obviously not getting from the publicized litterateurs of the best-seller list, from the compilers of fourth-rate historical novels which sell half a million copies, from the Broadway candy butchers known as playwrights, or from the sulky maestri of the little magazines.

To me the interesting point about Hollywood writers of talent is not how few or how many they are, but how little of worth their talent is allowed to achieve. Interesting—but hardly unexpected, once you accept the premise that writers are employed to write screenplays on the theory that, being writers, they have a particular gift and training for the job, and are then prevented from doing it with any independence or finality whatsoever, on the theory that, being merely writers, they know nothing about making pictures; and of course if they don't know how to make pictures, they couldn't possibly know how to write them. It takes a producer to tell them that.

I do not wish to become unduly vitriolic on the subject of producers. My own experience does not justify it, and after all, producers too are slaves of the system. Also, the term 'producer' is of very vague definition. Some producers are powerful in their own right, and some are little more than legmen for the front office; some—few, I trust—receive less money than some of the writers who work for them.

For my thesis the personal qualities of a producer are rather beside the point. Some are able and humane men and some are low-grade individuals with the morals of a goat, the artistic integrity of a slot machine, and the manners of a floorwalker with delusions of grandeur. In so far as the writing of the screenplay is concerned, however, the producer is the boss; the writer either gets along with him and his ideas (if he has any) or gets out. This means both personal and artistic subordination, and no writer of quality will long accept either without surrendering that which made him a writer of quality, without dulling the fine edge of his mind, without becoming little by little a conniver rather than a creator, a supple and facile journeyman rather than a craftsman of original thought.

It makes very little difference how a writer feels towards his producer as a man: the fact that the producer can change and destroy and disregard his work can only operate to diminish that work in its conception and to make it mechanical and indifferent in execution. The impulse to perfection cannot exist where the definition of perfection is the arbitrary decision of authority. That which is born in loneliness and from the heart cannot be defended against the judgment of a committee of sycophants. The volatile essences which make literature cannot survive the clichés of a long series of story conferences. There is little magic of word or emotion or situation which can remain alive after the incessant bone-scraping revisions imposed on the Hollywood writer by the process of rule by decree. That these magics do somehow, here and there, by another and even rarer magic, survive and reach the screen more or less intact is the infrequent miracle which keeps Hollywood's handful of fine writers from cutting their throats.

Hollywood has no right to expect such miracles, and it does not deserve the men who bring them to pass. Its conception of what makes a good picture is still as juvenile as its treatment of writing talent is insulting and degrading. Its idea of 'production value' is spending a million dollars dressing up a story that any good writer would throw away. Its vision of the rewarding movie is a vehicle for some glamor-puss with two expressions and eighteen changes of costume, or for some male idol of the muddled millions with a permanent hangover, six worn-out acting tricks, the build of a lifeguard, and the mentality of a chicken-strangler. Pictures for such purposes as these, Hollywood lovingly and carefully makes. The good ones smack it in the rear when it isn't looking.

3

For all this too there are colorable economic reasons. The motion picture is a great industry as well as a defeated art. Its technicians are now in their third generation, its investments are world-wide, its demand for material is insatiable.

The men with the money and the ultimate power can do anything they like with Hollywood—as long as they don't mind losing their investment. They can destroy any studio executive overnight, contract or no contract; any star, any producer, any director—as an individual. What they cannot destroy is the Hollywood system. It may be wasteful, absurd, even dishonest, but it is all there is, and no cold-blooded board of directors can replace it. It has been tried, but the showmen always win. They always win against mere money. What in the long run—the very long run—they can never defeat is talent, even writing talent.

It is, I am afraid, a *very* long run indeed. There is no present indication whatever that the Hollywood writer is on the point of acquiring any real control over his work, any right to choose what that work shall be (other than refusing jobs, which he can only do within narrow limits), or even any right to decide how the values in the producer-chosen work shall be brought out. There is no present guarantee that his best lines, best ideas, best scenes will not be changed or omitted on the set by the director or dropped on the floor during the later process of cutting—for the simple but essential reason that the best things in any picture, artistically speaking, are invariably the easiest to leave out, mechanically speaking.

There is no attempt in Hollywood to exploit the writer as an artist of meaning to the picture-buying public; there is every

attempt to keep the public uninformed about his vital contribution to whatever art the movies contains. On the billboards, in
the newspaper advertisements, his name will be smaller than that
of the most insignificant bit-player who achieves what is known
as billing; it will be the first to disappear as the size of the ad
is cut down toward the middle of the week; it will be the last
and least to be mentioned in any word-of-mouth or radio
promotion.

The first picture I worked on was nominated for an Academy
Award (if that means anything), but I was not even invited to the
press review held right in the studio. An extremely successful
picture made by another studio from a story I wrote used ver-
batim lines out of the story in its promotional campaign, but
my name was never mentioned once in any radio, magazine,
billboard, or newspaper advertising that I saw or heard—and I
saw and heard a great deal. This neglect is of no consequence to
me personally; to any writer of books a Hollywood by-line is
trivial. To those whose whole work is in Hollywood it is not
trivial, because it is part of a deliberate and successful plan to
reduce the professional screenwriter to the status of an assistant
picture-maker, superficially deferred to (while he is in the room),
essentially ignored, and even in his most brilliant achievements
carefully pushed out of the way of any possible accolade which
might otherwise fall to the star, the producer, the director.

4

If all this is true, why then should any writer of genuine
ability continue to work in Hollywood at all? The obvious reason
is not enough: few screenwriters possess homes in Bel-Air, illu-
minated swimming pools, wives in full-length mink coats, three
servants, and that air of tired genius gone a little sour. Money
buys pathetically little in Hollywood beyond the pleasure of
living in an unreal world, associating with a narrow group of
people who think, talk, and drink nothing but pictures, most of
them bad, and the doubtful pleasure of watching famous actors
and actresses guzzle in some of the rudest restaurants in the
world.

I do not mean that Hollywood society is any duller or more
dissipated than moneyed society anywhere: God knows it
couldn't be. But it is a pretty thin reward for a lifetime devoted

to the essential craft of what might be a great art . . . The superficial friendliness of Hollywood is pleasant—until you find out that nearly every sleeve conceals a knife. The companionship during working hours with men and women who take the business of fiction seriously gives a pale heat to the writer's lonely soul.

Beyond this I suppose there is hope; there are several hopes. The cold dynasty will not last forever, the dictatorial producer is already a little unsure, the top-heavy director has long since become a joke in his own studio; after a while even technicolor will not save him. There is hope that a decayed and make-shift system will pass, that somehow the flatulent moguls will learn that only writers can write screenplays and only proud and independent writers can write good screenplays, and that present methods of dealing with such men are destructive of the very force by which pictures must live.

And there is the intense and beautiful hope that the Hollywood writers themselves—such of them as are capable of it—will recognize that writing for the screen is no job for amateurs and half-writers whose problems are always solved by somebody else. It is the writers' own weakness as craftsmen that permits the superior egos to bleed them white of initiative, imagination, and integrity. If even a quarter of the *highly paid* screenwriters in Hollywood could produce a completely integrated and photographable screenplay under their own power, with only the amount of interference and discussion necessary to protect the studio's investment in actors and ensure a reasonable freedom from libel and censorship troubles, then the producer would assume his proper function of co-ordinating and conciliating the various crafts which combine to make a picture; and the director—heaven help his strutting soul—would be reduced to the ignominious task of making pictures as they are conceived and written—and not as the director would try to write them, if only he knew how to write.

Certainly there are producers and directors—although how pitifully few—who are sincere enough to want such a change, and talented enough to have no fear of its effect on their own position . . .

If there is no art of the screenplay, the reason is at least partly that there exists no available body of technical theory and practice by which it can be learned. There is no available library of screenplay literature, because the screenplays belong to the studios, and they will only show them within their guarded walls. There is no body of critical opinion, because there are no critics of the screenplay; there are only critics of motion pictures as entertainment, and most of these critics know nothing whatever of the means whereby the motion picture is created and put on celluloid. There is no teaching, because there is no one to teach. If you do not know how pictures are made, you cannot speak with any authority on how they should be constructed; if you do, you are busy enough trying to do it.

There is no correlation of crafts within the studio itself; the average—and far better than average—screenwriter knows hardly anything of the technical problems of the director, and nothing at all of the superlative skill of the trained cutter. He spends his effort in writing shots that cannot be made, or which if made would be thrown away; in writing dialogue that cannot be spoken, sound effects that cannot be heard, and nuances of mood and emotion which the camera cannot reproduce. His idea of an effective scene is something that has to be shot down a stair well or out of a gopher hole; or a conversation so static that the director, in order to impart a sense of motion to it, is compelled to photograph it from nine different angles.

In fact, no part of the vast body of technical knowledge which Hollywood contains is systematically and as a matter of course made available to the new writer in a studio. They tell him to look at pictures—which is to learn architecture by staring at a house. And then they send him back to his rabbit hutch to write little scenes which his producer, in between telephone calls to his blondes and his booze-companions, will tell him ought to have been written quite differently.

I have kept the best hope of all for the last. In spite of all I have said, the writers of Hollywood *are* winning their battle for prestige. More and more of them are becoming showmen in their own right, producers and directors of their own screenplays. Let us be glad for their additional importance and power, and not examine the artistic result too critically. The boys make good (and some of them might even make good pictures). Let us rejoice together, for the tendency to become showmen is well in the acceptable tradition of the literary art as practised among the cameras.

For the very nicest thing Hollywood can possibly think of to say to a writer is that he is too good to be only a writer.

Dec. 12, 1945
To: Charles W. Morton

. . . I should like to mention one error in this article[1] because it is the kind of thing I can never understand. It is the 9th line from the end of the piece. It reads: 'and not examine the artistic result too critically'. What I wrote was: 'and not too critically examine the artistic result' . . . It is obvious that somebody, for no reason save that he thought he was improving the style, changed the order of the words. I confess myself completely flabbergasted by the literary attitude this expresses, the assumption on the part of some editorial hireling that he can write better than the man who sent the stuff in, that he knows more about phrase and cadence and the placing of words, and that he actually thinks that a clause with a strong stressed syllable at the end, which was put there because it was strong, is improved by changing the order so that the clause ends in a weak adverbial termination.

Dec. 12, 1945
To: Charles W. Morton

I've owed you a letter for so darn long that I suppose you wonder whether I am still alive. So do I, at times . . . Let me report that my blast at Hollywood was received here in frozen silence . . . In view of the subject matter, and quite regardless of the reputation of the writer, and in view of the *Atlantic*, it seems to me reasonable to think that there was a suppression of the subject by request of the studio publicity heads . . . In various roundabout ways I heard that the piece was not received with favor. My agent was told by the Paramount story editor that it had done me a lot of harm with the producers at Paramount. Charlie Brackett[2] said: 'Chandler's books are not good enough, nor his pictures bad enough, to justify that article.' I wasted a

---

[1] *Writers in Hollywood.*
[2] Film director.

little time trying to figure out what that meant. It seems to mean that the only guy who can speak his mind about Hollywood is either (a) a failure in Hollywood, or (b) a celebrity somewhere else. I would reply to Mr Brackett that if my books had been any worse, I should not have been invited to Hollywood, and that if they had been any better, I should not have come . . .

Jan. 12, 1946
To: Alfred A. Knopf[1]

    . . . I no longer have a secretary because I no longer have a motion picture job. I am what is technically known as suspended. For refusing to perform under a contract which is not a proper expression of my standing in the motion picture business. I requested a cancellation, but was denied that. There is no moral issue involved since the studios have destroyed the moral basis of contracts themselves. They tear them up whenever it suits them. One of the troubles is that it seems quite impossible to convince anyone that a man would turn his back on a whopping salary—whopping by the standards of normal living—for any reason but a tactical manoeuvre through which he hopes to acquire a still more whopping salary. What I want is something quite different: a freedom from datelines and unnatural pressures, and a right to find and work with those few people in Hollywood whose purpose is to make the best pictures possible within the limitations of a popular art, not merely to repeat the old vulgar formulae.

    . . . No doubt I have learned a lot from Hollywood. Please do not think I completely despise it, because I don't. The best proof of that may be that every producer I have ever worked for I would work for again, and every one of them, in spite of my tantrums, would be glad to have me. But the overall picture, as the boys say, is of a degraded community whose idealism even is largely fake. The pretentiousness, the bogus enthusiasm, the constant drinking and drabbing, the incessant squabbling over money, the all-pervasive agent, the strutting of the big shots (and their usually utter incompetence to achieve anything they start

[1] Chairman, Alfred A. Knopf Inc.

out to do), the constant fear of losing all this fairy gold and being the nothing they have never ceased to be, the snide tricks, the whole damn mess is out of this world.

It is a great subject for a novel—probably the greatest still untouched. But how to do it with a level mind, that's the thing that baffles me. It is like one of these South American palace revolutions conducted by officers in comic opera uniforms— only when the thing is over the ragged dead men lie in rows against the walls and you suddenly know that this is not funny, this is the Roman circus, and damn near the end of a civilization.

May 30, 1946
To: James Sandoe
The Blue Dahlia, as you probably know by now, has been released in various places, including New York ... The best reviews I saw of it came from England, the worst from *The New Yorker*, but *The New Yorker* guy is only permitted to like one picture a year ...

Oct. 2, 1947
To: James Sandoe
... The panning of *The Blue Dahlia* in *New Writing* is all right with me. I agree with a lot of it. I have reached the happy state of being thoroughly insensitive to adverse criticism while glowing with pleasure at the other kind. If I were a letters-to-the-editor type guy, I should put in a little time contesting a couple of points, e.g., it is ludicrous to suggest that any writer in Hollywood, however obstreperous, has a 'free hand' with a script; he may have a free hand with the first draft, but after that they start moving in on him. Also, what happens on the set is beyond the writer's control. In this case I threatened to walk off the picture, not yet finished, unless they stopped the director putting in fresh dialogue out of his own head. As to the scenes of violence, I did not write them that way at all ... The broken toe incident was an accident. The man actually did break his toe, so the director immediately capitalized on it.

The real point at issue here is whether physical violence is worse than psychological violence. The element of burlesque is also overlooked. Where this critic throws his hand without knowing it is in calling the cutting of the picture bad. What he really means is that the direction was so bad that the cutting, which was very expert, was not able to conceal it. The best cutter in Hollywood cannot correct a botched job of directing; he can't make scenes flow when they are shot staccato, without reference to their movement on.film. If the cutter wants to make a dissolve to cover an abrupt transition, he can't do it unless he has the film to combine for the dissolve. If every foot of film in a scene is needed for the essential action, there is none over for a dissolve.

Take a simple example. Two characters are discussing a letter which one of them expects. They are in an apartment, a man and a girl. The man says: 'He's writing to me General Delivery. The letter's probably there now.' The girl says: 'Why don't you go down and get it?' The guy says: 'Will you be here when I get back?' The girl says: 'Sure', and smiles enigmatically.

The director, a bad director, holds on the enigmatic smile and holds long enough for a dissolve. He then shoots the exterior of the post office. Guy arrives in cab, pays cab, starts up stairs of post office. Close shot of entrance doors, guy starts in, scene in lobby, guy moves across, close shot of General Delivery window, guy goes up to it and asks for letter. Clerk looks through letters and hands him one, etc., etc.

Now the cutter knows that all this is bosh, dull, a holdover from the early days of the motion picture when the movement itself was exciting. All you really want is the General Delivery window and the guy receiving a letter. But the director has failed to deliver this scene by dissolving on the girl's enigmatic smile and making the audience wonder what she has up her sleeve. So they have that wiped out by a totally unnecessary series of shots showing arrival at the post office. The director has tried to make a point of something which is not at this time a point at all, and thrown the cutting mechanism out of gear. The point is whether a certain letter has come. A hand reaches across the counter and the guy takes the letter. That is all. But that is not what the preceding scene left you thinking about. You were thinking of what the girl would be up to while the guy was at the post office. And the poor cutter, to make his point, has to waste film to give the audience time to forget that. Not only that, but he has to make them look at dull film.

Hitchcock, the only time I met him, gave me a lecture on this kind of waste. His point was that Hollywood (and England, too) was full of directors who had not learned to forget about the Biograph. They still thought that because a motion picture moved it interested people. In the early days of the pictures, he said, a man went to visit a woman at her home. They were old flames, who had not seen each other for years. The director shot it this way:

The man took a taxi, he was seen riding along in the taxi, there was a view of the street and the house, the taxi stopped, the man got out and paid, he looked at the front steps, went up the steps, rang the bell, the maid answered, he said: 'Is Mrs Gilhooley in?' The maid said: 'I'll see, sir. What name shall I say?' The man said: 'Finnigan.' The maid said: 'This way, please.'

Inside house hallway, open door, maid stands at open door, man goes in, maid starts upstairs, man in living room looks around, lights a cigarette. Maid upstairs knocks on door, female voice calls 'Come in,' she opens door. Inside, maid says: 'Mr Finnigan to see you, ma'am.' Mrs Gilhooley says wonderingly: 'Mr Finnigan?' Then slowly, 'All right, Ellen, I'll be right down.' Goes to mirror, primps, enigmatic smile, starts out, shot of her descending stairs, entering living room after a slight embarrassed pause at door. Inside living room. She enters. Finnigan stands up. They look at each other in silence. Then they smile, slowly. Man, huskily: 'Hello, Madge. You haven't changed a bit.' Mrs Gilhooley: 'It's been a long time, George. A long, long time.'

And then the scene begins.

Every bit of this stuff is dead film, because every point, if there is a point, can be made inside the scene itself. The rest is just camera in love with mere movement. Cliché, flat, stale and today meaningless.

Well, I don't know why I run on about this. I suppose it's a sort of wonder at realizing that in spite of all the money, all the time, all the work, all the discussion and thought, there are still hardly any people who really know much about making pictures.

Dec. 16, 1947
To: Joseph Sistrom[1]

... Back in 1943 when we were writing *Double Indemnity* you told me that an effective motion picture could not be made of a detective or mystery story for the reason that the high point is the revelation of the murderer and that only happens in the last minute of the picture. Events proved you to be wrong, for almost immediately the mystery trend started, and there is no question but that *Double Indemnity* started it, although it was not exactly a mystery. You were right in theory as long as you were talking of the formal or English type of detective story, in which the solution of the mystery is the high point. The thing that made the mystery effective on the screen already existed on paper, but you somehow did not realize just where the values lay. It is implicit in my theory of mystery story writing that the mystery and the solution of the mystery are only what I call 'the olive in the martini', and the really good mystery is one you would read even if you knew somebody had torn out the last chapter.

... I look forward to discussing with you some means of changing the situation which makes the writing of pictures a second-rate and unsatisfying job to any writer who is capable of earning a living by writing for publication. I am quite sure the fault is not in the medium. I have just received a brochure about the Society of Authors, Playwrights and Composers in England and I am very interested to note that almost all the English screenwriters listed are either playwrights or novelists as well. Evidently these people do not regard screen writing as something only done by incompetent hacks or, when done by writers of any reputation, done rather callously just for the money. In England screen writing seems to be a respectable profession, just as it is in France. We have got to find a way to make it one in Hollywood because, I can assure you from the bottom of my heart that, unless this problem is solved, Hollywood will eventually lose its world leadership in picture making.

March 23, 1948
To: Joseph Sistrom

... I saw *Open City* again the other night. You always see

---

[1] Universal-International Pictures, Inc.

more the second time. I noticed, for example, that there is as much dialogue in the picture as in any of our more wordy specimens, but that this dialogue is so dynamically delivered that you don't get any impression of the action being slowed down. I am beginning to wonder whether the static quality of many pictures is not due simply to poor acting rather than to overwriting or unimaginative directing. Or, if I may correct myself, I am not beginning to wonder; I am convinced.

Nov. 26, 1948
To: Carl Brandt

. . . I haven't the least idea what they pay writers in England, nor at the moment in Hollywood. I averaged about $4000 a week on the Universal job, but I doubt if that kind of money could be had by me now.

I worked at M.G.M. once in that cold storage plant they call the Thalberg Building, fourth floor. Had a nice producer, George Haight, a fine fellow. About that time some potato-brain had decided that writers would do more work if they had no couches to lie on. So there was no couch in my office. Never a man to be stopped by trifles, I got a steamer rug out of the car and spread it on the floor and lay down on that. Haight coming in for a courtesy call rushed to the phone and yelled down to the story editor that I was a horizontal writer and for Chrissake send up a couch. However, the cold storage atmosphere got too quick, and I said I would work at home. They said Mannix had issued orders no writers to work at home. I said a man as big as Mannix ought to be allowed the privilege of changing his mind. So I worked at home and only went over there three or four times to talk to Haight.

I've only worked at three studios and Paramount was the only one I liked. They do somehow maintain the country club atmosphere there to some extent. At the writers' table at Paramount I heard some of the best wit I've ever heard in my life. I remember Harry Tugend's wonderful crack about a certain film star when Tugend was trying to be a producer and hating it. He said, 'You know this is a lousy job. You got to sit and talk to that birdbrain seriously about whether or not this part is going to be good for her career and at the same time you got to keep from being raped.' Whereat a rather innocent young man piped up: 'You mean to say she's a nymphomaniac?' Harry frowned off into distance and sighed and said slowly, 'Well, I guess she would be, if they could get her quieted down a little.' . . .

April 16, 1949
To: Alex Barris

    . . . The camera eye technique of *Lady in the Lake* is old stuff in Hollywood. Every young writer or director has wanted to try it. 'Let's make the camera a character'; it's been said at every lunch table in Hollywood one time or another. I knew one fellow who wanted to make the camera the murderer; which wouldn't work without an awful lot of fraud. The camera is too honest.

Sept. 4, 1950
To: Hamish Hamilton

    . . . I got myself involved in a film job doing a script for Alfred Hitchcock[1] and I don't seem able to do anything else while I'm at it. It's a silly enough story and quite a chore. Why am I doing it? Partly because I thought I might like Hitch, which I do, and partly because one gets tired of saying no, and someday I might want to say yes and not get asked. But it won't last beyond the end of this month, I think and hope.

    . . . The thing that amuses me about Hitchcock is the way he directs a film in his head before he knows what the story is. You find yourself trying to rationalize the shots he wants to make rather than the story. Every time you get set he jabs you off balance by wanting to do a love scene on top of the Jefferson Memorial or something like that. He has a strong feeling for stage business and mood and background, not so much for the guts of the business. I guess that's why some of his pictures lose their grip on logic and turn into wild chases. Well, it's not the worst way to make a picture. His idea of characters is rather

[1] *Strangers on a Train*, from Patricia Highsmith's novel of the same title.

primitive. Nice Young Man, Society Girl, Frightened Woman, Sneaky Old Beldame, Spy, Comic Relief, and so on. But he is as nice as can be to argue with. . .

EXTRACT FROM NOTES DATED 1950 ABOUT THE SCREENPLAY

Strangers on a Train

I nearly went crazy myself trying to block out this scene. I hate to say how many times I did it. It's darn near impossible to write, because consider what you have to put over:

(1) A perfectly decent young man agrees to murder a man he doesn't know, has never seen, in order to keep a maniac from giving himself away and from tormenting the nice young man.

(2) From a character point of view, the audience will not believe the nice young man is going to kill anybody, or has any idea of killing anybody.

(3) Nevertheless, the nice young man has to convince Bruno and a reasonable percentage of the audience that what he is about to do is logical and inevitable. This conviction may not outlast the scene, but it has to be there, or else what the hell are the boys talking about.

(4) While convincing Bruno of all this, he has yet to fail to convince him utterly so that some suspicion remains in Bruno's mind that Guy intends some kind of trick, rather than to go through with it in a literal sense.

(5) All through this scene (supposing it can be written this way) we are flirting with the ludicrous. If it is not written and played exactly right, it will be absurd. The reason for this is that the situation actually is ludicrous in its essence, and this can only be overcome by developing a sort of superficial menace, which really has nothing to do with the business in hand.

(6) Or am I still crazy?

The question I should really like to have answered, although I don't expect an answer to it in this lifetime, is why in the course of nailing the frame of a film together so much energy and thought are invariably expended, and have to be expended, in exactly this sort of contest between a superficial reasonableness and a fundamental idiocy. Why do film stories always have to have this element of the grotesque? Whose fault is it? Is it anybody's fault? Or is it something inseparable from the making of motion pictures? Is it the price you pay for trying to make a dream look as if it really happened? I think possibly it is. When you read a story, you accept its implausibilities and extravagances, because they are no more fantastic than the conventions of the medium itself. But when you look at real people, moving against a real background, and hear them speaking real words, your imagination is anaesthetized. You accept what you see and hear, but you do not complement it from the resources of your own imagination. The motion picture is like a picture of a lady in a half-piece bathing suit. If she wore a few more clothes, you might be intrigued. If she wore no clothes at all, you might be shocked. But the way it is, you are occupied with noticing that her knees are too bony and that her toenails are too large. The modern film tries too hard to be real. Its techniques of illusion are so perfect that it requires no contribution from the audience but a mouthful of popcorn.

Well, what has all this got to do with Guy and Bruno? What a silly question! You shouldn't have asked it. The more real you make Guy and Bruno, the more unreal you make their relationship, the more it stands in need of rationalization and justification. You would like to ignore this and pass on, but you can't. You have to face it, because you have deliberately brought the audience to the point of realizing that what this story is about is the horror of an absurdity become real—an absurdity (please notice because this is very important) which falls just short of being impossible. If you wrote a story about a man who woke up in the morning with three arms, your story would be about what happened to him as a result of this extra arm. You would not have to justify his having it. That would be the premise. But the premise of this story is not that a nice young man might in certain circumstances murder a total stranger just to appease a lunatic. That is the end result. The premise is that if you shake hands with a maniac, you may have sold your soul to the devil.

Sept. 27, 1950
To: Ray Stark[1]

... I haven't even spoken on the telephone to Hitchcock since the 21st August when I began to write the screenplay,[2] which was written in one day over five weeks. Not bad for a rather plodding sort of worker like myself. I don't know whether he likes it, or whether he thinks it stinks. The only method I have of deducing an answer to this question is that I was allowed to finish it ... Some of the scenes are far too wordy, partly because, as Woodrow Wilson once said, 'I didn't have time to write it shorter', and partly because I didn't know what Hitch was doing to the script himself ... It must be rather unusual in Hollywood for a writer to do an entire screenplay without a single discussion with the producer ...

Nov. 10, 1950
To: Hamish Hamilton

... Working with Billy Wilder on *Double Indemnity* was an agonizing experience and has probably shortened my life, but I learned from it about as much about screen writing as I am capable of learning, which is not very much. Like every writer, or almost every writer, who goes to Hollywood, I was convinced in the beginning that there must be some discoverable method of working in pictures which would not be completely stultifying to whatever creative talent one might happen to possess. But like others before me I discovered that this was a dream. Too many people have too much to say about a writer's work. It ceases to be his own. And after a while he ceases to care about it. He has brief enthusiasms, but they are destroyed before they can flower. People who can't write tell him how to write. He meets clever and interesting people, and may even form lasting

[1] Chandler's representative at the time.
[2] *Strangers on a Train.*

friendships, but all this is incidental to his proper business of writing. The wise screen writer is he who wears his second-best suit, artistically speaking, and doesn't take things too much to heart. He should have a touch of cynicism, but only a touch. The complete cynic is as useless to Hollywood as he is to himself. He should do the best he can without straining at it. He should be scrupulously honest about his work, but he should not expect scrupulous honesty in return. He won't get it. And when he has had enough, he should say goodbye with a smile, because for all he knows he may want to go back.

Nov. 22, 1950
To: Charles W. Morton

If you are so worked up about television, why don't you write the article yourself? And just whom should one be mad at, anyway? Who delivered television to the hucksters? And why blame the hucksters for being what they are? If we accept the theory, just to take a rough example, that the cosmetic racket is a respectable commercial enterprise, why should we get indignant about its advertising? If we think loud-mouthed comedians are funny instead of ineffably vulgar, why should we be surprised that shows are built around them? And if we think bad television shows are apt to corrupt the youth of this country, take a look at what goes on in the high schools.

To me television is just one more facet of that considerable segment of our civilization that never had any standard but the soft buck. Hasn't today and probably never will have . . .

Perhaps in some ways the worse television is, the better. A lot of people are looking at it, I hear, who had long since given up listening to radio. Perhaps enough of these people will realize after awhile that what they're really looking at is themselves. Television is really what we've been looking for all our lives. It took a certain amount of effort to go to the movies. Somebody had to stay with the kids. You had to get the car out of the garage. That was hard work. And you had to drive and park. Sometimes you had to walk as much as half a block to the theatre. Reading took less physical effort, but you had to concentrate a little, even when you were reading a mystery or a western or one of those historical novels, so-called. And every once in a while you were apt to trip over a three-syllable word. That was pretty hard on the brain. Radio was a lot better, but there wasn't anything to look at. Your gaze wandered around the room and you might start thinking of other things—things you didn't want to think about. You had to use a little imagination to build yourself a picture of what was going on just by the sound.

But television's perfect. You turn a few knobs, a few of those mechanical adjustments at which the higher apes are so proficient, and lean back and drain your mind of all thought. And there you are watching the bubbles in the primeval ooze. You don't have to concentrate. You don't have to react. You don't have to remember. You don't miss your brain because you don't need it. Your heart and liver and lungs continue to function normally. Apart from that, all is peace and quiet. You are in the poor man's nirvana. And if some nasty minded person comes along and says you look like a fly on a can of garbage, pay him no mind. He probably hasn't got the price of a television set.

Dec. 7, 1950
To : James Sandoe

. . . I haven't seen *Sunset Boulevard*, but I'm sure it's good in spite of *The New Yorker*. You should by all means catch *The Bicycle Thieves*, and if possible an English picture called *I Know Where I'm Going*, shot largely on the west coast of Scotland—the coast that faces the Hebrides. I've never seen a picture which smelled of the wind and rain in quite this way, nor one which so beautifully exploited the kind of scenery people actually live with, rather than the kind which is commercialized as a show place. The shots of Corryvreckan alone are enough to make your hair stand on end. (Corryvreckan, in case you don't know, is a whirlpool which, in certain conditions of the tide, is formed between two of the islands of the Hebrides.) But you'd better forget about the Hitchcock film, because I have seen the final script made up from what I wrote, but a good deal changed and castrated. It is, in fact, so bad that I am debating whether to refuse screen credit.[1]

[1] In the end Chandler took joint screen credit for the film, *Strangers on a Train*, with Czenzi Ormonde.

Nov. 7, 1951
To: Dale Warren

... You asked me how anyone can survive Hollywood? Well, I must say that I personally had a lot of fun there. But how long you can survive depends a great deal on what sort of people you get to work with. You meet a lot of bastards, but they usually have some saving grace. If you are a writer, most of your work is wasted it is true. And when it isn't, somebody else grabs most of the credit. A writer who can get teamed up with a director or producer who will give him a square deal, a really square deal, can get a lot of satisfaction out of his work. Unfortunately that doesn't happen too often. A really creative writer ought to become a director, which means that in addition to being creative he must also be very tough physically and morally. Otherwise by the time he has been kicked around enough to have learned how to write a script that can be shot, that is camera wise and not just writing, he has probably lost all his bounce.

If you go to Hollywood just to make money, you have to be pretty cynical about it and not care too much what you do. And if you really believe in the art of the film, it's a long-term job and you ought to forget about any other kind of writing. A preoccupation with words for their own sake is fatal to good film making. It's not what films are for. It's not my cup of tea, but it could have been if I'd started it twenty years earlier. But twenty years earlier of course I could never have got there, and that is true of a great many people. They don't want you until you have made a name, and by the time you have made a name, you have developed some kind of talent they can't use. All they will do is spoil it, if you let them. The best scenes I ever wrote were practically monosyllabic. And the best short scene I ever wrote, by my own judgment, was one in which a girl said 'uh huh' three times with three different intonations, and that's all there was to it.

Nov. 15, 1951
To: Carl Brandt

... The people who do a lot of worrying about what is going to happen to our civilization if everybody starts dropping atom bombs ought to be made to look at television for four hours every night for a space of say two weeks—look at it and listen to it. They might start worrying about something they could really help if they tried, because it is pretty obvious that the debasement of the human mind caused by a constant flow of fraudulent advertising is no trivial thing. There is more than one way to conquer a country. Sometimes when I wonder why I don't have a television show and get a little sore about it, I have the good grace to wonder if I could look myself in the eye if I did have one on the terms on which one must have one. But however toplofty and idealistic a man may be, he can always rationalize his right to earn money.

So by all means let's have a television show quick and long, even if the commercial has to be delivered by a man in a white coat with a stethoscope hanging around his neck, selling ergot pills. After all the public is entitled to what it wants, isn't it? The Romans knew that and even they lasted four hundred years after they started to putrefy.

Jan. 11, 1952
To: Dale Warren
   . . . Last night inveigled by the critics and the ballyhoo, although I should now know better, we went to see *A Place in the Sun.* This morning, looking through the *Variety* anniversary number, I see it is listed as the number 8 top grosser for 1951, three and a half million dollars domestic gross, which is very high for these times. So for once the New York critics and the public are agreed . . . And I despise it. It's as slick a piece of bogus self-importance as you'll ever see. And to mention it in the same breath with *A Streetcar Named Desire* seems to me an insult.

Streetcar is by no means a perfect picture, but it does have a lot of drive, a tremendous performance by Marlon Brando, and a skillful if occasionally rather wearisome one by Miss Vivien Leigh. It does get under your skin, whereas *A Place in the Sun* never touches your emotions once. Everything is held too long; every scene is milked ruthlessly . . . The chi-chi was laid on not with a trowel, not even with a shovel, but with a dragline. And the portrayal of how the lower classes think the upper classes live is about as ridiculous as could be imagined. They ought to have called it 'Speedboats for Breakfast'. And my God, that scene at the end where the girl visits him in the condemned cell a few hours before he gets the hot squat! My God, my God! . . . This slab of unreal hokum makes three and a half million dollars and *Monsieur Verdoux* was a flop. My God, my God! And let me say it just once more. My God!

Feb. 4, 1953

To: James Sandoe

. . . I thought *The Young and the Damned* was an interesting film, well photographed and directed. If you enjoy an afternoon gambolling among the garbage dumps of a big city, I suppose this is the sort of thing you would like (you being the general you here, not you in particular). It was the sort of sad and sordid film that culture bugs go pounding after full tilt, but which really doesn't add up to very much more than some parts of life are pretty dirty and nobody's doing anything much about it. As for your film critics . . . no one is right all the time; no one has to be. There are always films which you like for perhaps quite uncritical reasons. They happen to answer a mood; they happen to come close to some actual experience of the individual. I myself often like films the critics think are no good at all, and often find the films which critics praise extremely tired and laborious, and so forth and so on . . .

Feb. 14, 1955

To: Charles W. Morton

. . . The other night I looked at a television play called *Patterns* by Rod Serling; it is about a young engineer who was brought into the New York offices of some very large financial combine to replace an ageing but morally upright executive whom the boss is determined to get rid of. Little by little the older man comes to realize what is happening to him, and little by little the

young man comes to a boil with indignation at the petty mean-
ness and needless cruelty of the treatment the boss is handing
out to the older man, because he simply won't come straight out
and ask for his resignation. In the end the older man dies of a
heart attack ... and the young man goes in to see the boss with
the idea of breaking him into small pieces. The boss makes a
rather magnificent and well written defence in which he says that
his job is to drive men to heights of accomplishment, and if they
break in the process that is just too bad. There is the clear
implication that the executives and the employees exist for the
good of the business and that as individuals they simply don't
count.

If this is the thesis of big business management in our times,
it is also the thesis of Soviet communism. There is hardly a hair
between them. There is the same overdriving of the individual to
get the utmost efficiency out of him for the benefit of the firm
or the state or whatever you choose to call it, the same instantly
ruthless discarding of him the moment he begins to weaken, the
same contempt for the individual as a person, and reward and
admiration of him only as a tool of some vague purpose which
in our country seems to be the making of a lot of money for big
corporations and their stockholders and in Soviet Russia for
the protection of the State.

As you know, I have always wondered why intelligent men
occasionally become Communists, but it had never occurred to
me before that the basic philosophy underlying big business and
that underlying the Communist state were almost exactly the
same. The only difference I can see is that in Russia when you
begin to slip a little they either shoot you or send you to a forced
labor camp, whereas in the United States they ask for your
resignation or else force you to give it without being asked by
humiliating you beyond endurance.

Jan. 30, 1957
To: John Houseman [1]
   ... In *Lust for Life* you really made a masterpiece. Kirk's per-
formance in what might easily have been a monotonous and

---

[1] Film director.

tiresome role was something one hardly expects from a Hollywood actor, a complete surrender of himself to a part. I thought
it rather sublime. His walk was psychotic, that loose, swaggering
walk. He did everything perfectly, and I have no doubt that a
great deal of it was lost, and he must have known that. You
said once that '*Nobody Can Really Like an Actor!*' Well, perhaps not in some ways. But you do have to like an artist. You do
have to like Gielgud because of what he has done for the theatre,
and you do have to like Peggy Ashcroft because, although she is
rather plain, she is humble and has the most beautiful voice I
shall ever be allowed to hear. And you do have to like Kirk
Douglas as a man who can throw himself away and make a
very beautiful thing in so doing. After all, people like this don't
come with the mail.

Feb. 27, 1957
To: Edward Weeks
    ... When I wrote a couple of rather caustic things about Holly-
wood, writers warned me that I had destroyed myself, but I never
had a word of criticism from any important executive ... I think
Hollywood people are much underrated; they think, many of
them, what I think, but they just don't dare say it, and they are
really rather grateful to anyone who does. I always knew there
was only one way to deal with them. In any negotiations you
must be prepared to lay your head on the block. A writer never
has anything to fight with but whatever guts the Lord gave him.
He is always up against business organizations that have enough
power to destroy him in an hour. So all he can do is to try to
make them understand that destroying him would be a mistake,
because he may have something to give them.
    I found it quite wonderful to deal with the moguls. They
seemed so ruthless, they conceded nothing, they knew they could
throw me out, that in a sense I was nobody, that I said things to
them that a writer in Hollywood simply does not say to the big
bosses. But somehow or other they were too clever to resent it.
And in the end I almost think they liked me for it. At any rate,
they never tried to hurt me. And some of them are very clever
people. I wish I could write the Hollywood novel that has never

been written, but it takes a more photographic memory than I have. The whole scene is too complex and all of it would have to be in, or the thing would be just another distortion.

Apr. 16, 1957
To: Helga Greene

. . . Some of our TV is really very well done, but it has a soporific effect on me, after a certain time. If a film is *very* good I may stay awake, but I have slept through some of the most successful films ever made.

June 25, 1957
To: Edgar Carter

Thanks for your letter and the copy of the proposed contract with Goodson-Todman Enterprises.[1] The contract has me as goofy as a two-headed chimpanzee. I have all sorts of faults to find with it, although I understand perfectly that television is a world quite strange to me. By the way, have you noticed—I'm sure you have—that a good deal of the camera technique on TV is the sort of thing Hollywood was doing twenty years ago? I wonder why. But some of the stuff is damned good, nevertheless. The worst thing about it, except in the very best shows, is a sort of fluctuation in the lighting, and most of the direction seems to me quite below Hollywood standards, and yet the TV business is full of Hollywood people. There must be some technical reason for this.

I don't think anything will come of this contract, somehow, because these people think they can make the rules. In time, although perhaps not in my time, they will find that they can't. And I'd rather have no show at all than one which I think is making a sucker of me. When you are young and have a wife and children you have to accept things which I do not have to accept. I have no one and I can live the rest of my life on what I already have. And apart from that, I'm rather a pugnacious character. I think I proved that in Hollywood . . .

[1] A contract for a Philip Marlowe television program.

The television prices to writers are ridiculous. A few of them get real money, but these write original stuff. The average TV writer is strictly from hunger. That was why I thought I might do some work on the script, but you may think me wrong. I'd never be a good TV writer for the same reason that I was never a really good screen writer. I love words. It's true that they are more important, in TV, because otherwise the lunkheads would think nothing was happening and go out for a beer. Or else tune in on the wrestlers.

Feb. 25, 1959
To: Harris L. Katleman[1]

. . . For God's sake if you are going to pay any attention to my comments, please give me a little more time. I do indeed have a number of suggestions on the script, which is not brilliant but reads as if it might play well. First, I think the title is wrong. It is tepid and does not suggest the type of show you are making. I have tried out three or four titles in my mind but the best I have come up with is: 'Baby Sitter with a Gun' . . . the rest of my comments are about dialogue . . . Your writers in my opinion should not say things twice in the same speech. They should try to put bite into whatever is said. A great deal depends on the star and how he delivers lines, but a great deal also depends on the lines he is to deliver. If I am critical of any writer of the show, it is only because I know my character so well, so very much better than anyone else could.

[1] Executive Vice-President, Goodson-Todman Enterprises Ltd.

CHANDLER ON PUBLISHING

Jan. 11, 1945
To: Hamish Hamilton

Blanche Knopf sent me a copy of your letter to her of December 5th. It points up for me how little nowadays a writer seems to have to do with his publisher. I suppose this is largely because of the agent. Once in a while I hear from Alfred or Blanche Knopf. Their letters are always friendly but there is a sort of remoteness about the whole thing. I seem to remember in the rather dim past having received one letter from you.

Another thing that strikes me is that one publisher calls the other publisher's attention to what you term 'a magnificent boost in the *Book Society News*', and something by Desmond MacCarthy in the *Sunday Times*. But nobody ever tells the writer anything about these matters . . .

You say also 'I gather that he is a very big shot in Hollywood these days and might resent advice, whoever the sender may be and however good his intentions'. That really cuts me to the quick. I am not a big shot in Hollywood or anywhere else, and have no desire to be. I am, on the contrary, extremely allergic to big shots of all types wherever found and lose no opportunity to insult them whenever I get the chance. Furthermore, I love advice, and if I very seldom take it, on the subject of writing, that is only because I have received practically none except from my agent and he has rather concentrated on trying to make me write stuff for what we call the slick magazines over here . . .

Why not try me with a little advice some time? I am sure that I should treat yours with the greatest respect and should, in any case, like to hear from you.

Jan. 9, 1946
To: Hamish Hamilton

. . . I am wondering what is going to happen to the pocket book business. It looks to me, as an outsider, as if they would pretty soon run out of material unless they start using original material. The writer of mysteries will then be faced with the problem of deciding whether he would rather have the com-

paratively large advances and returns from the cheap trade—
now while he is hungry—or accept ten cents worth of so-called
prestige and live through the winter on a barrel of oatmeal like
John Shand. If his stuff is motion picture material he would
probably be well advised to bite on his knuckles for a while. But
if not—and the vogue for mysteries can't last forever, at least in
high-budget pictures—he might be better off to do business
direct with the pocket book people . . .

The tradition is all against any large sale of mysteries in their
original edition. And the publishers have co-operated in the
rental library swindle over a period of years with such infinite
good humour that even I, who realize the position of the author
and can afford to buy mysteries, very seldom do so, unless in cheap
reprint. To say that a book is not worth buying unless it is worth
re-reading is no answer. Practically no fiction now being published is worth re-reading and damn little of it worth reading
at all.

Early 1946
To: Hamish Hamilton
    . . . Someday I'd like to discuss with you why the publisher
has never been able to give the writer a decent living except in
cases of whopping success. It seems illogical to me. I could
understand it in the days of an extremely limited reading public,
but today it looks like economic failure. That a man whose
books are known to almost everyone he meets should not be
able to make quite a decent living out of those books strikes me
as an absurdity. There are too many damned middlemen in the
picture, I suppose.

As to my current effort,[1] it should be done not later than June,
unless I get mad and throw it away. It's kind of you to suggest
an advance. I've never accepted one on an unfinished work and
hope I never shall. I'm not rich by any means, but I'm far from
poor. I do envy the boys who worked in Hollywood in the days
when they could keep their money, though. I shall have paid
almost $50,000 income tax for last year. This is pretty awful for
a chap who was gnawing old shoes not too many years ago.

[1] *The Little Sister.*

March 8, 1947

To: James Sandoe

. . . I am a damn fool not to be writing novels. I'm still getting
about $15,000 a year out of those I did write. If I turned out a
really good one in the near future, I'd probably get a lot out of
it. Curiously enough my best public, relatively, is in England
where my publisher, in spite of the terrible shortage of paper, is
reissuing all my books. And over there the topflight critics, like
Desmond MacCarthy and Elizabeth Bowen, review them. Mac-
Carthy panned me, said the toughness was largely bluff (which
is true), but in view of the fact that he does only one article a
week and devoted it all to one of mine I am less concerned with
his strictures than with what he did with his space.

Oct. 6, 1946

To: Hamish Hamilton

. . . I never really solved my agent problem. I still feel much
the same about agents as a class: that they are often a nuisance
and sometimes do very stupid things. But living down here at
La Jolla, and not being able to face a regular secretary around
the house, I don't see how I could function without an agent.
The thing about agents that really annoys me is not that they
make mistakes but that they never admit them.

Dec. 20, 1946

To: H. N. Swanson

. . . This is to thank you very, very much for your Christmas
gift of the little radio.

From the shape of it, I gathered that it was to be placed on a
bookshelf. I have therefore placed it between Roget's *Thesaurus*
and Bartlett's *Quotations*, and the cretinous dialogue of 'When
a Girl Marries' coming out from between those two books certainly gives me a laugh.

My wife said (paraphrased slightly), 'Why the hell should
Swanson keep on giving you presents when you don't do a

damned thing for him except cause him a lot of worry, and especially when you give him nothing in return?'

I am therefore going to look for a pair of twelve-hundred-year-old Ming vases to present to you on your next birthday, and I hope they will be large enough to be used as receptacles for your discarded clients.

May 15, 1947
To: Erle Stanley Gardner

... If the publisher were really the author's or agent's friend and represented him as he should, it would be fine, but I don't think in general that the publisher is. My feeling is that the publisher ought to be able to recognize some saleable and meritorious quality in books early enough in the game to help convince the public and to help promote the books, rather than wait around for a lot of unknown disconnected individuals scattered over the face of the country to find out for themselves that such and such a writer is a good writer and to say so often and loud enough, and in sufficient numbers, to create for him some sort of vogue. I think the publisher should be able to contribute to this vogue to get it started.

June 2, 1947
To: Dale Warren

... I have always hated the book clubs and I have always thought that the publisher grabbed far too much of the reprint and subsidiary rights to the books he published. The fact that he will occasionally make concessions to an established writer does not alter his practice towards unestablished writers. The publisher could justify himself perhaps, but he won't give any figures out. He won't tell you what his books cost him, he won't tell you what his overhead charge is, he won't tell you anything. The minute you try to talk business with him he takes the attitude that he is a gentleman and a scholar, and the moment you try to approach him on the level of his moral integrity he starts to talk business.

May 11, 1948
To: Carl Brandt

Come Michaelmas, or thereabouts, I shall be in need of a literary agent. The purpose of this is to inquire whether your office would be interested.

At the moment there is nothing much to do . . . I have a mystery novel half finished.[1] The writing is of an incomparable brilliance, but something has went wrong with the story. An old trouble with me. The brain is very, very tired. I have lately finished a screenplay for Universal-International, want to finish this mystery and do another novel which has a murder in it but is not a mystery. Monday I am going north for a month. What I want to do and what I do are not always of the same family.

You are a stranger to me and I can't very well let my hair down but neither should I want you to be too much in the dark. I am not a completely amiable character any more than I am a facile and prolific writer. I do most things the hard way and I suffer a good deal over it. There may not be a lot of mileage left in me. Five years of fighting Hollywood has not left me with many reserves of energy . . .

May 13, 1949
To: Hamish Hamilton

. . . I don't know what's happening to the writing racket in this country. I get an offer of $1200 a year for the use of my name on the title of a new mystery magazine, *Raymond Chandler's Mystery Magazine*. I have nothing to do with the magazine, no control over the contents and no contact whatever with the editorial policy. They are not even faintly aware that the offer is an insult and that for a writer to trade on his reputation without putting something into the pot is not permissible. You can sell your work in any way you please, you can subdivide it and sell it in small pieces, but your standing with the public, high or low, you do not own—you hold it in trust.

I'm aware that apparently reputable people do not agree with me. I am told they take money for puffing books (I have been

[1] *The Little Sister*.

offered some), and they go on autographing tours as a matter of course, they talk at book fairs, they are very occasionally photographed as Men of Distinction holding a glass of blended whisky that I should be almost afraid to pour down the drains, for fear of corroding the metal . . . I don't want to be revoltingly old-school-tie, but it does seem to me that a line has to be drawn, and I am even willing to argue that you can rule out ethics and you would still, if you had any vision, have to draw that line as a matter of policy. But such is the brutalization of commercial ethics in this country that no one can feel anything more delicate than the velvet touch of a soft buck.

Oct. 15, 1949
To: Bernice Baumgarten
    . . . I'm pretty sore about the *Newsweek* project—sore at myself, really, not any anyone else, because I let myself be taken for a ride again on that tricky steed, publicity. After getting the treatment from *Time* several years ago I should have known better. But I was assured by the Houghton Mifflin publicity man that *Newsweek* was not like that. So you give them everything they want, talking yourself silly and exhausting yourself with posing for God knows how many pictures, get reproductions of older pictures made for them and in the end not only do they not give you anything they promised, but they don't even review the book at all.

    What hurts here is a sense of guilt unrewarded, like the pickpocket who gets an empty wallet.

June 14, 1950
To: Dale Warren
    . . . It never occurred to me that you would want me to send you a copy of my novelette.[1] *Cosmopolitan* has just rejected it, so I feel rather deflated. It appears they are having some kind of change in trend or tone, or whatever they call these things in a magazine. Why the hell can't they once in a while reject

          [1] *Professor Bingo's Snuff.*

something just because it stinks? 'Dear Sir: Your story *Midnight at Dawn* has been carefully read by our editorial staff. We are returning it herewith and suggest that you use it to line a bureau drawer.'

May 22, 1950
To: Hardwick Moseley

I have a note from Bernice Baumgarten saying that Houghton Mifflin would like a formal consent from me to the terms for your arrangements for reprint editions of *The Little Sister* and *The Simple Art of Murder*. Please take this as my consent. Please send me my end of the take as soon as possible as our cat needs a new basket.

I had of course planned originally to republish these books myself. A close friend (and close is the word I want) has a small hand press and a fair supply of deckle-edged vellum, and also a font or so of 24-point Goudy Lombardic capitals. We thought we could turn out something quite nice, say in a limited edition of nine copies, handsomely autographed by the author during a rare moment of comparative sobriety, and retailing at about $65 a copy. We were quite confident of the result, but I shall not specify what result . . .

June 23, 1950
To: Hamish Hamilton

Your Paris trip sounds like a typical publisher's jaunt, every meal an interview, and authors crawling in and out of your pockets from morning till night. I don't know how publishers stand these trips. One writer would exhaust me for a week. And you get one with every meal. There are things about the publishing business that I should like, but dealing with writers would not be one of them. Their egos require too much petting. They live over-strained lives in which far too much humanity is sacrificed to far too little art. I think that's why I decided years ago that I should never be anything but an amateur. If I had the talent to be first-class, I would still lack the hard core of selfishness which is necessary to exploit that talent to the full. The creative artist seems to be almost the only kind of man that you could never meet on neutral ground. You can only meet him as an artist. He sees nothing objectively because his own ego is always in the foreground of every picture. Even when he is not talking about his art, which is seldom, he is still thinking about it. If he is a writer, he tends to associate only with other writers and with the various parasitic growths which batten on writing. To all these people literature is more or less the central fact of existence. Whereas, to vast numbers of reasonably intelligent people it is an unimportant sideline, a relaxation, an escape, a source of information, and sometimes an inspiration. But they could do without it far more easily than they could do without coffee or whisky.

Nov. 15, 1950
To: Edgar Carter

Thanks for those big fat checks you have been sending me. They make quite a difference in my life. Extra spoonful of grape-nuts in the morning.

Will be in Los Angeles Nov. 27th (so planned anyhow) and will be happy to buy you and Swanie[1] or you without Swanie a lunch (eon) at some flashy rendezvous of the lower classes (i.e. writers, bit players, unsuccessful agents, and producers and directors employed by Republic, Monogram, P.R.C., and other smaller studios like Paramount).

I am having a feud with Warners. I am having a feud with the gardener. I am having a feud with the man who came to assemble a Garrard changer and ruined the L.P. records. I have several feuds with the TV people. Let's see who else—oh, skip it. You know Chandler. Always griping about something.

Jan. 9, 1951
To: Hamish Hamilton

. . . I have taken the liberty of sending you an Italian translation of *The Little Sister* in the hope that you will glance over it

[1] H. N. Swanson.

and tell me whether I am right in my opinion that it is a perfectly
abominable job of translating, full of outright mistakes (to
determine which you need not read beyond the first two or three
pages) and also making no attempt whatever to render my kind
of writing into an equivalent sort of Italian, although I'm quite
sure that such an Italian style must be well developed, just as in
French. In their cast of characters they make mistakes so stupid
as to indicate an extreme carelessness in the whole production.
And as for the picture on the cover, I think it would be regarded
as revoltingly crude even by a pulp magazine here. There is no
point in this sort of thing. It would be better for me not to have
my books published in Italian at all if this is the most I can
expect.

May 15, 1951
To: Freeman Lewis[1]
   Thanks for sending me your new edition of *Farewell, My
Lovely* . . . Is it permissible to wonder why the people who do
illustrations and covers can't pay some attention to the text?
The bedspring shown in your cover illustration is entirely wrong,
since it is a type of spring which is very light and would be useless as a weapon. If your illustrator had taken the trouble to
read merely a few lines at the top of page 144 in the book, he
might not have made a fool of himself and incidentally of me,
since the kind of spring I was writing about would be a very
efficient weapon, almost as efficient as a blackjack. The kind he
illustrated would be of no use at all. Also, he ought to take a
look at a hospital bed sometime and see what these so-called
springs are made of and how they are put together.

June 19, 1951
To: Richard H. Dana[2]
   You have sent me a massive hunk of galleys of a book al-
legedly by one Charles W. Morton, an Omaha Bostonian who

[1] Executive Vice-President Pocket Books Inc.
[2] Promotion Manager, J. B. Lippincott Co.

fiddles around with *The Atlantic Monthly* in some obscure capacity . . . You are in a frantic rush. You are holding the presses on the jacket in case I might care to get hysterical and call Mr Morton the greatest American humorist since Hoover. So I am supposed to drop everything, including the week's washing and ironing and such feeble attempts as I may make to earn a living, and dedicate myself to your noble purpose. You have probably been stalling around with this book for six months until somebody lit a fire under your chair, and now you are climbing up and down the walls yodelling like a Swiss tenor, because, forsooth, 'the jackets must go to press without fail next week, be sure to send your comment along the fastest way'.

I know you publishers. You send the proofs off by air express and I sit up all night correcting them and send them back the same way. And the next thing anybody hears about you, you're sound asleep on somebody's private beach in Bermuda. But when anybody else has to do something, it's rush, rush, rush. I may read these galleys and I may not. I may make a comment about them, and I may not. Perhaps I'll go out and cut the back lawn instead. I have some begonias to plant and some roses to spray, and we have a new Siamese kitten which takes up quite a lot of my time. And let me tell you something else. There's an article of mine on the way to *The Atlantic Monthly*[1] and the reception that gets will have a great deal of influence on the reception that Mr Charlie Morton's compendium of idle verbiage gets from me.

July 5, 1951
To: Charles W. Morton
    . . . As to this business of pre-publication plugs on bookjackets, where do you get this bitter sweet stuff? I wasn't writing to you but to a man at Lippincott's. Evidently somebody with an important name dropped dead or got jailed at the last moment, so he had to root around in the weeds for a substitute; so I just had a little fun with him, meaning no harm to anyone. Secretly of course I was delighted that he hit me when I didn't have time to think, because I hate the whole lousy racket. The

[1] *Ten Per Cent of Your Life.*

proper time to praise a writer is after his book has been published, and the proper place to praise him is in something else that is published. You must be well aware that there is practically a stable of puff merchants back in your territory who will go on record over practically anything including the World Almanac, provided they get their names featured. A few names occur with such monotonous regularity that only the fact of their known success as writers keeps one from thinking that this is the way they earn their groceries.

My personal reaction to complimentary remarks on dust jackets, other than those quoted from reviews, is to refuse to have anything to do with the book enclosed in the jacket. But that's only personal, and of course I don't claim to be the most amiable character in the world. Over in England they carry this quote business (though not pre-publication so much) to the point where it is absolutely meaningless. The currency of praise has been so depreciated that there is nothing to say about a really good book. It has all been said already about the second, third and fourth rate stuff.

I'm glad you find something of interest in my piece about agents.[1] I knew it was much too long and I knew I should have to cut the hell out of it, and if you're willing to do that, I'm delighted. No need to show me any cut version in advance of publication; I'm perfectly satisfied to have you handle it in whatever way seems right to you.

Dec. 17, 1951
To: Charles W. Morton

... As for that article about agents, I think now, after reading your proof, that I was too nice to them. But when I opened the morning paper one morning last week, I saw that it had finally happened: somebody shot one. It was probably for the wrong reasons, but at least it was a step in the right direction.

---

[1] *Ten Per Cent of Your Life.*

TEN PER CENT OF YOUR LIFE

(Published in *The Atlantic Monthly*, Feb. 1952)

Among all those quasi-professional businesses which like to refer to their customers as clients the business of literary agenting is probably the most enduring and the most adhesive. Technically, you can fire your agent; it is a sticky operation, but a determined man can achieve it. It really ends nothing. Long after your agent has been gathered to his fathers, you may be paying commissions to his estate on some transaction with which he had hardly any contact, something purely automatic that arose out of something else long before.

There is nothing wrong with this. It is the way the agent gets his pay. But writers as a class are apt to be a cantankerous and not particularly lovable set of people; they have the egotism of actors without either the good looks or the charm. However much they are paid, they never think they are paid enough. They resent it that other people make money out of the work they, the writers, do alone and unaided. The agent creates for himself a vested interest in a writer's entire professional career. However much you pay him, he is never paid off. What really galls you on the raw is not how much commission the agent collects, but that the account is never closed. The agent never receipts his bill, puts his hat on and bows himself out. He stays around forever, not only for as long as you can write anything that anyone will buy, but as long as anyone will buy any portion of any right to anything that you ever did write. He just takes ten per cent of your life.

Perhaps the sensible thing is to get it over with and admit that throughout the history of commercial life nobody has ever quite liked the commission man. His function is too vague, his presence always seems one too many, his profit looks too easy, and even when you admit that he has a necessary function, you feel that this function is, as it were, a personification of something that in an ethical society would not need to exist. If people could deal with one another honestly, they would not need agents. The agent creates nothing, he manufactures nothing, he distributes nothing. All he does is cut himself a slice off the top. Possibly there are agents who dislike the commission method of payment as much as the most contentious writer, and would gladly change it into something else, if there were anything else to change it into. The writing profession itself is far too speculative and uncertain to permit of any system of fixed fees for the selling of its products. The struggling writer simply wouldn't have the money to pay the bill, and the successful one would very rapidly become aware that what he was charged was more nearly determined by the size of his income than by the amount of time and effort that went into the service rendered to him. That is obviously true of professions much more strictly administered than agency. Furthermore, the agent did not invent the percentage method of payment, nor does he monopolize it. He has a lot of company, including various taxing authorities and including the writer himself if he is a writer of books, since royalties are merely commissions by another name.

Perhaps the three most valuable attributes of an agent are his emotional detachment from a very emotional profession, his ability to organize the bargaining power of his clients, and his management of the business side of a writer's career. As to the first of these, I do not suggest that the agent is callous or hard-boiled, but merely that he is, and has to be, realistic in a thoroughly commercial sense. If you do a bad job, he will not tell you it is good; he will merely suggest its badness in the nicest possible way.

Next, the agent creates and maintains a competitive atmosphere without which the prices paid for literary material would be a mere fraction of what they are today. In Hollywood, where this is carried to its extreme limits, literary material is offered simultaneously to the entire market, and an offer received from one prospective purchaser is immediately used as a basis for needling all the others. The New York literary agent has not carried the system this far; the book and magazine publishers still insist that what is offered to them for sale, while they consider it, shall for the time being be offered to no one else. The rule is not absolute; there are various genteel ways of evading it without causing too much acrimony. The more powerful the magazine, the more rigidly it can enforce the rule. But however rigidly it is enforced, the editor considering material submitted by an agent is aware that the agent knows the going price; the editor's offer must come within trading distance of this, or the material will be withdrawn. The agent knows how to say no without slamming the door. He can take risks, because his risks are averaged. And if, as I suppose occasionally happens, he loses a sale by pressing too hard, the client will never know why he lost it. There will always be another reason.

The truly commanding reason for any writer to deal through an agent nowadays is the enormous complexity of the literary business. A writer operating alone, even with the assistance of a secretary, would be so snowed under by correspondence and paper work, filing and digesting contracts, so confused by the ramifications of copyright, that either he wouldn't know where he stood or he wouldn't have any time left for writing. Many very successful writers have only the foggiest notion of what, legally and contractually speaking, has happened to the products of their brains. They don't know the elements of the financial side of their business. They don't know what they own, what they have sold, whom they have sold it to, nor on what terms, nor when the payments are due, nor whether in fact payments that are past due have been received. They trust their agents to look after all that and take what their agents send them without scrutiny or mistrust.

Such people would be very easy to swindle, and it is a high tribute to the agency profession that with so many suckers to deal with, so few agents have ever been caught doing anything dishonest. If the ethical standards of agency are declining, and I think they are, and I think it is inevitable that they should, it is remarkable that their dollars-and-cents honesty in dealing with their clients has so seldom been attacked. The decline I mentioned is not a question of individuals stealing money, but of something in the nature of a personal service profession turning into a hard-boiled business, and a pretty big business at that.

The old-line literary agent still exists, but he is slipping. He was a pretty useful fellow. In addition to his obvious functions of knowing markets and prices and having the tenacity to go through a long list of them before giving up, he acted as a clearing house for information. He was a post office, and he was a buffer. He guarded the writer in many matters of detail in connection with contracts and the sale of subsidiary rights. He gave fairly sound business advice. In those somewhat rare cases where he had the ability to recognize quality beyond mere saleability, he encouraged and helped the writer to improve himself in his profession. If he made mistakes, they were usually not too costly, because his operations, taken one at a time, were rather modest. As a Hollywood operator of my acquaintance put it, 'Those boys bring their lunch'. The literary agent collected money, forwarded royalty reports, and kept the writer's affairs in some kind of order. Most writers were quite satisfied with this service.

This kind of agent, if I may say so without rancor, had inevitable faults, some of which were the price of his virtues. He was always persuading his writers to adapt themselves to the big smooth-paper magazines in which a few genuine talents have survived but far more have perished. The reason was not discreditable, since the agent had no security of tenure and demanded no contract for a term of years. If he wished to make money out of you, he would naturally try to channel your talents into the most immediately lucrative field. It would have been unfair to expect him to realize that this was not in the long run the most lucrative field for every writer. If he did realize this, the agent had no guarantee that he would be around when the long run paid off. He read himself half blind in a search for saleable material and for talent which he might with good luck build into a money-making capacity; at which point some Hollywood agent would be very apt to steal it from him.

Another of his faults was that he took in rather too much territory. He demanded the right to represent you in fields which he did not understand and could not properly cover: motion picture, radio, television, the stage, and the lecture platform. In these he would make split-commission deals with specialists where he had to, but he would rather not, because he needed the money. When he did make split-commission deals, he was apt to select a second-rate practitioner not powerful enough to steal his client. This could, and did, result in serious mishandling of his client's interest. But against his faults must be set one commanding virtue: he spent a large part of his time and effort in the service of unknowns whose aggregate commissions would not pay his office rent. And he did so in the sure and certain knowledge that if and when they became known and successful, they were quite likely to slam the door in his face without so much as a thank you.

This type of agent has gradually been driven towards the

fringes of his profession because of the same complexities which forced the working writer to have an agent in the first place. If the agent has the resource and ability to avoid this fate, he will be forced into a much more elaborate organization, and into a system of alliances with the high pressure specialists who operate in the other media to which writers contribute either directly or by the adaptation of their material to other forms. To stay even with these boys, the agent has to spend money and look as if he had it to spend. He has to have competent help and adequate space in a good office building. His life becomes expensive. His long distance telephone bills cost him as much as his entire overhead used to cost. And as his overhead rises, his availability to new or unknown writers decreases. He can still recognize talent without a name, but it takes an awful lot of it to convince him that he can afford the slow, expensive toil of a build-up. He will still, for sound reasons, handle a prestige writer who isn't making much money. But if you are just a promising beginner scratching a meagre living from the tired soil, he will send you a polite note of regret. He can afford to wait until you have made a name, because when you do you will have to come to him anyway.

So, whether he likes it or not, the beginner will be forced to accept the services of a small agent as unsure and almost as uninformed as himself. Or he may even fall into the clutches of one of those racketeers of hope, calling themselves agents, whose real income is from reading fees and from such charges as they can impose on their 'clients' for editing and revising work which any reputable commission man would know in the beginning to be hopeless.

The point about the small agent who is genuinely an agent is precisely that he is small. You take him only because you cannot get someone bigger and better. You know it, and he knows it. You will stay with him only as long as you cannot do better, and he will keep you as a client only as long as you are un-important. There is no loyalty because there is no permanence. From the first your relationship with him will be ambiguous. And yet in later years, if you are what is known as successful, you may look back on this small agent with a touch of nostalgia. He was a simple fellow, insecure like yourself. A twenty dollar commission meant a lot to him, because he needed the money, and he couldn't afford to take chances. That story he sold to a pulp magazine might, with a little careful polishing, have made *Cosmopolitan* or *Red Book*. But the big market was a gamble, and here was a pulp magazine with money in its hand, and the agent's secretary bothering him for something on account of her overdue salary.

You didn't blame him and wouldn't have, even if you had known what was in his mind. You needed the money too. Besides, you rather liked the guy. More often than not he typed his own letters, just as you had to, and they were nice warm encouraging letters. In a simpler world you and he might have been good friends. But of course he could never have got you that deal with MGM.

This brings me, not too eagerly, to the orchid of the profession—the Hollywood agent—a sharper, shrewder, and a good deal less scrupulous practitioner. Here is a guy who really makes with the personality. He dresses well and drives a Cadillac—or someone drives it for him. He has an estate in Beverly Hills or Bel-Air. He has been known to own a yacht, and by yacht I don't mean a cabin cruiser. On the surface he has a good deal of charm, because he needs it in his business. Underneath he has a heart as big as an olive pit. He deals with large sums of money. His expenses are tremendous. He will buy you a meal at Romanoff's or Chasen's with no more hesitation than is necessary for him to tot up the commissions he has made out of you in the last six months. He controls expensive talent, since with rare exceptions he is not exclusively an agent for writers. This gives him prestige in dealing with people who are starved for talent in spite of having a great deal of money to buy it with.

He is rough and tough and he doesn't care who knows it. He may think up an entirely new kind of deal and put it over in the face of great opposition. He will seldom make a bad deal for fear of not making any deal at all. His prestige as a negotiator is at stake, and he is not moved by the consideration of earning a commission to the extent that he will allow himself to be beaten in a trade. He operates in a hard world.

The Hollywood agent pays a big price for his ability and toughness as a trader. He is a huckster of talent, but talent as such he seldom respects or even understands. He is concerned solely with its market value. Quality does not interest him, only the price tag. Even within the narrow limits of his own activities, he cannot tell the good from the bad, merely the expensive from the cheap. He scurries around the studios and the restaurants and the night clubs, his ears reaching for gossip and his eyes always restlessly seeking some new or important face. It is a part of his business to know what is going on, since many of his most successful operations have depended on a piece of inside information which was in effect nothing more than backstairs gossip. If a studio wants to buy something, he must know why and for what purpose and on whose instructions, and whether the front office negotiator has a blank check or has been ordered not to purchase unless purchase is cheap.

No writer operating in his own interest could deal with this situation, even if the structure of the motion picture industry would allow him to, which it will not, because in Hollywood deals are made by word of mouth even though the elaborate contracts which embody them may take weeks to write. When made they must be final, although legally either party can withdraw up to the moment the contract is signed. To achieve finality the reputation and word of an agent must be involved. In the lush days of Hollywood there is no question but that many agents made far too much money. Ten per cent on the sale of a piece of literary property might be fair enough, but ten per cent of the salary earned during a seven-year employment contract came pretty close to larceny.

Since the same hard-boiled way of doing things prevailed in radio and prevails now in television, it was only natural that the once personal, kindly, and intimate relationship between an author and his commission man became a question of dealing more or less at arm's length with someone you never entirely trusted and often did not trust at all. The fat profits to be made in Hollywood and in radio brought a new kind of operator into the business—a sharpshooter with few scruples, whose activities spread over the whole field of entertainment. The law allowed him to incorporate, which, in my opinion, was a fatal mistake. It destroyed all semblance of the professional attitude and the professional responsibility to the individual client. It permitted a variety of subtle maneuvers whereby the agent could make a great deal more money after taxes, and it allowed him to slide, almost unobserved, into businesses which had nothing to do with agency. He could create packaging corporations which delivered complete shows to the networks or the advertising agencies, and he loaded them with talent which, sometimes under another corporate name, he represented as an agent. He took his commission for getting you a job, and then he sold the job itself for an additional profit. Sometimes you knew about this, sometimes you didn't. In any case the essential point was that this operator was no longer an agent except in name. His clients and their work became the raw material of a speculative business. He wasn't working for you, you were working for him. Sometimes he even became your employer and paid you a salary which he called an advance on future commissions. The agency part of his operations was still the basic ingredient, since without control of talent, he had no bricks to build his wall, but the individual meant nothing to him. The individual was just merchandise, and the 'representing' of the individual was little more than a department of an entertainment trust—a congeries of powerful organizations which existed solely to exploit the commercial value of talent in every possible direction and with the utmost possible disregard for artistic or intellectual values.

Such trusts, and it is fair to call them that regardless of whether they meet an exact legal definition, cover the whole field of entertainment. Their clients include actors, singers, dancers, mouth organ players, trainers of chimpanzees and performing dogs, people who ride horses over cliffs or jump out of burning buildings, motion picture directors and producers, musical composers, and writers, in every medium including those quaint old-fashioned productions known as books. The organizations maintain publicity departments, travel bureaus, hotel reservation facilities, and for a small additional commission (or perhaps for none if you are important enough to them) they will manage your private business affairs, keep your books, make out your income tax returns, and get you your next divorce. Of course you don't have to become their client, but the inducements are glittering. And if they reduce you to a robot, as eventually they will, they will usually be very pleasant about it, because they can always afford to employ well-dressed young men who smile and smile.

Old-line New York literary agents can hardly look forward with pleasure to the prospect of becoming department managers in some big, impersonal industry whose only motivating force is the fast buck. They have been for the most part serious and reputable people. Nevertheless, they have to eat, and preferably high on the joint where the meat is tasty. To do this, they must deal with the entertainment industry and with the talent trusts that feed it. And you can't deal with sharpers without becoming a little of a sharper yourself. The more distinguished practitioners may be able to keep their independence for a time; they may still deal scrupulously with their clients as individuals; they may still be the spark of successful and even distinguished literary careers. But the talent trusts are snapping at their heels in greed for commissions and in their desire for the control and manipulation of every ingredient that the increasingly vast entertainment industry must use. Where the money is, there will the jackals gather, and where the jackals gather something usually dies.

Probably the literary agents do not agree with my gloom. Having dealt in the past on fairly level terms with the big publishing combines and with the predatory but always uncertain and bewildered moguls of Hollywood, they think they can still deal on level terms with any and all concentrations of power. Naturally, I hope the agents are right. I pray they may be right. Any working writer who does otherwise is either an imbecile or already corrupted beyond repair.

Feb. 13, 1952
To: Miss Wilma Shirley Thone[1]
. . . Your experience with the 'agent' you mention must by this time have taught you what to expect from the sort of people who solicit unknown or unestablished writers as clients. The woods are full of them and will continue to be full of them as long as the country is full of would-be writers who are willing to pay them unearned fees in the faint but desperate hope that somehow, somewhere they can sell something to a reputable magazine.

It may sound harsh, but a beginning writer is better off without an agent until he or she has had enough stuff published in

[1] Of Clyde, Ohio.

some decent magazine to interest a real agent, not a faker. When
that stage is reached an agent is worth while, because he will get
you better prices through knowing what prices are possible, he
will protect your rights in a way which you would probably
not know how to protect them yourself, and he may make sales
down side streets which you would not think of trying. But if
he represented the struggling writer who was just trying to break
in, how on earth could he make a living?

March 10, 1952
To: H. N. Swanson
What do you mean, do a trailer plugging a picture named
The Ragged Edge? You want I should be a man of indistinction
or something sitting behind a borrowed desk, looking straight
into the camera and giving a spiel? Or is it that I should write
the stuff for fifty dollars a week maybe, like a publicity man?
I think that Sherlock Holmes tie you sent me has gone to your
head. Seriously, the only thing about this proposition, if you
could call it a proposition, that interests me is the fact that anybody would want me to do it. They're crazy anyhow. I have
about as much publicity value as a fuzzy caterpillar. After five
and a half years in La Jolla I don't think I even got my name in
the local paper.

Nov. 14, 1952
To: Mr Sheppard[1]
Whatever happened to my photographs, those that were
taken on October 6th last by the Russian-Armenian lady in the
smock and the Apache-style coiffure? You remember the proofs
were to have been sent to you by the following Friday.
Experience has taught me to be very sensitive about photographs. I am no fuzzy chicken and I can be made to look pretty
ghastly. All questions of personal vanity apart, I am convinced
as a member of the reading public that bad photographs are
bad business.

[1] Of Hamish Hamilton Ltd.

I don't think publishers pay enough attention to this sort of thing. I do think, and positively, that a poor photograph is worse than none at all. In his writing, if he is going to get anywhere, an author has to present the public with an attractive personality. It may be and often is an artificial personality, something the author as a human specimen cannot live up to. But time and time again publishers will destroy the effect the author has managed to achieve in his writing by presenting a photographic study of him as a conceited ape or a flat-faced homunculus whom you would not on his looks think capable of a BBC talk about the sex life of a caterpillar . . .

Undated, 1954
To: Hardwick Moseley
The Bantam Books operation is okay by me if I don't have to sign that warranty. I never heard of such impudence. The big networks used to demand that sort of warranty and I always refused to sign it and never did. No one has ever attacked me so far and yet in every book I have written there is what is described by my more perceptive friends as a 'thinly disguised portrait of some notorious local character'. In every case the thinly disguised etc. has been a portrait of someone I didn't even know existed. In *The High Window* I had an Italian mortician on Bunker Hill who was a political boss on the side. Well, whaddaya know, there actually was an Italian mortician on Bunker Hill who was a political boss, and a pretty crooked one, on the side. But I never heard of him. I invented him. I suppose it's an old story. And yet when you do use some really notorious person as a model nobody spots it.

March 1, 1954
To: Paul Brooks[1]
. . . Some day someone ought to explain to me the theory behind dust jacket designs. I assume they are meant to catch the eye without offering any complicated problems to the mind, but

[1] Editor, Houghton Mifflin Co.

they do present problems of symbolism that are too deep for
me. Why is there blood on the little idol?[1] Why is the idol there
at all? What is the significance of the hair? Why is the iris of the
eye green? Don't answer. You probably don't know either.

March 23, 1954
To: Hardwick Moseley

I'm sick as a dog, thank you, with one of those lousy virus
infections the doctors have invented to cover up their ignorance.
I missed seeing Paul Brooks two weeks ago and I'm still rocking.
I also missed a *Time* photographer who insisted on a picture . . .
There is no worse murderer than a newspaper flash gun artist.
They did one of me in London that made me look like Grandma
Moses and I swore I'd never have another. (By the way, where
did you get that beastly thing you put in your spring list?)

You'd better do a damn sight better with *The Long Good-Bye*
than you did with *Little Sister*. I realize the appalling situation,
but I also realize that the publishers are not indefinitely going to
be able to make their profits, if any, by their share of the re-
prints. Writers of forgettable fiction will simply be forced into
the paper-back market. How the hell can you expect anyone to
pay dollars three for a mystery novel? I might be the best writer
in this country, and with two exceptions I very likely am, but
I'm still a mystery writer. For the first time in my life I was reviewed as a novelist in the London *Sunday Times* (but Leonard
Russell is a friend of mine and may have leaned a little out of
kindness). I was discussed on the BBC by as addled a group of
so-called intellectuals (among them Dilys Powell hardly got a
word in) as ever had soup on their vests. But over here?

It may interest and even sadden you to know that I receive a
larger income from Europe, especially England, than from the
U.S.A. in spite of the exchange situation. Your December statement was a whimper from the morgue. Your total sales of *Little
Sister* (which you hope to equal with this last thing and have
not at the time of writing, obviously) are less than 17,000 copies.
The English sales for the same period were almost 30,000.

[1] On the jacket of *The Long Good-Bye*.

April, 1954

To: The Editor, *The Third Degree*

I disagree with Helen McCloy's[1] rules for handling fan letters, as published in a recent issue of *The Third Degree*.

The idea that writers of fan letters are psychopathic is judging the general by the exceptional. A few of them are, of course. If I get a letter (I haven't lately) from a lady in Seattle who says she likes music and sex and practically invites me to move in, it is safe not to answer it. If you get a letter from a schoolboy asking for an autographed photo to hang in his den beside the photographs of such distinguished personalities as Hedy Lamarr, the Emperor Franz Josef and Dr Crippen, you ignore that too. And occasionally a fan letter is a pitch for a free copy of a book—you can always tell by the letter itself.

Intelligent people write intelligent letters. I've had them from all over the world—and at least two-thirds of them have been polite and friendly and rather diffident. I know that answering them can be a real economic problem for a real best-seller, but it never has been for me—I'm not that popular a writer. And I strongly object to Miss McCloy's dictum that the fan-letter writer is ipso facto abnormal or psychopathic. He may be just lonely, just generous, or just someone who finds pleasure in letter-writing.

Aug. 10, 1954

To: Dale Warren

. . . The reviews of *Long Good-Bye* sound much better than the sales which are, so far as I know, about one quarter of what they were in England . . . It's a weird business all right. You put out a novel over there at 12/6 and nobody buys it but the library unless it's by somebody who is an automatic best seller, like Daphne du Maurier. You put out the same book at 10/6 and you sell 30,000 copies. The difference is two shillings, and for two shillings in London you can't even get a decent seat in a movie theatre. Over here the publisher puts out a mystery novel for $3.00 which he knows is too much for the public, although not nearly enough from his point of view, and to try to make the merchandise look elegant, he prints it well on good paper,

[1] Author of crime fiction.

binds it well and adds an expensive jacket. I guess nobody knows how much the public would pay for a book, willingly, outside of the best-seller list and the snob appeal (pay for a book just because they want to read it, that is) but my guess would be about fifty cents tops.

After all I don't buy novels very often, not even those which might be supposed to have a special interest for me. From the point of view of the time and trouble and expense that goes into the making of them, books are cheap, very cheap at current prices, but they're not cheap for the fellow who is just looking for something to read. Far from it. And not cheap even if they're good enough to read a second time. I don't know the answer to this problem and I don't suppose you do. All I know is that I'm a member of the reading public as well as a writer, and that I don't buy mystery novels for three dollars even though I might be able to afford it. If I want to read one, I get it at the rental library. If I like it very much, I probably buy it when it comes out in the paperback and read it a second time.

This country through its enormous talent for manufacture has worked itself into an economy of overproduction, which is probably a permanent economy. Half the world is starving, or at any rate badly underfed, yet we have to have a new refrigerator and a new automobile every year or so. If we don't, we feel inferior because we are made to feel inferior. The kind of economy we have can only continue to exist if there is an enormous artificial wastage of manufactured products. We get that kind of waste in a war. In time of peace you have to try to create it artificially by advertising. In the publishing business you can't do that because there is no trade-in. I bleed for you, in more senses than one.

Sept. 1, 1956
To: Roger Machell

. . . Jamie wrote me a long and pleasant letter about covers and misprints and some great artist (for covers) whom many had tried to bribe away from him. This incorruptible genius designed the cover for *The Long Good-Bye*. I still don't like it. Houghton Mifflin's covers tend to an extravagance of design which is supposed to suggest something rather than hit you on the nose with

it. Even Paul Brooks, their senior editor, didn't know what the
last cover was supposed to mean, but it looked rich.

As to misprints, I think the strange lingo I write is a bit tough
on English proof-readers and some of the things I write are
probably changed deliberately by some typesetter or proof-
reader of the printer's because they think *I* have made a mistake.
For instance on Page 11, line eight, there appears the word
'wag', quite meaningless in context. The real word was 'vag',
short for vagrant; in this state and in many others a vagrant or
person without visible means of support and without a fixed
address can be picked up and given thirty days. But of course
whoever changed it (unless it was a mistake in my script) didn't
know what a 'vag' was and substituted 'wag'.

Oct. 26, 1956
To: Hamish Hamilton

. . . Roger and I had some growling about your covers, but it
was all amiable and I haven't changed my opinion in the least.
Have you ever looked at the dust jacket of *The Little Sister*, for
example? It portrays a dessicated (can't spell—desiccated)
schoolteacher or librarian of some 38 or 40 years of age, about
as sexy as a rat trap. Yet this little girl was young, and without
her glasses or with smarter ones, looked good enough to fumble
with. Someday, just for the hell of it, a dust jacket artist ought to
submit to the excruciating agony of reading the damn book.

Jan. 14, 1957
To: Helga Greene

. . . Books are very difficult here. The publisher insists on
getting half of the reprint rights and many quite good writers of
mystery and adventure stories and other fiction of what is regarded as hammock-reading sell directly to the paperbacks and
get all the royalties. But I don't feel that I lose much by dealing
with a publisher, since he can bargain much more strongly with
the reprint people than I could, gets much larger advances than
the chaps who go direct to them, and although the returns on

library editions aré poor by comparison with England—instead
of being three times they are about half—there is some prestige
in being published by a firm which does not have a detective
or mystery story list. Also, they are very nice people. I am going
to try to get a 70-30 per cent on the paperbacks next time. No
agent could get it, because it would at once become common
knowledge and the agent, here anyhow, would at once use it as a
bargaining point for other clients. Whereas if I could get it on
my reputation and standing, I'd keep it to myself.

Oct. 5, 1958
To: Hardwick Moseley
  . . . I still think American publishers are crazy not to bring
out cheap editions from the original plates, but I suppose you
have your reasons. One question I'd like to ask is why I never,
but never, see any book of mine on the paperback stands. There
is a tobacco shop in La Jolla that has two enormous stands with
hundreds of paperbacks—but nothing by Chandler. I'm beginning to think that the goof on the panel truck, who seems to
have absolute control of what he puts on the stands, doesn't like
me. I can go into almost any bookstore in London and find a
complete set of Penguins plus the paperbacks Jamie Hamilton's
firm now put out themselves. Here, only at very long intervals
do I ever see a book of mine. I know they have a system now of
republishing at intervals with a different cover design, but how
the hell can they sell the books to capacity if they are not available to buyers?

CHANDLER ON CATS

Chandler on Cats

March 19, 1945
To: Charles W. Morton

. . . A man named Engstead took some pictures of me for *Harper's Bazaar* a while ago (I never quite found out why) and one of me holding my secretary in my lap came out very well indeed. When I get the dozen I have ordered I'll send you one. The secretary, I should perhaps add, is a black Persian cat, 14 years old, and I call her that because she has been around me ever since I began to write, usually sitting on the paper I wanted to use or the copy I wanted to revise, sometimes leaning up against the typewriter and sometimes just quietly gazing out of the window from a corner of the desk as if to say, 'The stuff you're doing is a waste of time, bud'.

Her name is Taki (it was originally Take, but we got tired of explaining that this was a Japanese word meaning bamboo and should be pronounced in two syllables), and she has a memory such as no elephant ever tried to have. She is usually politely remote, but once in a while will get an argumentative spell and talk back for ten minutes at a time. I wish I knew what she is trying to say then, but I suspect it all adds up to a very sarcastic version of 'You can do better!'

I've been a cat lover all my life (have nothing against dogs except that they need such a lot of entertaining) and have never quite been able to understand them. Taki is a completely poised animal and always knows who likes cats, never goes near anybody that doesn't, always walks straight up to anyone, however lately arrived and completely unknown to her, who really does. . . . She has another curious trick (which may or may not be rare) of never killing anything. She brings 'em back alive and lets you take them away from her. She has brought into the house at various times such things as a dove, a blue parrakeet, and a large butterfly. The butterfly and the parrakeet were entirely unharmed and carried on just as though nothing had happened. The dove gave her a little trouble and had a small spot of blood on its breast, but we took it to a bird man and it was all right very soon. Just a bit humiliated. Mice bore her, but she catches them if they insist and then I have to kill them. She has a sort of tired interest in gophers, and will watch a gopher hole with some attention, but gophers bite and after all who the hell wants a gopher anyway? So she just pretends she might catch one if she felt like it.

She goes with us wherever we go journeying, remembers all the places she has been to before and is usually quite at home anywhere. One or two places have got her—I don't know why. She just wouldn't settle down in them. After a while we know enough to take the hint. Chances are there was an axe murder there once and we're much better somewhere else. The guy might come back. Sometimes she looks at me with a rather peculiar expression (she is the only cat I know who will look you straight in the eye) and I have a suspicion that she is keeping a diary, because the expression seems to be saying: 'Brother, you think you're pretty good most of the time, don't you? I wonder how you'd feel if I decided to publish some of the stuff *I've* been putting down at odd moments.' At certain times she has a trick of holding one paw up loosely and looking at it in a speculative manner. My wife thinks she is suggesting we get her a wrist watch; she doesn't need it for any practical reason—she can tell time better than I can—but after all you gotta have some jewelry.

I don't know why I'm writing all this. It must be I couldn't think of anything else or—this is where it gets creepy—am I really writing it at all? Could it be that—no, it must be me. Say it's me. I'm scared.

Aug. 9, 1948
To: James Sandoe
I am fascinated by the cat that brings snakes into the house. Our cat, who is 17 years old and pretty lazy now, used to do things like that . . . She is a black Persian. What kind is yours? And how many have you? We have never been able to have another, because Taki wouldn't let us. We picked up a stray kitten in the desert once and tried to bring it into the house, but she got so mad she vomited. So the poor kitten had to sleep in the garage and eat outdoors until we found a home for it. Can't have a dog either. Can't have anything but fish. She's indifferent to fish. She's horribly spoiled. The last time we went away she

knocked the cook's glasses off and when we came back she spat
at me and wouldn't speak to us for two days.

Sept. 20, 1948
To: Charles W. Morton

    . . . Did I send you a picture of our cat? I asked the cat and
she said the hell with Boston, she wouldn't have her picture
there . . . So I said they publish and edit the *Atlantic* in Boston
what's supposed to be the most intellectual periodical in the
country except the avant garde stuff that nobody reads except
the guys that write in it. The cat said, the hell with the *Atlantic*
too, the last piece she tried to read in it was something about
England (the hell with England) and by a guy working for some
college or other as some kind of teacher and the guy don't know
the difference between each other and one another. No wonder
we got illiterates running the country and guys that think *Abie's
Irish Rose* is a novel.

    You say you would take a piece about our cat, God forgive
you. Try and get a piece about our cat. We didn't have this cat
seventeen years in order for some freeloader to say God forgive
him he'd even take a piece about her for his goddam parish
magazine. Any time he would get a piece about our cat or by our
cat or even just okay'd by our cat, he would be hanging upside
down from the chandelier with his foot in his mouth. The hell
with him, our cat says. And if you don't like it, see her lawyer.

Sept. 23, 1948
To: James Sandoe

    Our cat is growing positively tyrannical. If she finds herself
alone anywhere she emits blood curdling yells until somebody
comes running. She sleeps on a table in the service porch and
now demands to be lifted up and down from it. She gets warm
milk about eight o'clock at night and starts yelling for it about
7.30. When she gets it she drinks a little, goes off and sits under a
chair, then comes and yells all over again for someone to stand
beside her while she has another go at the milk.

When we have company she looks them over and decides almost instantly if she likes them. If she does she strolls over and plops down on the floor just far enough away to make it a chore to pet her. If she doesn't like them she sits in the middle of the living room, casts a contemptuous glance around, and proceeds to wash her backside. In the middle of this engaging performance she will stop dead, lift her head without any other change of position (one leg pointing straight at the ceiling), stare off into space while thinking out some abstruse problem, then resume her rear-end job. This work is always done in the most public manner.

When she was younger she always celebrated the departure of visitors by tearing wildly through the house and ending up with a good claw on the davenport, the one that is covered with brocatelle and makes a superb clawing, as it comes off in strips. But she is lazy now. Won't even play with her catnip mouse unless it is dangled in such a position that she can play with it lying down. I'm going to send you her picture. It has me in it, but you'll have to overlook that.

Cats are very interesting. They have a terrific sense of humor and, unlike dogs, cannot be embarrassed or humiliated by being laughed at. There is nothing in nature worse than seeing a cat trying to provoke a few more hopeless attempts to escape out of a half-dead mouse. My enormous respect for our cat is largely based on a complete lack in her of this diabolical sadism. When she used to catch mice—we haven't had any for years—she brought them alive and undamaged and let me take them out of her mouth. Her attitude seemed to be, 'Well, here's this damn mouse. Had to catch it, but it's really your problem. Remove it at once.' Periodically she goes through all the closets and cupboards on a regular mouse-inspection. Never finds any, but she realizes it's part of her job.

Dec. 19, 1948
To: Dale Warren
    ... Of course you can show the script to Charlie Morton. Our correspondence is developing a very fancy tone of suppressed fury. It all started with an unfortunate remark he made about

our cat. He is evidently, in spite of his many gifts, one of those people who can't tell one cat from another. Our cat no more resembles the ordinary scrap-fed put-out-at-night feline than Louis B. Mayer resembles a clerk in a Bronx delicatessen store (or is that an unfortunate comparison?). Let me correct that and say our cat is to the ordinary cat what an Alfa-Romeo sports two-seater is to a Model A. Ford business coup, or a Rolls Silver Wraith to a wheelbarrow . . . I've written an article for Charlie but I'm afraid to send it to him . . .

Christmas, 1948
From: Taki Chandler to Mike Gibbud, Esq., a Siamese Cat of imperfect blood line, acknowledging an unsolicited Christmas greeting
Dear Mike:
   This is to thank you for your card and good wishes, which I reciprocate, although I do not reciprocate the somewhat excessive familiarity of your mode of address, since we have not, so far as I recall, been formally introduced. As to your suspicions of your 'old lady' (do try to get rid of these palsy-walsy mannerisms) they are probably quite unfounded and due to an inferiority complex which in turn is the product of your mixed blood. But don't worry about these things. This is an age of heraldic inferiority. A bend sinister is no more a disgrace today than it was in the Middle Ages. Your father may have been a gentleman, even if your mother was no lady. Your rat tail is all the fashion now. I prefer a bushy plume, carried straight up. You are Siamese and your ancestors lived in trees. Mine lived in palaces. It has been suggested to me that I am a bit of a snob. How true! I prefer to be.
   Come around sometime when your face is clean and we shall discuss the state of the world, the foolishness of humans, the prevalence of horsemeat, although we prefer the tenderloin side of a porterhouse, and our common difficulty in getting doors opened at the right time and meals served at more frequent intervals. I have got my staff up to five a day, but there is still room for improvement.
   As for your parting greetings: 'Happy mouse hunting', you

are, I trust, a little drunk. Cats of our lineage do not hunt mice.

Dec. 4, 1949
To: James Sandoe

Max Miller[1] found a cat the other day with a coyote trap on its foot. We tunnelled through some manzanita to get it and the poor damn cat's foot was all maggots, must have been wearing the trap for days and days. So gentle and no scratching or yelling when we took the trap off. I'm haunted by its almost inevitable end because I can't find the owner. It still has two toes and is doing fine at the vet's, but I can't give it a home and what the hell can I do? A great big affectionate tom cat all scarred up with many battles, not a whimper in its character, and no place to go, no one who cares to give it a home.

Dec. 16, 1949
To: James Sandoe

The cat that was caught in the trap is all right. They have named him King Two-Toes. They have removed his virility because he has been in enough fights and his right foot is no good for fighting any more. And he has a home. He hasn't just got a home, he has a real home, too.

Jan. 26, 1950
To: Hamish Hamilton

I said something which gave you to think I hated cats. By gad, sir, I am one of the most fanatical cat lovers in the business. If you hate them, I may learn to hate you. If your allergies hate them, I will tolerate the situation to the best of my ability. We have a black Persian cat nearly 19 years old which we would not exchange for one of the topless towers of Manhattan.

[1] Author living in La Jolla.

Raymond Chandler with Taki. Photograph by
John Engstead, Beverly Hills. *Reproduced
by courtesy of* Harper's Bazaar.

Dec. 15, 1950
To: H. N. Swanson

Our little black cat had to be put to sleep yesterday morning. We feel pretty broken up about it. She was almost 20 years old. We saw it coming, of course, but hoped she might pick up strength. But when she got too weak to stand up and practically stopped eating, there was nothing else to do. They have a wonderful way of doing it now. They inject nembutal into a vein in the foreleg and the animal just isn't there any more. She falls asleep in ten seconds. Pity they can't do it to people.

Jan. 9, 1951
To: Hamish Hamilton

... Our Christmas was not a particularly happy one, since we lost our black Persian cat that had been with us for almost twenty years, and was so much a part of our lives that even now we dread to come into the silent empty house after being out at night. It happened that Elmer Davis, whom you may perhaps know, lost his white Persian cat, General Gray, just a little before. And I had so much feeling for him (although Taki was not then sick enough for us to be really worried about her) that I had to write to him and commiserate. All my life I have had cats and I have found that they differ almost as much as people, and that, like children, they are largely the way you treat them except that there are a few here and there who cannot be spoiled. But perhaps this is true of children also. Taki had absolute poise, which is a rare quality in animals as well as in human beings. And she had no cruelty, which is still a rarer quality in cats. I have never liked anyone who disliked cats, because I've always found an element of acute selfishness in their dispositions. Admittedly, a cat doesn't give you the kind of affection a dog gives you. A cat never behaves as if you were the only bright spot in an otherwise clouded existence. But this is only another way of saying that a cat is not a sentimentalist, which does not mean that it has no affection.

Jan. 10, 1951
To: James Sandoe

Thanks for letter and Christmas card. I didn't send any this year. We were a bit broken up over the death of our black Persian cat. When I say a bit broken up I am being conventional. For us it was tragedy . . .

Feb. 5, 1951
To: Hamish Hamilton

Thank you for all you say about cats and your friends who are cat-lovers. After a while I think we shall get another cat, or preferably two cats. Elmer Davis says he and his wife have decided not to have another, because it would be likely to out-live them. That seems to me a curious point of view. He must be feeling rather old. By that analogy children should never have parents, women should never marry men ten years older than themselves, nobody should desire to possess a horse or in fact anything which one day one might lose. Woe, woe, woe (I think I am quoting Ezra Pound more or less) in a little while we shall all be dead. Therefore let us behave as though we were dead already.

Oct. 31, 1951
To: James Sandoe

. . . How are all your cats? We have a new black Persian who looks exactly like our last one, so exactly that we have to call him by the same name, Taki. He is going to be a very large fellow I think when he gets his full growth, as he weighs eight pounds at seven months. I had a Siamese kitten for a while, but he chewed everything to pieces and was so much trouble to handle that I had to give him back to the breeder. I felt rather bad about it, because he was an affectionate little devil and full of life. But he chewed up blankets, chewed up my clothes, and he would have chewed up all the furniture. We just couldn't let him run loose, and a cat who can't run loose in our house has no business in it. We never let them run loose in the street, but in the house they own everything.

CHANDLER ON FAMOUS CRIMES

Chandler on Famous Crimes

Dec. 14, 1951
To : Carl Brandt

... The *American Weekly* suggestion strikes me as quite down my alley *in principle*, as the negotiators say ...

The choice of the case is very difficult, since the really good ones have been written up so much and all the best cases that I'm really familiar with are English. Three of the best of all time, and certainly my three favorites, because of their huge elements of doubt, their strange characters and the richness of their background, are : the Wallace case, which I would call The Impossible Murder; the Maybrick case, or Why Doesn't an Arsenic Eater Know When He's Eating Arsenic; and the Adelaide Bartlett case, or The Man Who Didn't Get Up Half an Hour Early for Breakfast. The Wallace case is the nonpareil of all murder mysteries, but it has been done to a turn by Dorothy Sayers,[1] and whole books have been written about it. It is still not completely analysed, but the sort of analysis which remains to be done would probably not appeal to *The American Weekly*. The Maybrick case is just too damn difficult. Even the facts are in dispute. In the Wallace case an important fact is in dispute, a question of time. It is vital to the extent that if it had been decided one way Wallace would not have been convicted, and yet if it had been decided the other way the circumstances are all in favor of Wallace's innocence. I call it the impossible murder because Wallace couldn't have done it, and neither could anyone else. The Adelaide Bartlett case is relatively simple to tell, although completely goofy. It has a happy ending—the lady was found not guilty, although I personally think she was guilty. But she was not found not guilty on the strength of the evidence but on the strength of a great lawyer. I suppose the most celebrated American case is the Lizzie Borden case, but it certainly does not come under any such heading as 'The True Murder Mystery I Wish I'd Created'. Its fascination is its extreme gruesomeness against a background of extreme respectability. The real mystery is not who committed the murders (I don't think there is very much doubt about that now) but how in

[1] In *Anatomy of Murder*.

hell, granted the people concerned, such a thing could ever have
happened. The only one of these I could write about in the space
allotted would be the Adelaide Bartlett case, and that might not
interest them.

The kind of case you want is one which *is* a genuine mystery,
that is to say one which could not now be solved but on which
enough data exist to make a strong logical argument either
way; or else one which really was solved but only by a peculiar
and interesting chain of circumstances. The case should not be
sordid or repulsive. It should not be too remote in time. It should
not show up incompetent or downright crooked police methods
(as for example in the Oscar Slater case). It should not, like the
William Desmond Taylor case, be a mystery merely because
there was no adequate investigation at all. It should be a case in
which the accused, whether found innocent or guilty, had a good
run for his money and was not simply railroaded. And it should
preferably be a case in which a slight shifting of emphasis might
have made the trial go the other way. Or else, as I said before,
the chain of clues should in itself be fascinating. That's another
way of saying that it should be a case which would have been
worth writing as fiction.

Jan. 16, 1952
To: James Sandoe
    . . . As to the cases you were good enough to dig up and men-
tion, there seems to be a misunderstanding in your mind, for
which I suppose I must be to blame, to the effect that I wanted
a poisoning case in particular. I did not. I just wanted any good
murder case of which a detailed account was available. An
open-and-shut case is no good unless the detective work was
especially intricate and brilliant, or some strange chance brought
about the solution. I don't want any sordid cases except in the
sense that all murders are a bit sordid. I prefer a case which
can still be argued about. Except for the Lizzie Borden case,
which has been done to death, all the good ones I can think of
are English. I don't know why that is unless that there is a more
solid tradition of writing them up in England. I'm not just
going to do a rehash of somebody else's already adequate

account, and neither am I going to dig through old newspaper files, even if I knew where they were. It has to be a case on which I have or could acquire some individual ideas. I think a case like the Wynekoop case in Chicago is the sort of thing. But where does one go to find a transcription of the trial and an account of the investigations? It was written up in the book of Chicago Murders, but I can't work from that. This, like the Starr Faithfull case, has the necessary enigma.

THE MAYBRICK CASE

The Maybrick case, one of the most celebrated in legal history, is still a matter for discussion.

At the time of her trial in July 1889, *Florence Maybrick (née Chandler), an American, had for eight years been married to James Maybrick, a prosperous Liverpool cotton broker; she was* 26 *and he was* 50; *they had two children. Earlier that year Mrs Maybrick became intimate with a man named Brierley and stayed with him in a London hotel. On May* 11 *Maybrick died after an intermittent illness with acute intestinal disturbances. He had been taken violently ill nine days previously after eating a lunch his wife had prepared for him.*

Florence Maybrick was arrested, tried, and convicted; but her sentence was commuted to penal servitude for life and in 1904 *she was released. She died in South Kent, Connecticut, in* 1941 *at the age of* 88.

The verdict has frequently been assailed as a miscarriage of justice. The presiding judge had suffered a stroke and was not always in possession of his faculties; and although a certain amount of arsenic was found in Maybrick there was no actual proof that it had killed him, or that his wife had given it to him. On the other hand her innocence was never clearly established.

Chandler's keen interest was aroused partly by the lack of evidence as to the cause of Maybrick's death and partly because of the coincidence that, before her marriage, Mrs Maybrick had borne the same name as his mother—Florence Chandler.

April 5, 1948
To: James Sandoe

. . . Just read *The Trial of Florence Maybrick* in the Notable British Trials Series and I think I should very much indeed like to see Levy's analysis of the case entitled, apparently, *The Necessity for Criminal Appeal Illustrated from the Maybrick Case*. I have also read Patrick Quentin's piece, *The Last of Mrs Maybrick*, in the Pocket Book of True Crime Stories, edited by Anthony Boucher.[1]

Frankly, I am wondering whether Patrick Quentin ever read *The Trial of Mrs Maybrick*. He refers to the judge's summing-up as 'a two-day harangue of impassioned malignity and misogyny. In one of the most biased speeches ever to come from the English Bench, he referred to poor Mrs Maybrick as "a horrible woman" and branded her as the epitome of all that was vile.' These remarks are not made about that summing-up at all, so far as I can see. The reference to Mrs Maybrick as 'that horrible woman' escaped my eye completely, as did also the malignity and misogyny.

The only real criticism H. B. Irving[2] makes of the summing-up is that the judge did not again at the end, as he did at the beginning, remind the jurors that it was not proved beyond doubt that Maybrick died of arsenic poisoning. Yet if he had pointed this up again at the end, it would have amounted to inviting the jury to bring in a verdict of not guilty; and I don't think the judge was convinced Mrs Maybrick wasn't guilty. Neither do I think he was convinced she *was* guilty. I think it was one of the very few cases of this sort in which the judge himself was uncertain. His remarks about the defect then existing in criminal law which forbade the accused to take the stand in her own defence and submit to questioning and cross-examination seem to me to indicate that he felt this was the only way in which this particular puzzle could have been resolved.

In the summing-up, the judge (or the court reporter more likely) made a few mistakes in dates and a rather serious mistake in the quantity of arsenic. Nevertheless the judge's respect for the facts is in marked contrast with Patrick Quentin's very casual treatment of them. For instance he says 'Her star witness, Mr James Heaton, the chemist from whom Mr Maybrick had so

---

[1] Critic and author of crime fiction.
[2] In the Notable British Trials series.

constantly purchased his swig of *liquor arsenicalis* . . .' This is assuming a fact which was never positively proved. The defense tried very hard to show that Maybrick had a continuous record as an arsenic eater and it was apparently a fact that there was a lot of arsenic in the house. So much so in fact one wonders why Mrs Maybrick had to go out and buy flypapers containing arsenic; the judge very carefully pointed this out. If there was all this arsenic, why did Maybrick have to go to a drug store to buy it in small doses as a pick-me-up? As a matter of fact there was no competent proof that Maybrick had recently been taking arsenic; but if he had wanted to take it, he had it in the house, and didn't have to go elsewhere to buy it.

Since Maybrick was known to have a lot of stomach trouble, and at the pertinent time was suffering from a severe intestinal upset, what is so absurd in supposing that his wife fed him a little arsenic to make sure he wouldn't get over it? The effect of even a very small dose of arsenic on a man in that condition would be catastrophic; that may very well be why such a small dose killed him, if it *was* the arsenic that killed him. But the Home Secretary makes the very admirable point that even if she did give him arsenic, there is no clear evidence that that *was* what killed him. He might have died anyway, not through any lack of ambition or efficiency on her part, but simply because he was already so far gone that arsenic had no decisive effect on the result.

I am genuinely puzzled myself. I believe this case is worth the kind of close analysis that Dorothy Sayers gave to the Julia Wallace case.[1] I might even have patience to do it myself. After all, my mother's married name was Florence Chandler . . .

May 12, 1948
To: James Sandoe
. . . The Maybrick case grows more and more confusing. In a purely legal sense there is little question but that the woman should not have been convicted of murder, since it was never proved beyond reasonable doubt that Maybrick died as the result of the administration of arsenic. Yet even here one has to

[1] Included in *Anatomy of Murder.*

consider the morality of the case, the legal and judicial morality, with reference to the times. In 1889 criminal justice was not the barbarity it was in 1840, but neither was it as enlightened as it is today.

The question that intrigues me is: what did the man die of? Since arsenic was found in him, it must be assumed that he took it either himself, or it was given him by Mrs Maybrick at his request without her knowing what she was doing, or given him by Mrs Maybrick deliberately . . . Assuming for the moment that no-one poisoned him and that he did not poison himself and that the amount of arsenic in his system was not fatal and could not have been fatal, what I want to know is what did he die of? Did you ever hear of anyone dying of acute gastritis, idiopathic in origin, where there were no perforating ulcers? . . . Certainly people do die of food poisoning once in a while, but the medical picture of the case is apparently no more characteristic of food poisoning than it is of arsenic poisoning.

The whole case is a tragedy of bad judicial procedure, but this was not the fault of the judge, who could not change it at will. The judge did make mistakes, but so did everyone else, and he did call attention to the defects, the very grave defects, in the procedure of a criminal trial which then existed and which were afterwards, I don't know when, remedied.

Aug. 8, 1948
To: Dale Warren
. . . By a very odd coincidence I have been fussing with the Maybrick case myself for quite a while. I am pretty well convinced the dame was guilty. Want to get into a fight with me?

I never saw her confessional, by the way; by this I assume you do not mean her statement in court, but some later document. One point not clear to me, and I think it is very important, is when she knew that her letter to Brierley had been intercepted . . . I think the judge thought her rather more likely to be guilty than innocent, but the confusion in his mind was certainly not all due to incipient insanity. It rides through the whole case.

Sept. 2, 1948

To: Dale Warren

. . . To me the real joker about the Maybrick business is the beautiful inconsistency of the defense. The guy didn't die of arsenic poisoning; he had been eating it by the spoonful ever so long and he took it himself.

Of course the medical work was atrocious, by our standards. It would have been quite possible to demonstrate not only whether or no he was a chronic and recent eater of arsenic, but how long he had been using it.

Well, this could go on forever. The question will never be really settled now. It might be interesting, but hardly worth the effort, to construct the evidence on the theory that she was guilty. After all, it's only been done the other way. It always is. Nobody ever writes a book about a famous case to prove that the jury brought in the right verdict.

FROM CHANDLER'S WORKING NOTES

Pro and con Maybrick

Pro

1. Mrs Maybrick was the instance of the doctor being summoned.
2. The doctors had no suspicion of arsenic until they heard it had been suggested.
3. Maybrick was an arsenic eater and ought to have suspected arsenic himself. He said nothing to suggest that he did.
4. The course of the illness was not typical of arsenic poisoning.
5. Mrs M. made no attempt to conceal the flypapers.
6. There was white arsenic in the house, so she didn't need the flypapers.
7. She had, long before M.'s fatal illness, tried to get some doctor to stop Maybrick's poison-eating habits.
8. She had previously used an arsenical face wash.
9. The medical evidence cancels out.
10. M. died of sub-acute poisoning, if he died of arsenic at all. If Mrs M. had poisoned him, the chances were all in favor of her giving him a whacking great dose of which he would

have died much more quickly than eight or nine days. She was not an experienced poisoner . . . the determination of a minimum fatal dose would have been extremely difficult.

11. She made no attempt to hide the poisoned meat juice or to give it to him.
12. Her character does not suggest the cold-blooded callousness of the poisoner. Considering the circumstances of her life the affair with Brierley hardly suggests an utterly depraved character . . .

Con

1. She had a very powerful motive and what looked like a very fine opportunity.
2. Rebutting 7 above, the fact that he took arsenic and was known to dose himself with various poisonous drugs would suggest the relative safety of killing him with an overdose. A situation existed which could be taken advantage of . . . If a man you want to kill is a poison-eater, the simplest way to kill him would be to make him eat too much of his own poison. That is so obvious that a really clever murderer might have avoided it just because it was obvious. Florence M. does not appear to have been that clever.
3. The letter to Brierley is damning. She called M. sick unto death . . . at a time when the doctors did not regard him as dangerously ill at all . . .
4. During the vomiting period nothing was kept that might be analysed . . .
5. However unclandestinely she handled the bottle of poisoned meat juice (the one into which at his request—her story— she put some of 'his powder') it is difficult to reconcile this incident with a theory of her innocence; surely she would have told a friendly doctor about his wanting 'his powder' . . . there *was* a friendly doctor and she could certainly have got to him somehow . . .
6. The course of his sickness very clearly suggests sub-acute poisoning and slow death by exhaustion and impairment of the heart action . . . it does not suggest accidental food

poisoning. This talk about too much brandy and getting wet is all nonsense; a man in substandard health exposed to wet and cold and too much alcohol would normally develop pneumonia or at the very best a severe cold and fever.

7. The small quantity of arsenic recovered from his body can be at least partly explained by the lapse of time after he took it. Arsenic once it gets past the stomach is gathered in the liver and circulated with the blood stream. The longer a person lives after taking what turns out to be a fatal dose, the less you would find in the vital organs.

8. There was an attempt to show that the arsenic found in the dish M. used at his office to heat his lunch was in the glaze. This is a typical overstrained defence attempt to create a technical and innocent explanation of something which can be much better explained by the known facts that Mrs M. prepared this food, that this was the day when he got his dose and that it was most likely arsenic in this food that killed him. Granted that it would be possible to show the presence of arsenic in a glazed enamel saucepan; in *some* quantity it might be possible to show its presence almost anywhere—in paint, in the handle of a toothbrush, in the metal of the front door knob; to release that arsenic requires the operation of certain acids. If these acids were present in food, a lot of people would have had arsenic poisoning by this time.

9. F.M.'s shock and prostration after M.'s death appear superficially to be in her favor, but are they really? She didn't love this man; he was not a lovable person; it is pretty obvious that he was unfaithful to her on the one hand and that he was sexually a damn unsatisfactory husband on the other. Yet she was knocked galley-west. Why? It is reasonable to suggest that she poisoned him . . . and she collapsed from terror at the realization that she was probably going to be found out.

10. Florence had motive, means and opportunity to kill her husband. She probably, if guilty, did not for a moment realize how cruel those means were nor how much and long he would suffer. A lot of murderers have been broken up by finding their victims so hard to kill . . .

Conclusions

Nevertheless, and in spite of the above, she should not have been convicted. The element of doubt existed and it should have been resolved in her favor, because that is the law. The case against her never amounted to more than heavy suspicion. It was never proved that she gave him arsenic or that she knew there was any in the house, apart from the flypapers . . . It was never really proved that he died from the effects of arsenic. The strongest point against her to a jury was probably the letter to Brierley . . . and the strongest point in her favor should have been that M. never at any time even hinted at arsenic as the cause of his illness . . . He was hardly the type to keep quiet out of altruistic motives. In view of his past medical history and habits I find this absence of any reference to arsenic the strangest thing in the case.

I think she poisoned him; and that by pure chance she gave him what was perhaps the smallest dose that could kill him. But it is not proved. She was entitled to an acquittal.

THE CRIPPEN CASE

In July 1910 *human remains were discovered beneath the cellar of Dr Hawley Harvey Crippen's house at Hilldrop Crescent, London. Dr Crippen, who had left England a few days before with his mistress, Ethel Le Neve, for Canada, was apprehended at sea on the S.S.* Montrose, *wireless telegraphy having been used for the first time in the pursuit of a wanted man. Crippen was brought to trial at the Old Bailey in October and found guilty of the murder of his wife Cora (known as Belle Elmore) by hyoscin poisoning. He was executed in November, 1910. Ethel Le Neve was acquitted after a separate trial as an accessory after the fact.*

Filson Young, in his Introduction to The Trial of Hawley Harvey Crippen *in the Notable British Trials Series, writes: 'We may consider Crippen a hateful man; but nobody who came in contact with him was able to say so'; and this aspect of crime—the likeable murderer—was the one that interested Chandler.*

Dec. 6, 1948
To: James Sandoe
. . . I wanted Crippen because I was interested in Marshall
Hall's theory that Crippen did not commit murder at all, but
gave his wife an accidental overdose of hyoscin, a drug not then
fully understood, for reasons I'll go into another time. You can't
help liking this guy somehow. He was one murderer who died
like a gentleman . . .

Dec. 15, 1948
To: James Sandoe
. . . The Marshall Hall theory attributed to the Crippen case
in Filson Young's introduction is not, if my memory is any good
at all, the same Marshall Hall theory expounded by Edward
Marjoribanks' life of Hall. According to Filson Young, Crippen
gave his wife five grains of hyoscin to curb her sexual enthu-
siasm. According to Marjoribanks, the idea was that Le Neve
. . . although carrying on an affair with Crippen, was a very con-
ventional-minded lower-middle-class girl who was ashamed of
hotel assignations. Crippen wanted to bring her home, and to
achieve that got in the way of doping the buxom Belle Elmore
to eliminate her temporarily and that he accidentally gave her
a fatal dose. Realizing that he could never get away with the
explanation of this once the affair Le Neve came out (and they
always do), he proceeded as though he had murdered her.
 I don't want to write an essay on every case you send me, but
there are a couple of very queer things about this case. I cannot
see why a man who would go to the enormous labor of de-
boning and de-sexing and de-heading an entire corpse would
not take the rather slight extra labor of disposing of the flesh
in the same way, rather than bury it at all. He has been criticized
for running away, on the ground that Inspector Dew was satisfied and would have dropped the matter if only Crippen had
stood his ground. I can't believe that. I think Scotland Yard
would have had a good try at finding Belle Elmore, if alive, and
not finding her would have come to the old digging routine.
 The second thing I can't understand is his telling of his wife's
death. Why? What did he gain? Why not let it stand that she
had decamped and stay with that?

The third is why a man of so much coolness under fire should have made the unconscionable error of letting it be known that Elmore had left her jewels and clothes and furs behind. She was so obviously not the person to do that.

Here was a man who apparently had the means and opportunity and even the temperament for a perfect crime, and he made all sorts of mistakes which usually are not the result of stupidity but of panic. But Crippen didn't seem to panic at all. He did many things which required a very cool head. For a man with a cool head and some ability to think he also did many things which simply didn't make sense.

Jan. 24, 1949
To: James Sandoe
   . . . I don't think I want to read the Penge case; it is too damn cruel and sordid. One needs a little touch of something out of the ordinary in these trials, even if it's only out of the ordinary idiocy. The good Kate Webster determined to cash in on the furniture, Mrs Rattenbury's rat race around the whisky bottles on the night of the murder, Fox's hair smelling of smoke and the exact timing of his murder to get the insurance, the Crippen friend's account of the Crippen menage . . . poor old Knowles with his revolver and his bottle on his fleabitten couch in that stinking African jungle and the fat Mrs Knowles saying 'Look!'
. . . one almost sympathizes with him for putting a bullet into her backside. These are the things that make murder cases fascinating.

THE WALLACE CASE

In 1931 William Herbert Wallace, a 35-year-old Liverpool insurance agent, was tried for the murder of his wife Julia. It was alleged that he had battered her to death, and his main defence was an alibi to the effect that an unknown man calling himself R. M. Qualtrough had made a telephone appointment with him for the time of the murder, but that he had been unable

*to find the address of 25 Menlove Gardens East which Qual-
trough had given. He had returned home to find his wife dead.
Wallace was convicted. On appeal, however, the verdict was reversed, evidence of his guilt being held insufficient, and he was
released; but he died two years later of cancer.*

Nov. 21, 1949
To: James Sandoe
   ... Sending *The Wallace Case*[1] back today. Rowland makes it
as dull as Wallace himself must have been.
   Three or four little points struck me:
   (1) Why had Wallace, a man who travelled Liverpool widely
on his rounds, no map of the city? It's the first place I would look
for a strange address.
   (2) Why would he not want to know something about this
Qualtrough merely for selling purposes? An insurance man would
have certain sources of information.
   (3) When, in the course of his vain search for Menlove Gardens East he went to a newsvendor's shop and asked her where
the street was and then to look up her accounts to see if she delivered papers to that address, why did he not mention the *name*
to the newsvendor? Qualtrough was apparently an uncommon
name in those parts.
   (4) The prosecution attempted to make something of the fact
that the gas jet Wallace lit in the living room, where his wife's
body was lying, was not the nearest to the door, and why did he
not light the most accessible jet? The defense pooh-poohed this
on the ground that when you live in a house with gaslight you
habitually light the same burner on entering a room. My point
here is, who says the one he lit was the habitual burner, who
besides Wallace himself?
   To some slight extent all these points are against Wallace, but
they are too slight to mean anything. It's a very unsatisfactory
case, because you feel that if the police and medical work had
been any good there wouldn't have been any chance of Wallace
getting away with it, if he was guilty, or of being arrested and
tried if he was innocent. The doctor sits around for hours timing

[1] By John Rowland.

the rigor mortis, but never records the temperature of the room or the loss of heat by the body. He never examines the stomach contents to see how far digestion has proceeded. There is no search for strange fingerprints . . . and no scrapings from Wallace's fingernails. There is a lot of magoozlum about blood splashes, but we end up with a very vague idea about how much and how far.

It also seems to be assumed even by the prosecution that Wallace could not have had more than twenty minutes in which to batter his wife to death, put out the fire, go upstairs and get cleaned up if he had his clothes on and get dressed if he had not, get his blood-pressure back to normal and appear perfectly calm and composed on a tram several blocks away. The number of blows struck shows a frenzy of either fear or hate, since the first blow was fatal, but the judge was the only one to point out that a man may plan a murder very coolly and yet lose his head in the execution of it. But this man got his head back again awfully damn quick . . .

FROM CHANDLER'S WORKING NOTES

Notes on the Julia Wallace Case

. . . But if you assume Qualtrough to be the murderer, let's see where that puts us. The motive must be robbery, because nothing else makes any sense . . . But if it is robbery, the only thing to steal is Wallace's collections. So Qualtrough has to know when they will be worth stealing, although he is unlucky this particular night. He has to know how and when to make that phone call and just what to say to interest Wallace; just what address to give, Menlove Gardens East, assuming rightly that Wallace knows . . . there are Menlove Gardens and will take it for granted that Menlove Gardens East will be near Menlove Gardens West . . . Is it possible to believe that Qualtrough knew so much about Wallace, and Wallace knew so little about Qualtrough? He has to know the Wallaces and their affairs pretty damn well. But it doesn't seem that *anybody* knew the Wallaces that well.

Dorothy Sayers seems to feel[1] that what was written in Wallace's diary after his trial and conviction and the reversal of the conviction has considerable significance in proving his innocence. I'm not convinced. I feel that with a man of Wallace's type a diary is the only outlet. And as a very occasional diarist I also feel that the moment a man sets his thoughts down on paper, however secretly, he is in a sense writing for publication. ... There is nothing quoted from Wallace's diary after the trial which ... I could not imagine a guilty man writing in the circumstances. There is such a thing as remorse; there is such a thing as the wish to believe that the irrevocable had never happened ...

Wallace has posed to himself as a stoic; in his behavior after the murder there is something more than pose. In his diary he clings to the last shred of pride he has—his pride in this stoical behavior, the last stability of a ruined life.

The Wallace case is unbeatable; it will always be unbeatable.

The Bartlett Case

In 1875 Edwin Bartlett, a London provision merchant, married a twenty-year-old French girl, Adelaide de la Tremoille. They settled in Pimlico, London, and in 1883 made the acquaintance of a Wesleyan minister, the Rev. George Dyson. Dyson acted as tutor to Adelaide, and when Bartlett made a new will leaving everything unconditionally to his wife Dyson was appointed executor. Dyson's relations with Adelaide became increasingly friendly and Bartlett, who held eccentric views on marriage, seemed to have no objection to this.

Chandler, in his notes on this case, writes:

'A portrait of Adelaide Bartlett printed in the Notable British Trials does not suggest that she was a raging beauty. She had rather a large mouth with prominent lips, an ordinary sort of nose, big dark eyes and heavy dark eyebrows, and a great cluster of curly dark hair worn low over the forehead. She might have poisoned forty people or none. The portrait we have of the Rev. George Dyson shows an enormous soup-strainer mustache,

[1] *Anatomy of Murder.*

the point of which hung down below what he had in the way of a chin, large stupid cowlike eyes, and a face with as much character as a bowl of gravy.'

When Bartlett died on New Year's Eve, 1885, from drinking liquid chloroform, Adelaide was arrested and tried for his murder. Sir Edward Clarke, after a brilliant defense, secured her acquittal. On this Chandler writes:

'Some persons tried for murder are acquitted because they are shown to be so clearly innocent that one wonders why they were ever brought before the court. Some are acquitted because although they are almost certainly guilty some vital element of proof is lacking. And a very rare few are acquitted because a great lawyer is able to convince a jury that the means of murder itself is so unprecedented and so difficult as to amount to a technical impossibility. If Edwin Bartlett had died of the results of any of the ordinary poisons, Adelaide would have been duly convicted and hanged. But Edwin Bartlett died of chloroform poisoning. And chloroform is neither tasteless, odorless, instantaneous, nor easy to administer. It had never, so far as the then records showed, been successfully used in a homicide. To use it as a murder weapon amounted to a medical miracle, and on the medical evidence for the prosecution Adelaide Bartlett was acquitted.'

Chandler was proud of his medical knowledge, and it was this fact of 'murder by medical miracle', together with Adelaide's acquittal, that particularly intrigued him about the Bartlett case.

Compiled from two letters
Feb. 20, 1951 and July 30, 1952
To: James Sandoe

. . . I have been having another look at the Adelaide Bartlett case, God knows why. I think one of its most confusing elements is that Sir Edward Clarke's defense was so brilliant, in contrast to the rather uninspired defense of Maybrick and Wallace, that you are almost fooled into ignoring the facts. But the facts, if you look them straight in the eye, are pretty damning. For example:

Edwin Bartlett died of drinking liquid chloroform. Adelaide, his wife, had liquid chloroform procured for her surreptitiously by Dyson the clergyman, who if not actually her lover in a technical sense was certainly doing some very high-powered necking ... Edwin was an unattractive and unnecessary husband and was a dope as well. If he died she got Dyson and Edwin's money. Edwin's health was excellent in spite of his constant complaining. It was more than usually good the night before he died. His insomnia was supposed to have been severe, but is not consistent with his hearty appetite. . . . There are three principal arguments against her guilt.

(1) Her nursing care seemed genuine and fairly self-effacing.

(2) She urged a quick post-mortem and herself scouted the chance of his having taken the chloroform himself.

(3) The difficulty of poisoning Edwin by this method was enormous, according to medical testimony, and there was no previous record of murder by this means.

But assuming her guilt, the first argument is meaningless ... how else has any poisoner ever acted? As to the second argument, there is no reason to assume, as the judge did, that she *knew* a delay in the post-mortem would be in her favor. He didn't die of jugged hare. There was bound to be an investigation. If you know that and if you have murdered him, how best can you look innocent? The way she did. The judge disposed of the third argument. If she murdered him, it was by a method which had one chance in twenty of succeeding. But she didn't know that. To her it may have looked easy.

The insomnia makes me laugh. I have had insomnia—quite severe insomnia. I did not want a big meal of jugged hare. I did not want a supper of oysters and cake. I did not want a haddock for breakfast—a large haddock—so badly that I would have been willing to get up an hour earlier in order to start eating. I think this guy was a neurotic insomniac. That is to say, if he didn't feel as fresh as a daisy in the morning, he said he hadn't slept more than twenty minutes the night before.

But if I don't believe his insomnia was severe, I can't believe he would be desperate enough to take the chloroform himself. Apart from murder, this seems to me to be the only possibility. And it is not a very convincing one ...

You have to try to conjecture how Adelaide would have behaved if she had come into the front room and found the man dead, knowing that she had given him chloroform with his consent and that was probably what had killed him. Why in the world couldn't she have said that she got the chloroform so that Edwin would sniff some on his handkerchief, enough to make him drowsy, and that evidently he had got too much or else he had recklessly drunk some—and that she had got it surreptitiously for him because she didn't want to hurt Dr Leach's feelings?

It seems to me she would quite easily have got away with that. It would have been straightforward and simple and the bottle of chloroform would have been right there in the room. Of course old Bartlett would have said she had poisoned his son, and a lot of people wouldn't have believed the story, but enough would have believed it to create a reasonable doubt.

It makes a neat little problem all right. Personally, I think she murdered him. I think she gave him enough chloroform to sniff to make him just a little woozy and indifferent and then gave him a drink of it mixed with brandy. The doctors say that if he had been quite unconscious his swallowing would not be working. But they also seem to think that if he had swallowed it while he was conscious he would have thrown it up. What they really mean is that they would, or you would, or I would. Edwin is a little bit different from us. You can feed anything to Edwin, and all he wants is to get up an hour early the next morning and start eating more. I think the man had a stomach like a goat. I think he could digest sawdust, old tin cans, iron filings and shoe leather. I think he could drink chloroform just like you and I could drink orange juice.

Anyhow any argument against his being able to retain it in his stomach is nonsense, because he did retain it in his stomach; so the only real argument is against the difficulty of getting it down his throat. And in Edwin's case that doesn't seem to me a very strong argument. He probably thought he was drinking ginger wine . . .

CHANDLER ON HIS NOVELS, SHORT STORIES AND PHILIP MARLOWE

Chandler on His Novels, Short Stories, and Philip Marlowe

1939 PLAN OF WORK TAKEN FROM CHANDLER'S NOTEBOOK

(Notes in brackets are additions in his handwriting dated April, 1942)

Since all plans are foolish and those written down are never fulfilled, let us make a plan, this 16th day of March, 1939, at Riverside, California.

For the rest of 1939, all of 1940, spring of 1941, and then if there is no war and if there is any money to go to England for material.

Detective novels

Law is Where You Buy It
Based on *Jade, the Man Who Liked Dogs, Bay City Blues*.[1] Theme, the corrupt alliance of police and racketeers in a small California town, outwardly as fair as the dawn.
(*Farewell, My Lovely*)

The Brasher Doubloon
A burlesque on the pulp novelette, with Walter and Henry. Some stuff from *Pearls Are a Nuisance*[1] but mostly new plot.
(Written 1942 but as a novel with Phil Marlowe, to be published under the title *The High Window*)

Zone of Twilight
A grim witty story of the boss politician's son and the girl and the blending of the

---

[1] These are all titles of stories by Chandler.

upper and underworlds. Material, *Guns at Cyrano's, Nevada Gas*[1]

(Dated, I'm afraid, by events)
If advisable, try *Goldfish*[1] for material for a fourth

Dramatic novel　　　*English Summer*

A short, swift, tense, gorgeously written story verging on melodrama, based on my short story. The surface theme is the American in England, the dramatic theme is the decay of the refined character and its contrast with the ingenuous, honest, utterly fearless and generous American of the best type
(Still hoping to do this, April, 1942)

Short-long stories

*Seven from the Stars
Seven from Nowhere*

*Seven Tales from
Nowhere*

(And still praying I
may someday do
these)

A set of six or seven fantastic stories, some written, some thought of, perhaps one brand new. Each a little different in tone and effect from the other. The ironic gem *The Bronze Door*, the perfect fantastic atmosphere story *The Edge of the West*, the spooky story *Grandma's Boy*, the farcical story *The Disappearing Duke*, the Allegory Ironic *The Four Gods of Bloon*, the pure fairytale *The Rubies of Marmelon*. The three mystery stories should be finished in the next two years, by end of 1940. If they make enough for me to move to England and to forget mystery writing and try *English Summer* and the Fantastic Stories, without worrying about whether these make money, I tackle them. But I must have two years' money ahead, and a sure market with the detective story when I come back to it, if

[1] These are all titles of stories by Chandler.

I do. If *English Summer* is a smash hit, which it should be, properly written, written up to the hilt but not overwritten, I'm set for life. From then on I'll alternate the fantastic and the dramatic until I think of a new type. Or may do a suave detective just for the fun.

To this Cissy added:

Dear Raymio, you'll have fun looking at this maybe, and seeing what useless dreams you had. Or perhaps it will not be fun.

Feb. 19, 1939
To : Alfred A. Knopf

Please accept my thanks for your friendly letter and please believe that, whether you wrote to me or not, I should have written to thank you for the splendid send-off you are trying to give me . . .

I have only seen four notices, but two of them seemed more occupied with the depravity and unpleasantness of the book[1] than with anything else . . . I do not want to write depraved books. I was aware that this yarn had some fairly unpleasant citizens in it, but my fiction was learned in a tough school and I probably didn't notice them much. I was more intrigued by a situation where the mystery is solved more by the exposition and understanding of a single character, always well in evidence, than by the slow and sometimes long-winded concatenation of circumstances. That's a point which may not interest reviewers of first novels, but it interested me very much.

The Big Sleep is very unequally written. There are scenes that are all right, but there are other scenes still much too pulpy. Insofar as I am able I want to develop the objective method— but slowly—to the point where I can carry an audience over into a genuine dramatic, even melodramatic, novel, written in a very vivid and pungent style, but not slangy or overly vernacular. I realize that this must be done cautiously and little by little, but

[1] *The Big Sleep*, published by Knopf and Hamish Hamilton, 1939.

I think it can be done. To acquire delicacy without losing power, that's the problem.

Aug. 23, 1939
To: Blanche Knopf [1]

The effort to keep my mind off the war has reduced me to the mental age of seven. The things by which we live are the distant flashes of insect wings in a clouded sunlight . . .

If I could write another 12,000 words I should have a draft of a book finished. I know what to write, but I have momentarily mislaid the urge. However, by the end of September there should be something for you to wrinkle your very polite nose at. It's rather a mixed up mess. It will take me a month to shape it up. The title, if you should happen to approve, is *The Second Murderer*.[2] Please refer to *King Richard III*, Act I, Scene IV. Sanders[3] has been impressing on me the dire necessity of so contriving a detective story that it might be serialized. This is only horse sense, even though good serials seldom make good novels. I do not think this particular opus is the one he is looking for. I'm not sure anyone is looking for it, but there's a law against burning trash up here during the fire hazard.

Oct. 17, 1939
To: George Harmon Coxe

I have never made any money out of writing. I work too slowly, throw away too much, and what I write that sells is not at all the sort of thing I really want to write . . .

I sold a story to the *Saturday Evening Post* recently.[4] I didn't think much of the story when I wrote it—I still don't know whether it is any good. When I read it in print I thought it was, but print can be so deceiving. On the other hand one of my oldest friends took the trouble to write me two pages telling me how lousy it was.

[1] President, Alfred A. Knopf Inc.
[2] Published as *Farewell, My Lovely*, 1940.
[3] Sydney A. Sanders, Chandler's literary agent at the time.
[4] *I'll be Waiting.*

June 27, 1940
To: George Harmon Coxe

The title of my book is not *The Second Murderer*. I used that for a while as a working title, but I didn't like it . . . I didn't know it had been announced under that name. When I turned the manuscript in they howled like hell about the title (*Farewell, My Lovely*) which is not at all a mystery title, but they gave in. We'll see. I think the title is an asset. They think it is a liability. One of us has to be wrong.

March 15, 1942
To: Blanche Knopf

Your letter, kind and charming as always, reaches me at a very bad time. I'm afraid the book is not going to be any good to you.[1] No action, no likeable characters, no nothing. The detective does nothing. I understand that it is being typed and will be submitted to you, and I'm not sure that is a good idea, but it is out of my hands . . . About all I can say by way of extenuation is that I tried my best and seemed to have to get the thing out of my system. I suppose I would have kept tinkering at it indefinitely otherwise.

The thing that rather gets me down is that when I write something that is tough and fast and full of mayhem and murder, I get panned for being tough and fast and full of mayhem and murder, and then when I try to tone it down a bit and develop the mental and emotional side of a situation, I get panned for leaving out what I was panned for putting in the first time.

April 3, 1942
To: Alfred A. Knopf

. . . As to the title, let me say at once that whatever I might think or like or not like I am not going to set my opinion against yours. The title, *Brasher* or *Brashear Doubloon*, was the origin of the story, but that's not important. I never thought of your

[1] *The High Window*. Chandler's first title for this was *The Brashear Doubloon*.

idea that booksellers might pronounce Brasher as brassiere. I can see the point now.

Brasher, more commonly Brashear, is an actual name. There was an Ephraim Brashear or Brasher, and he actually did make this coin for the State of New York in 1787. It is not the most valuable American coin, but except possibly the 1822 five-dollar gold piece it is the only one existing in sufficient numbers, and being of sufficient value, to be of any use for my purpose. There are a couple of small towns named Brashear and also a Brasher Falls. However, all this, which gives the title a hard reality to me, is nothing to the bookseller.

I have not the ingenuity to devise the sort of intricate and recondite puzzle the purest aficionados go for. The title might lead them to expect a type of story they are not getting. But that again is really your problem . . . All I can think of along this line at the moment is *The Lost Doubloon, The Lost Doubloon Mystery, The Stolen Coin Mystery, The Rare Coin Mystery.* All rather pedestrian. I'd like something with a bit more oomph.

April 5, 1942
To: Blanche Knopf
    P.S. How about *The High Window*? It is simple, suggestive and points to the ultimate essential clue.

Feb. 8, 1943
To: Alfred A. Knopf
    Thank you for yours of January 14th and it was friendly, understanding and welcome, as always. Thank you also for the two-bit edition of *The Big Sleep*. I looked into it and found it both much better and much worse than I had expected—or than I had remembered. I have been so belabored with tags like tough, hardboiled, etc., that it was almost a shock to discover occasional signs of almost normal sensitivity in the writing. On the other hand, I sure did run the similes into the ground.

    I hope to get a book out fairly soon.[1] I am trying to think up a good title for you to want me to change.

    [1] *The Lady in the Lake.*

Jan. 26, 1944
To: James Sandoe

... Somewhere put away with my papers in storage I have a complete list of all the stuff I ever published in this country. All my earlier stories were written for *Black Mask* when Joe Shaw was editor. The Avon Book Co. is bringing out a 25 cent edition in the spring sometime containing five of these novelettes.¹ If they sell them they will probably publish others. As to your being able to obtain these old pulp magazines with stuff of mine in them, I doubt it very much. A friend of mine has been trying to build up a collection for years and has offered as much as two dollars a copy without any success.

Oct. 12, 1944
To: Charles Morton

... The article or diatribe or whatever on screen writing² is just something I should like to do, but I cannot set a date for it at all. I am roughly halfway through a Marlowe book³ and may not get to the other for some time. I wish I could, but I am a fellow who writes 30,000 words to turn in five, and that is a lot of work. I do most certainly agree with you that it does even a writer no harm to use his stagnant brain once in a while in thought about something or other, and I am not deterred by any financial considerations at all. But I am getting old, my cerebrum squeaks against my cerebellum and I have to write some kind of a book before they forget me. A man of talent would write it in a month, a man of ability without talent in two months, and a genius would not write it at all. But it will take me about three more just to get a first draft.

Nov. 20, 1944
To: Charles Morton

... P. Marlowe is acting up, I have had many interruptions,

¹ *Finger Man.*
² *Writers in Hollywood.*
³ *The Little Sister.*

and also a long-drawn-out wrangle with Paramount about a contract. I wish I had one of these facile plotting brains, like Erle Gardner or somebody. I have good ideas for about four books, but the labour of shaping them into plots appalls me.

Jan. 7, 1945
To: Dale Warren

I finally unearthed your kind letter from a tangled mass of correspondence dating back to the Civil War, spurred on by your letter in the *Atlantic* about my little tirade.[1]

The *Atlantic* article has got me into a lot of trouble. Mr P. Marlowe, a simple alcoholic vulgarian who never sleeps with his clients while on duty, is trying to go refined on me. 'What the hell', he said, 'do you mean by keeping me in the basement all this time? Here you are unmasked as a guy who can write English—after a fashion—so get busy and write about me.' I can imagine the result. I suppose if I write another article in the *Atlantic* he will demand spats and a monocle and start collecting old pewter.

There are certain disadvantages in attracting attention, even the small amount that has come my way. People start telling you how to do things and then you start trying to do them that way. All I wanted to do when I began writing was to play with a fascinating new language, to see what it would do as a means of expression which might remain on the level of unintellectual thinking and yet acquire the power to say things which are usually only said with a literary air. I didn't really care what kind of story I wrote; I wrote melodrama because when I looked around me it was the only kind of writing I saw that was relatively honest and yet was not trying to put over somebody's party line. So now there are guys talking about prose and other guys telling me I have a social conscience. P. Marlowe has as much social conscience as a horse. He has a personal conscience, which is an entirely different matter.

There are people who think I dwell on the ugly side of life. God help them! If they had any idea how little I have told them about it! P. Marlowe doesn't give a damn who is President;

[1] The essay, *The Simple Art of Murder*.

neither do I, because I know he will be a politician. There was even a bird who informed me I could write a good proletarian novel; in my limited world there is no such animal, and if there were, I am the last mind in the world to like it, being by tradition and long study a complete snob. P. Marlowe and I do not despise the upper classes because they take baths and have money; we despise them because they are phoney.

Feb. 26, 1945
To: Hamish Hamilton
　. . . *The Lady in the Lake*, incidentally, has been sold to M.G.M. and I am supposed to go there to work on it in July. I am hoping to finish a Marlowe story[1] in the time between that and the conclusion of my present assignment, which is an original story for the screen called *The Blue Dahlia*.

Aug. 18, 1945
To: James Sandoe
　. . . Am working on a screen treatment of *The Lady in the Lake* . . . The last time I'll ever do a screenplay of a book I wrote myself. Just turning over dry bones.

Aug. 24, 1945
From an interview with Irving Wallace in Los Angeles
　. . . Inspirations? All of my novels started from some known or unknown fact. Most of my work came from knowing or hearing of an inside news story that could not be published. Then fiction took over.

　How I work? No regular hours. Can't keep them. Start in morning and go as long as I can. I work very fast, but I work for the waste-basket. I never revise phrase by phrase and line by line. Instead I rewrite entire things I don't like. I work on typewriter for novels, but at studio I dictate. I've written 5000 words at one

[1] *The Little Sister.*

sitting, and I always write final draft. The faster I write the better my output. If I'm going slow I'm in trouble. It means I'm pushing the words instead of being pulled by them. I'm one writer who never says I have a terrific idea for a story. I don't get ideas. Sometimes I get a situation and develop it mechanically. I'm a poor plotter and bad at construction. I never write plots down but work them out in my head, never completely, but in advance of the words I'm writing. I'm best when I know my ending, always try to, though rarely know intermediate steps.

Marlowe just grew out of the pulps. He was no one person.

Apr. 9, 1946
To: Anthony Boucher[1]
... My own stories would all have to be rewritten, as they are no longer 'fitten'. I used to be a pretty fancy bloke with the language, have since learned the bitter lesson (of which Gatsby is a fine example) that where you find a particularly sweet bit of description you are rather more than not likely to find a place where the author dodged a scene. Anyhow, regardless of the condition of my old fantastic stories,[2] I'm not sure I want them in a magazine. I've always thought I might eventually drag together enough to make one of those slim volumes and browbeat my publisher into publishing it at a dead loss. One of my few remaining ambitions is to make publishers lose money . . .

May 30, 1946
To: Hamish Hamilton
When and if you see the film of *The Big Sleep* (the first half of it anyhow) you will realize what can be done with this sort of story by a director with the gift of atmosphere and the requisite touch of hidden sadism. Bogart, of course, is also so much better than any other tough-guy actor. As we say here, Bogart can be

[1] Boucher had written Chandler about a new magazine he and J. Francis McComas were bringing out.
[2] *The Bronze Door*, etc.

tough without a gun. Also he has a sense of humour that contains that grating undertone of contempt. Ladd is hard, bitter and occasionally charming, but he is after all a small boy's idea of a tough guy. Bogart is the genuine article. Like Edward G. Robinson, all he has to do to dominate a scene is to enter it.

Oct. 6, 1946
To: Hamish Hamilton

'A new Philip Marlowe story . . . tentatively called *The Little Sister*, and dealing with some rather queer characters in Hollywood, not to mention an innocent little girl from Kansas, who may or may not be quite as innocent as she looks.'

That's about all I could tell you at the moment. I have what you people call a 'thing' about discussing or writing about anything I haven't licked. I'm never sure I shall lick it. I might blow up completely and shelve the whole project. My title may not be very good. It's just the best I can think of without straining. I have peculiar ideas about titles. They should be rather indirect and neutral, but the form of words should be a little unusual. I haven't achieved this here. However, as some big publisher once remarked, a good title is the title of a successful book. Nobody would have thought *The Thin Man* a great title. *The Maltese Falcon* is, because it has rhyme and rhythm and makes the mind ask questions . . .

March 8, 1947
To: James Sandoe

No, I am not working on a story of murder without detection. I have such a story in mind, but have not got down to it yet. I am working, or was, on another Marlowe,[1] because for business or professional reasons I think the guy is too valuable to let die out. My next job, however, is to do a job for Universal on one of the most unusual deals ever made in Hollywood, or so I am told. They pay me a large sum of money and a percentage of the picture to write them a screenplay, and they only

[1] *The Little Sister.*

get the picture rights. The unusual feature is that they do *not* employ me, but merely agree to buy the motion picture rights to something I write in my own way and without any supervision.[1]

Oct. 27, 1947
To: Hamish Hamilton

... I finished the first draft of my screenplay[1] and the way I went on anyone would think I was building a pyramid ... Now I have to polish it, as they say. Which means leave out half and make what is left hammier. This is a very delicate art, and about as fascinating as scraping teeth.

March 13, 1948
To: Hamish Hamilton

... I am sending you two volumes of stories for you to look at. These are entitled *Red Wind* and *Spanish Blood*. There are ten stories in this collection, all of which but one are novelettes of 15,000 words or over. The exception is the short story called *I'll Be Waiting* which was published in the *Saturday Evening Post*. My suggestion as to the best of these stories is *Red Wind*, *I'll Be Waiting*, *Goldfish*, *Spanish Blood* and *Pearls are a Nuisance*.

I don't for a moment think these should be published by you in such a way as to suggest to anyone they are new material. I was thinking of some kind of reprint edition.[2]

May 7, 1948
To: Frederick Lewis Allen

... Auden's piece about detective stories[3] was brilliant in the

[1] *Playback*, never produced by Universal-International. Chandler's last novel, published in 1958, was based on this script.
[2] Some of these stories were included in the volume *The Simple Art of Murder*, with the famous essay of this title, published in 1950. Hamish Hamilton have reissued them as two volumes, *Pearls are a Nuisance* and *Smart-Aleck Kill*, in 1958. Others were published by Penguin Books in the volume *Trouble is My Business* in 1950.
[3] *The Guilty Vicarage*, by W. H. Auden, *Harper's Magazine*, May, 1948.

clear cold classical manner. But why drag me in? I'm just a fellow who jacked up a few pulp novelettes into book form. How could I possibly care a button about the detective story as a form? All I'm looking for is an excuse for certain experiments in dramatic dialogue.

Here I am halfway through a Marlowe story and having a little fun (until I got stuck) and along comes this fellow Auden and tells me I am interested in writing serious studies of a criminal milieu. So now I look at everything I put down and say to myself, Remember, old boy, this has to be a serious study of a criminal milieu. Are you serious? No. Is this a criminal milieu? No, just average corrupt living with the melodramatic angle over-emphazised, not because I am crazy about melo-drama for its own sake, but because I am realistic enough to know the rules of the game.

A long time ago when I was writing for the pulps I put into a story a line like 'He got out of the car and walked across the sun-drenched sidewalk until the shadow of the awning over the entrance fell across his face like the touch of cool water.' They took it out when they published the story. Their readers didn't appreciate this sort of thing—just held up the action.

I set out to prove them wrong. My theory was that the readers just *thought* they cared about nothing but the action; that really, although they didn't know it, the thing they cared about, and that I cared about, was the creation of emotion through dia-logue and description. The things they remembered, that haun-ted them, was not, for example, that a man got killed, but that in the moment of his death he was trying to pick a paper clip up off the polished surface of a desk and it kept slipping away from him, so that there was a look of strain on his face and his mouth was half open in a kind of tormented grin, and the last thing in the world he thought about was death. He didn't even hear the death knock on the door. That damn little paper clip kept slipping away from his fingers.

June 30, 1948
To: Charles W. Morton
    I ain't neither a languid correspondent. I'm trying to mop up

a mystery novel and every time I start writing letters there goes
a day. Seems as if I have to keep my mind impure of all extra-
neous matters in order to deal adequately with blood and sex.
I'm a small man in a big world, and my hair is turning gray
rapidly . . .

Aug. 10, 1948
To: Hamish Hamilton
    The trouble with the Marlowe character is he has been written
and talked about too much. He's getting self-conscious, trying
to live up to his reputation among the quasi-intellectuals. The
boy is bothered. He used to be able to spit and throw the ball
hard and talk out of the corner of his mouth.
    I am trying desperately to finish *The Little Sister* and should
have a rough draft done almost any day I can get up enough
steam. The fact is, however, that there is nothing in it but style
and dialogue and characters. The plot creaks like a broken
shutter in an October wind.

Aug. 19, 1948
To: Hamish Hamilton
    . . . The position as to *The Little Sister* is roughly that I have
on paper in the rough about 85,000 words and lack two or three
scenes at the end. But I have a very, very tired mind . . .
    The story has weaknesses. It is episodic and the emphasis
shifts around from character to character and it is, as a mystery,
over-complicated, but as a story of people very simple. It has
no violence in it at all; all the violence is off stage. It has menace
and suspense, they are in the writing. I think some of it is beautifully written, and my reactions to it are most unreliable. I
write a scene and I read it over and think it stinks. Three days
later (having done nothing in between but stew) I re-read it and
think it is great. So there you are. You can't bank on me.
P.S. It contains the nicest whore I ever didn't meet.

Dec. 15, 1948
To : James Sandoe

The reason you don't find me on Knopf's spring list is that I am not being published by him this time, but by Houghton Mifflin. The very innocuous title, in case I haven't told you, is *The Little Sister*. From a severely technical point of view it is not a good mystery. It is easy for me to say I don't care, but I really do, because I should like to write one that was if I could have all the other things in it too.

Jan. 23, 1949
To : Dale Warren

[Re *The Little Sister*.] I hate explanation scenes and I learned in Hollywood that there are two rules about them. (1) You can give only a little at a time, if there is much to give. (2) You can only have an explanation scene when there is some other element, such as danger, or love-making, or a character reversal suspected. Suspense of some sort, in one word. But pictures and books are different, naturally. For one thing, the picture people seem to me to confuse plot and construction, which I regard as two entirely different things, as different as tactics and strategy.

March 21, 1949
To : Hamish Hamilton

. . . I remember several years ago when Howard Hawks was making *The Big Sleep*, the movie, he and Bogart got into an argument as to whether one of the characters was murdered or committed suicide. They sent me a wire asking me, and dammit I didn't know either . . .

Apr. 10, 1949
To : James Sandoe

. . . I see nothing to worry about in a dick picking up a letter in a handkerchief, to preserve the fingerprints, if any. There might be excellent reasons for picking up a letter with a handkerchief: not to preserve a print, because on paper, if there was one at all, it would not easily wipe off, as it would on metal, but to avoid putting more prints on it and thus making more work for the lab men. I remember once reading a dissertation by a ballistics expert making game of silencers and saying that the first shot with one would jam the mechanism of an automatic. I had at the moment a photograph of a silenced Colt Woodsman .22 which was used in several theatre stickups in Massachusetts.

Apr. 16, 1949
To: Alex Barris, replying to questions

. . . Marlowe development of character used in novelettes, first named in *Big Sleep*.[1] I believe *Farewell, My Lovely* would be called the best of my books, *The High Window* the worst, but I have known people who would pick any of them as against the others. In some ways my last, not yet published, is the best.[2] But I'll never again equal *The Big Sleep* for pace nor *Farewell, My Lovely* for plot complication. I probably don't want to; the time comes when you have to choose between pace and depth of focus, between action and character, menace and wit. I now choose the second in each case.

Do I read my stuff when published? Yes, and at very great risk of being called an egotistical twerp, I find it damn hard to put down. Even me, that knows all about it. There must be some magic in the writing after all, but I take no credit for it. It just happens, like red hair. But I find it rather humiliating to pick up a book of my own to glance at something, and then find myself twenty minutes later still reading it as if someone else had written it.

May 3, 1949
To: James Sandoe

Houghton Mifflin seem to want to publish a trade edition

[1] Chandler originally thought of calling Marlowe Mallory. At his wife's suggestion the name became Marlowe.
[2] *The Little Sister.*

collection of my old stories. I tried to argue that they had been around enough and were only pulp writing anyhow but they insist that they should be published and that 'there is nothing like them anywhere'. This I doubt very much.

I think I am going to have to do a little rewriting on *The Little Sister* and I dread it. In the end I was faced with the choice between a clear but boring explanation of who shot who, and more or less letting it hang in air on the theory that who cared anyway, it wasn't and couldn't pretend to be a proper mystery story. But the subconscious has been at work chiding me. As a constructionist I have a dreadful fault; I let characters run away with the scenes and then refuse to discard the scenes that don't fit. I end up usually with the bed of Procrustes. The system works if one is hitting on all twelve, but I've a few leaky spark-plugs now. But I do (since this damn letter is already impossibly egotistic) have one great advantage. I still regard myself as an amateur and insist on having some fun out of my work.

May 14, 1949
To: James Sandoe
    . . . I never thought of mentioning the radio program . . . I have nothing to do with it except to complain to my agent and to collect a weekly royalty. Your friends who speak highly of it must be radio fans . . . The character (let us keep this a secret or they might stop paying me) has about as much relation to Philip Marlowe as I have to Winnie the Pooh.

June 22, 1949
To: Hamish Hamilton
    . . . Yesterday afternoon I airmailed a set of corrected proofs of *The Little Sister* to you. My God, what a writer suffers with proofs . . . In spite of this there were scenes here and there that stood up wonderfully well. To say little and convey much, to break the mood of the scene with some completely irrelevant wisecrack without entirely losing the mood—these small things for me stand in lieu of accomplishment . . .

Sept. 14, 1949
To: James Sandoe

... What you note as my tendency to gag[1] is undoubtedly the effect of Hollywood which I struggled against to the best of my ability, but it takes more than one book to slough it off. It comes from that noxious habit of writing lines for actors which are overpointed for effect, so that the line is really said to the audience rather than to a character in the play. Of course Shakespeare does it too, does it all the time. He just does it better.

Sept. 15, 1949
To: Dale Warren

As to the comment you kindly quoted from me about *The Little Sister*. I disagree that this story is much the best. I think *Farewell, My Lovely* is the top and that I shall never again achieve quite the same combination of ingredients. The bony structure was much more solid, the invention less forced and more fluent, and so on. Writers who get written about become self-conscious. They develop a regrettable habit of looking at themselves through the eyes of other people. They are no longer alone, they have an investment in critical praise, and they think they must protect it. This leads to a diffusion of effort. The writer watches himself as he works. He grows more subtle and he pays for it by a loss of organic dash. But since he often achieves a real success in the commercial sense just about as he reaches this stage of regrettable sophistication he fools himself into thinking that his last book is his best. It isn't. Its success is the result of a slow accumulation. The book which is the occasion of success is more often than not by no means the cause of it.

Oct. 14, 1949
To: James Sandoe

... *The Little Sister* has had some wonderful reviews, but I don't think it is going too well. The advance sale was less than 10,000 and with this sort of book there are not many reorders.

[1] In *The Little Sister*.

In a couple of big bookstores in San Diego I couldn't even find the damn thing. Was much too diffident to ask about it. It's the only book of mine I have actively disliked. It was written in a bad mood and I think that comes through.

Nov. 8, 1949
To: Bernice Baumgarten
  I should admire to have your list of my stories for that book.[1] I'd like to leave off *The Bronze Door* because I'd like to do a group of fantastic stories in which it would belong, if they ever got published (or written, you will add). These stories, about ten of them, longish short stories, would all be about murder in some sense, or the elimination of some annoying person, all more or less fortuitously through the happening on a magic means of doing it, all realistic in tone, with a dash of humor, and all in the nature of a spoof on some type of murder story. I am poking at one now which is a sort of reductio ad absurdum of the locked-room puzzle.[2] I'm willing to take advice about *Blackmailers Don't Shoot* and *Smart-Aleck Kill*. The second I think is weakish, the first too full of massacres. But it has some good scenes. I know you haven't the original version of *Pick-Up On Noon Street*, Maurice Diamond of the Avon people had it and lost it. He published a version of this story in some paperback monthly or other, but this was the whitewashed version in which five or six characters originally Negroes were made white at the insistence of some magazine editor. Just to show the ethical standards of these taboo merchants, he objected to certain people being colored but insisted on keeping the brief scene in the Negro whorehouse.

Nov. 19, 1949
To: James Sandoe
  . . . The omnibus of my stories is to come out in the fall of 1950.[3] I am now trying to remove the Nazi element from a story

[1] *The Simple Art of Murder.*
[2] *Professor Bingo's Snuff.*
[3] *The Simple Art of Murder.*

called *No Crime in the Mountains* and also the bits of description I swiped for a book.[1] I don't know why I bother. I guess I have an affection for the story because I have or had an affection for the Big Bear Lake country which I knew very well indeed about ten years ago.

Nov. 20, 1949
To: Dale Warren

... The Marlowe radio show has gone so soft that even old ladies like it now. Who said mystery programs were sadistic? This one is about as sadistic as a frosted marshmallow sundae ...

Oct. 9, 1950
To: James Sandoe

... As to the introduction of the name of Marlowe into some of the stories[2] where he had not originally appeared, there might possibly have been a base commercial motive at work here (in the mind of the publisher, I mean, I am far above such things myself) but also there was the idea that, although he wasn't called Marlowe until *The Big Sleep*, he certainly had his genesis in two or three of the novelettes; and he probably hadn't changed any more relatively between, say, *Finger Man* and *The High Window* than he will have changed between *Finger Man* and the next one I turn out in which, by God, I am for once going to get by with a single murder, and even that a little doubtful.

Jan. 4, 1951
To: Dale Warren

... I don't know how good your French is, but I don't understand the French title[3] of *The Little Sister*, even with the assistance of what is perhaps the best French-English dictionary

[1] *The Lady in the Lake.*
[2] *The Simple Art of Murder.*
[3] *Fais pas ta Rosière.*

published, Harraps. *Rosière* is defined as a maiden to whom was awarded the wreath of roses and a small dowry for virtuous conduct. But the particular application here throws me.

Feb. 3, 1951
To: Carl Brandt
Thanks for the Japanese translations. I thought them very well done—didn't you—especially the illustrations? You have to read this stuff standing on your head to get the full effect.

Apr. 19, 1951
To: Mr D. J. Ibberson
It is very kind of you to take such an interest in the facts of Philip Marlowe's life. The date of his birth is uncertain. I think he said somewhere that he was thirty-eight years old, but that was quite a while ago and he is no older today. This is just something you will have to face.

He was not born in a Midwestern town but in a small California town called Santa Rosa, which your map will show you to be about fifty miles north of San Francisco. Santa Rosa is famous as the home of Luther Burbank, a fruit and vegetable horticulturist, once of considerable renown. It is perhaps less widely known as the background of Hitchcock's picture *Shadow of a Doubt*, most of which was shot right in Santa Rosa. Marlowe has never spoken of his parents and apparently he has no living relatives. This could be remedied if necessary. He had a couple of years of college, either at the University of Oregon at Eugene, or Oregon State University at Corvallis, Oregon. I don't know why he came to Southern California, except that eventually most people do, although not all of them remain. He seems to have had some experience as an investigator for an insurance company and later as investigator for the district attorney of Los Angeles County. This would not necessarily make him a police officer nor give him the right to make an arrest. The circumstances in which he lost that job are well known to me but I cannot be very specific about them. You'll have to be satisfied with the information that he got a little too efficient at a time and in a place where efficiency was the last thing desired by the person in charge.

He is slightly over six feet tall and weighs about thirteen stone eight. He has dark brown hair, brown eyes, and the expression 'passably good looking' would not satisfy him in the least. I don't think he looks tough. He can be tough. If I ever had an opportunity of selecting the movie actor who could best represent him to my mind, I think it would have been Cary Grant. I think he dresses as well as can be expected. Obviously he hasn't very much money to spend on clothes, or on anything else for that matter. The horn-rimmed sun-glasses do not make him distinctive. Practically everyone in Southern California wears sun-glasses at some time or other. When you say he wears 'pajamas' even in summer, I don't know what you mean. Who doesn't? Were you under the impression that he wore a night-shirt? Or did you mean that he might sleep raw in hot weather? The last is possible, although our weather here is very seldom hot at night.

You are quite right about his smoking habits, although I don't think he insists on Camels. Almost any sort of cigarette will satisfy him. The use of cigarette cases is not as common here as in England. He definitely does not use book matches, which are always safety matches. He uses either large wooden matches, which we call kitchen matches, or a smaller match of the same type which comes in small boxes and can be struck anywhere, including on the thumb-nail if the weather is dry enough. In the desert or in the mountains it is quite easy to strike a match on your thumb-nail, but the humidity around Los Angeles is pretty high.

Marlowe's drinking habits are much as you state. I don't think he prefers rye to bourbon, however. He will drink practically anything that is not sweet. Certain drinks, such as Pink Ladies, Honolulu cocktails, and crême-de-menthe highballs he would regard as an insult. Yes, he makes good coffee. Anyone can make good coffee in this country, although it seems quite impossible in England. He takes cream and sugar with his coffee, not milk. He will also drink it black without sugar. He cooks his own breakfast, which is a simple matter, but not any other meal. He is a late riser by inclination, but occasionally an early riser by necessity. Aren't we all?

I would not say that his chess comes up to tournament standard. I don't know where he got the little paperbound book of tournament games published in Leipzig, but he likes it because he prefers the continental method of designating the squares on the chess board. Nor do I know that he is something of a card-player. This has slipped my mind. What do you mean, he is 'moderately fond of animals'? If you live in an apartment house, moderately is about as fond of them as you can get. It seems to me that you have an inclination to interpret any chance remark as an indication of a fixed taste.

As to his interest in women as 'frankly carnal', these are your words, not mine. I should say his attitude toward women is that of any reasonably vigorous and healthy man who does not happen to be married and probably should have been long since. . . . Marlowe cannot recognize a Bryn Mawr accent because there is no such thing. All he implies by that expression is a top-lofty way of speaking. I doubt very much that he can tell genuine old furniture from fakes. And I also beg leave to doubt that many experts can do it either, if the fakes are good enough. I pass the Edwardian furniture and Pre-Raphaelite art. I just don't recall where you get your facts.

I would not say that Marlowe's knowledge of perfume stops at Chanel Number 5. That again is merely a symbol of something that is expensive and at the same time reasonably restrained. He likes all the slightly acrid perfumes, but not the cloying or overspiced type. He is, as you may have noticed, a slightly acrid person. Of course he knows what the Sorbonne is, and he also knows where it is. Of course he knows the difference between a tango and a rumba, and also between a conga and a samba, and he knows the difference between a samba and a mamba, although he does not believe that a mamba can overtake a galloping horse. I doubt if he knows the new dance called a mambo, because it seems to be only recently discovered or developed.

Now let's see, how far does that take us? Fairly regular film-goer, you say, dislikes musicals. Check. May be an admirer of Orson Welles. Possibly, especially when Orson is directed by someone other than himself. Marlowe's reading habits and musical tastes are just as much a mystery to me as they are to you, and if I tried to improvise, I'm afraid I'd get him confused with my own tastes. If you ask me why he is a private detective, I can't answer you. Obviously there are times when he wishes he were not, just as there are times when I would rather be almost anything than a writer. The private detective of fiction is a fantastic creation who acts and speaks like a real man. He can be completely realistic in every sense but one, that one sense being that in life as we know it such a man would not be a private detective. The things which happen to him might still happen to him, but they would happen as the result of a peculiar set of chances. By making him a private detective, you skip the necessity for justifying his adventures.

Where he lives: in *The Big Sleep* and some earlier stories he apparently lived in a single apartment with a pull-down bed, a bed that folds up into the wall and it has a mirror on the under side of it. Then he moved into an apartment similar to that occupied by a character named Joe Brody in *The Big Sleep*. It may have been the same apartment, he may have got it cheap because a murder had taken place in it. I think, but I'm not sure, that this apartment is on the fourth floor.

It contains a living room which you enter directly from the hallway, and opposite are French windows opening on an ornamental balcony, which is just something to look at, certainly not anything to sit out on. Against the right-hand wall as you stand in the doorway is a davenport. In the left-hand wall, nearest to the hallway of the apartment house, there is a door that leads to an interior hall. Beyond that, against the left-hand wall, there is this oak drop-leaf desk, an easy chair, etc.; beyond that, an archway entrance to the dinette and kitchen. The dinette, as known in California apartment houses, is simply a space divided off from the kitchen proper by an archway or a built-in china closet. It would be very small, and the kitchen would also be very small.

As you enter the hallway from the living room (the interior hallway), you would come on your right to the bathroom door and continuing straight on you would come to the bedroom. The bedroom would contain a walk-in cupboard or closet. The bathroom in a building of this type would contain a shower in the tub and a shower curtain. None of the rooms is very large. The rent of the apartment, furnished, would have been about sixty dollars a month when Marlowe moved into it. God knows what it would be now. I shudder to think.

As to Marlowe's office, I'll have to take another look at it sometime to refresh my memory. It seems to me it's on the sixth floor of a building which faces north, and that his office window faces east. But I'm not certain about this. There is a reception room which is a half-office, perhaps half the space of a corner office, converted into two reception rooms with separate entrances and communicating doors right and left respectively. Marlowe has a private office which communicates with his reception room, and there is a connection which causes a buzzer to ring in his private office when the door of the reception room is opened. But this buzzer can be switched off by a toggle switch.

He has not, and never has had, a secretary. He could very easily subscribe to a telephone answering service, but I don't recall mentioning that anywhere. And I do not recall that his desk has a glass top, but I may have said so. The office bottle is kept in the filing drawer of the desk—a drawer, standard in American office desks (perhaps also in England) which is the depth of two ordinary drawers, and is intended to contain file folders, but very seldom does, since most people keep their file folders in filing cases. It seems to me that some of these details flit about a good deal.

His guns have also been rather various. He started out with a German Lüger automatic pistol. He seems to have had Colt automatics of various calibers, but not larger than .38, and when last I heard he had a Smith & Wesson .38 special, probably with a four-inch barrel. This is a very powerful gun, although not the most powerful made, and has the advantage over an automatic of using a lead cartridge. It will not jam or discharge accidentally, even if dropped on a hard surface, and it is probably just as effective a weapon at short range as a .45 caliber automatic. It would be better with a six-inch barrel, but that would make it more awkward to carry. Even a four-inch barrel is not too convenient, and the detective branch of the police usually carries a gun with only a two-and-a-half inch barrel.

This is about all I have for you now, but if there is anything else you want to know, please write to me again. The trouble is, you really seem to know a good deal more about Philip Marlowe than I do, and perhaps I shall have to ask you questions instead of your asking me.

Oct., 1951
To: Mr Inglis
   ... I don't think my friend Philip Marlowe is very much concerned about whether or not he has a mature mind. I will admit to an equal lack of concern about myself . . . If being in revolt against a corrupt society constitutes being immature, then Philip Marlowe is extremely immature. If seeing dirt where there is dirt constitutes an inadequate social adjustment, then Philip Marlowe has inadequate social adjustment. Of course Marlowe is a failure and he knows it. He is a failure because he hasn't any money. A man who without physical handicaps cannot make a decent living is always a failure and usually a moral failure. But a lot of very good men have been failures because their particular talents did not suit their time and place. In the long run I guess we are all failures or we wouldn't have the kind of world we have. But you must remember that Marlowe is not a real person. He is a creature of fantasy. He is in a false position because I put him there. In real life a man of his type would no more be a private detective than he would be a university don. Your private detective in real life is usually either an ex-policeman with a lot of hard practical experience and the brains of a turtle or else a shabby little hack who runs around trying to find out where people have moved to.
   I think I resent your suggestion that Philip Marlowe has contempt for other people's physical weakness. I don't know where you get the idea, and I don't think it is so. I am also a little tired of the humorous suggestions that have been made that he is always full of whiskey. The only point I can see in justification of that is that when he wants a drink he takes it openly and doesn't hesitate to remark on it. I don't know how it is in your part of the country, but compared with the country club set in my part of the country he is as sober as a deacon.

May 14, 1952
To: Bernice Baumgarten
   I'm sending you today a draft of a story which I have called *The Long Good-Bye*. It runs 92,000 words. I'd be happy to have your comments and objections and so on. I haven't even read

the thing, except to make a few corrections and check a number of details that my secretary queried. So I am not sending you any opinion on the opus. You may find it slow going.

It has been clear to me for some time that what is largely boring about mystery stories, at least on a literate plane, is that the characters get lost about a third of the way through. Often the opening, the mise en scène, the establishment of the background, is very good. Then the plot thickens and the people become mere names. Well, what can you do to avoid this? You can write constant action and that is fine if you really enjoy it. But alas, one grows up, one becomes complicated and unsure, one becomes interested in moral dilemmas, rather than in who cracked who on the head. And at that point perhaps one should retire and leave the field to younger and more simple men. I don't necessarily mean writers of comic books like Mickey Spillane.

Anyhow I wrote this as I wanted to because I can do that now. I didn't care *whether the mystery was fairly obvious*, but I cared about the people, about this strange corrupt world we live in, and how any man who tried to be honest looks in the end either sentimental or plain foolish.

May 25, 1952
To: Bernice Baumgarten
You will have received my wire by now and I hope it has been in time to stop the script from being copied and to withhold same from Jamie Hamilton. I thank you for your letter and needless to say I regret having sent the script out when I did. I was just too impatient to get rid of it. I knew the character of Marlowe had changed and I thought it had to because the hardboiled stuff was too much of a pose after all this time. But I did not realize that it had become Christlike, and sentimental, and that he ought to be deriding his own emotions . . .

I'll take a quick trip through the script when I get it back and then lay it aside for long enough to get perspective. I've always wanted to do that. I was never able to. I was always afraid that if I did I would junk the whole thing when I came back to it. I'm not afraid of that now. I know that whatever errors of emphasis or plot and so on the story contains it is fundamentally all right for me. I've never ridden with a loose rein before. That may be more of a trick than I know.

Curiously enough, I seem to have far fewer doubts about this story than I had about *The Little Sister*. Why that is I haven't the remotest idea. It has been said, I think, that writers always like the wrong things in their own work.

June 10, 1952
To: Hamish Hamilton

Thank you for your note. And bless your heart, old thing, I'm not depressed in the least. Feeling quite chipper, in fact. I am rather disgusted, because I made it clear that the script I sent East was no more than a corrected first draft by which I meant corrected as to most of the typographical and other errors. I am a rapid but inaccurate typist and my writing is very hard to read. Most of the points Bernice criticized in detail would have been changed automatically on revision and a great many that she did not criticize . . .

When I get through the script again and am fairly well satisfied with it, or as satisfied as I can presently hope to be, I shall send you a copy direct . . . I have changed the title to *Summer in Idle Valley*. That was the original title which I carried for a long time. Then it occurred to me that the first hundred pages of the script didn't contain any reference to this title. But what of it? I liked the title because it had a romantic flavor and was not pretentious.

Some titles stick close to their subject, some touch it tangentially and in one spot. The title of *The Big Sleep* was only justified on the last page or two of the book. The kind of title I dislike most is the typical murder novel title, such as *The Case of the Seasick Monkey* or *The Corpse With the Freckled Teeth* or *The Affair at Fiddler's Green* and so on.

Be of good cheer. I don't mind Marlowe being a sentimentalist, because he always has been. His toughness has always been more or less a surface bluff, a point which Desmond MacCarthy made a long time ago.

July 20, 1952
To: Bernice Baumgarten

Thanks for note, but I see no reason why you should, even as a matter of form, apologize for speaking what was in your mind. You were probably, almost certainly, right. One never knows what sort of impact a letter will make, since one never knows the mood or very much of the circumstances in which it will be read. Complete tact requires more knowledge than is given to us. It was all my fault anyway, as I've said. My present trouble is that I don't know where I am at, don't know whether there is anything in all this mess worth salvaging or whether it would be cleverer to throw it away and start fresh. I am not much good at tinkering or revising. I lose interest, lose perspective, and whatever critical sense I have is dissipated in trivialities such as whether it is better to put in 'he said' or let the speech stand alone.

My kind of writing demands a certain amount of dash and high spirits—the word is gusto, a quality lacking in modern writing—and you could not know the bitter struggle I have had the past year even to achieve enough cheerfulness to live on, much less put in a book. So let's face it; I didn't get it into the book. I didn't have it to give.[1]

Jan. 5, 1953
To: H. N. Swanson

. . . I got out the two scripts of the thing I did for Universal, *Playback*, and read them. The first . . . seemed to me much the better of the two, although the ending is no good . . . I think it would make a fairly good story, but the difficulty of adapting it as a novelette with Philip Marlowe as the main character is that so much of the best action takes place outside the ken of the dick. I don't mean that it's impossible, but the result, if achieved, would have very little of the original in it except a few of the characters and a basic situation of a girl who has narrowly escaped taking the rap for a murder she didn't commit, and then gone a long way off to try to hide under a different name and suddenly found herself in a situation so similar to the original

[1] *The Long Good-Bye* was written during the illness of Chandler's wife, Cissy.

catastrophe that she doesn't dare to give an account of herself, especially as it looked as though the second guy who was murdered was using his knowledge of her identity to blackmail her.

March 14, 1953
To: H. N. Swanson

. . . *Playback* is getting a bit tired. I have 36,000 words of doodling and not yet a stiff. This is terrible. I am suffering from a very uncommon disease called (by me) atrophy of the inventive powers. I can write like a streak but I bore myself. That being so, I could hardly fail to bore others worse. I can't help thinking of that beautiful piece of Sid Perelman's entitled *I'm Sorry I Made Me Cry*[1] . . .

May 11, 1953
To: Hamish Hamilton

. . . As to my own efforts, I should say I am about four-fifths of the way through *Summer in Idle Valley* which I no longer like as a title, almost completely rewritten because of my unfortunate inability to edit anything . . . Every now and then I get stuck on a chapter and then I wonder why. But there's always a reason and I have to wait for the reason to come to me. I got about halfway through the other book[2] before I decided that that needed a very drastic revision also . . .

May 26, 1953
To: Hamish Hamilton

. . . As to my delivering a script to you by mid-July, I don't see anything against it at all. It looks to me now pretty easy, but I would remind you that you haven't seen it, and when I first showed a draft of the story to Brandt & Brandt they were far

[1] Published in *The New Yorker*, autumn 1952; published in book form in *Bite on the Bullet*, by S. J. Perelman (U.S. title *The Road to Miltown*).
[2] *Playback.*

from enthusiastic about it. Of course I have rather drastically rewritten the thing, but I'm still the same guy; if I can do it wrong once, I can do it wrong again. Proceed therefore with caution.

As to the title, I don't see how you can agree that *Summer in Idle Valley* is not an ideal title when you don't know what the book is about. If you mean that it doesn't suggest a murder mystery, I don't think my other titles did very much either.

My original title for *Summer in Idle Valley* was *The Long Good-Bye*, which is perfectly apt, but I was a little put off by the idea that there were numerous titles with the same sort of cadence and the word 'long' in them.

June 26, 1953
To: Hamish Hamilton

. . . That was one of the most charming and encouraging letters I have ever received . . . To say that I don't welcome compliments—come off it, Jamie. Everyone loves them, the more fulsome the better. . . . Pittsburgh Phil:[1] either you have heard of this character or you haven't. He was the kingpin killer of the Brooklyn murder mob. His real name was Harry Strauss and he was a bit of a dandy. He loved his work. I mean he actually enjoyed killing people on contract, usually by strangulation and then forty or fifty with the ice pick to make sure. His method of strangulation was very artistic in that he liked to truss the victim up in such a way that he strangled himself trying to get loose. He was electrocuted with a sneer on his face . . .

Aug. 3, 1953
To: H. N. Swanson

. . . I had a story in the *Post*[2] once, and the history of it was rather amusing and illuminating. It was a story called *I'll Be Waiting* and Sanders[3] showed it to the then editor, who liked

[1] Referred to in *The Long Good-Bye.*
[2] *The Saturday Evening Post.*
[3] Chandler's literary agent at the time.

it with reservations . . . They wanted certain changes made—
they wanted certain things more soft or romantic or whatever
it was—so I sat down to try to work out these changes and finally
did do them. And then they published the story exactly as it had
originally been written.

March 23, 1955
To: Hardwick Moseley

. . . I leave for England April 12th and have a return leaving
Southampton Sept. 23rd if I live that long; I also have half a book
written and hope to finish it over there.[1] The scene is La Jolla
and a local columnist has already spilled the beans (why beans?)
on that and the citizenry are about equally divided between
dragging me behind a chariot and the more commonplace
method of shooting me with an arbalest. Unfortunately for them
the local police force is very much on my side.

Apr. 19, 1956
To: Hamish Hamilton

. . . I have a very difficult time in retaining a set of my books.
You should know that an author must re-read his books about
every six months to avoid the danger of writing one over again.

June 19, 1956
To: Helga Greene

. . . I love fantastic stories and have sketches of perhaps a
dozen that I should love to see in print . . . one about a man who
got into fairyland but they wouldn't let him stay. Another about
a princess who traded her tongue for a ruby and then was sorry
and it had to be retrieved. One about a young society novelist
whose father was a magician and kept making a duke disappear
so his son could make love to the duchess.

[1] *Playback.*

Jan. 31, 1957

To: Helga Greene

... I haven't touched the book yet,[1] but I shall have it finished when I come to England. It's not difficult, it's just that I think I may have outgrown this kind of thing. I did my whack for the mystery story, and many writers, although not all, concede that I did manage to recreate a worn-out medium, and that, but for me, they would hardly be able to exist. The problem is what to write ... Many years ago I wrote a story about an American at an English country cottage. I haven't looked at it for twenty years, but I came on it while looking through boxes in the storeroom here. And strangely, without any conscious intention, I had used a variation of the situation as a part of *The Long Good-Bye*. I guess the only reason I still have it is that Cissy thought it wonderful. I am going to make a few changes, not many, and send it to you for your opinion. It's the sort of writing that I could never have got anywhere with in the beginning, but once one has a reputation one may be permitted to step out of character occasionally.

Apr. 30, 1957

To: Helga Greene

... Have finished the story[2] and am sending it to you herewith. It is about 8500 words long, not the best length commercially. It may not be commercial at all, but I enjoyed writing it and re-writing it very much. It's a rather exquisite bit of writing, possibly a little too exquisite, but, hell, can't a man spread himself once in a while? ... If anything seems wrong to you, not only from the point of view of writing and story, but from the point of view of English usages or anything else, I hope you will tell me.

... The difficulty about making a play from it, if you think it has any chance that way, is that the two women never meet. Also, would the Lord Chamberlain stand for the end of the scene between Faringdon and Lady Lakenham? I hope I'm safe on this name. I couldn't find any such title in Whitaker ...

[1] *Playback.*

[2] *English Summer.* This story has never been published. Chandler never actually attempted to turn it into a play.

Plays, I think, need tight construction and clear, not too complicated, line. But I am, by nature, a rather discursive writer who falls in love with a scene or a character or a background or an atmosphere. Once I wrote a description as an attempt to find out whether purely through the tone of the description I could render a state of mind. I may fail dismally at playwriting, but I'd certainly like to try. The one thing I can write is dialogue, but for the stage that is not enough, is it?

May 25, 1957
To: Helga Greene

... I now think *English Summer would* make a play, but only the basis ... I think after a while I shall attempt a rough draft of a play with the idea in mind that here is an American who thinks he is in love with a very refined English lady who has about as much sex as a capon, but he doesn't know that and he hasn't really planned to seduce her. Her husband, a good-natured but hopeless drunk, invites him to stay in the country. He (the hero) realizes almost at once that she is just a decoration. He runs into a woman of an entirely different type who throws herself into his arms because she needs a man but is hardly low enough to accept any man she doesn't like. After this the 'hero' finds that the apparent icicle has killed her husband, quietly and very competently (and her reasons will always be a little obscure) and makes sure that the American knows it, and is sure that he will protect her from the consequences because she knows he is that sort of man. She is probably not in love with him and is probably incapable of love, but all the same she thinks and hopes in her own mind that there is such a thing and that it might come to her from the right man. The American can do nothing but sacrifice himself, if necessary, to save her ... He feels lost in a society he doesn't quite understand, and among people he will never understand, but he nevertheless can't just walk out. He has to do something. He has, according to his code and mine, incurred an obligation, and we Americans are a sentimental and romantic sort of people, often wrong of course, but when we have that feeling we are willing to destroy ourselves rather than let someone down. To me this is a theme for a play ... the essence of drama is there . . . I'll probably try to write the play anyhow because a writer who feels he has a theme will have a go at it, even if it ends in the waste-paper basket . . .

I haven't finished the Marlowe book[1] in the sense that it is not ready to be copied, but it will be in two or three weeks or less. The middle part of it is a bit confused as though I were not sure at the time which plot line I might follow. Also, I have re-written the ending. It was good, but it was just a little soft. I wanted to inject a little toughness into it. I didn't want Marlowe crying all over the place because someone was in love with him. It's just a question of rewriting a few scenes, ejecting a certain amount of overwritten stuff and so on.

May 19, 1958
To: Marcel Duhamel[2]

If you leave out Chapter XII,[3] you leave me with an unre-solved character who has been played up too much to be dropped unceremoniously. You also leave me without an adequate plant for the last chapter: the telephone call from Paris. As to the $5000 which Marlowe refused from the hotel, knowing it was an indirect bribe from Brandon, a man who had committed two criminal acts—namely disposing of a body and hiring a gunman to frighten Goble away—if Marlowe had taken that money he would have been an accessory after the fact. In any case, even if Marlowe is at times hard boiled, he is always extremely scrupulous.

Oct. 1, 1958
To: Helga Greene

. . . My short story[4] is about a man who tried to get out of the Syndicate organization, but he knew too much, and he got a tip that a couple of pros were being sent to wipe him out. He has no one to turn to for help, so he goes to Marlowe. The problem

---

[1] *Playback.*
[2] Editor of the 'Série Noire' published by Gallimard.
[3] *Playback.*
[4] *The Pencil.*

is what can Marlowe do without getting in front of the guns himself. I have some ideas and I think the story would be fun to
write. Needless to say, if the killers fail, others will take care of
them. You don't fail the Syndicate and go on living. The disci-
pline is strict and severe, and mistakes are simply not tolerated.
The only Syndicate boss who was ever convicted of murder was
Lepke Buchhalter, at one time head of Murder Inc. in Brooklyn
and head of a 'protection' racket in New York. These boys all
have good business fronts and very clever although crooked
lawyers. Stop the lawyers and you stop the Syndicate . . .

Oct. 4, 1958
To: Wilbur J. Smith, University of California, Los Angeles[1]
    The only difference I can think of between the English and
American editions[2] is a name. It was one of those curious things;
they have happened to me twice; you make up a name and find
it really exists. I have an unpleasant elderly man I called Lee
Kinsolving. It turned out there was a Bishop of Boston with this
name, so in the American edition it was changed to Cumberland.
In the English edition the publisher did not think it necessary to
change it . . .

Oct. 11, 1958
To: Helga Greene
    . . . I get up around five o'clock, have tea, work until eight-
thirty or so, and then go back to the typewriter. The story[3] is
drudging ahead but I'll probably have to rewrite it and sharpen it
up. The basic idea is too damned serious to be witty about. That
has a tendency to cramp me. Yet it is rather a good idea and has
never been done to my knowledge: one man trying to save
another from a couple of professional killers, and a man who is
only barely worth saving at that. The thing could not run less

----

[1] There is a Raymond Chandler section in the Special Collections Department of the University of California Los Angeles.
[2] *Playback.*
[3] *The Pencil.*

than 10,000 words, but this is a good length for some magazines, which put out what they call one-shot 'book-length' stories.

Oct. 30, 1958
To: Hardwick Moseley
  ... Thank you for your suggestion that if I do a book every fourteen months or so I might be able to endow a Negro college, but as a matter of fact I should prefer to spend the money taking lovely ladies to dinner. I have begun a new novel laid in Palm Springs.[1] I can't yet tell whether it is going to be any good.
  If you do get out to California this winter I shall be happy to come and see you wherever it is most convenient for you, although naturally I would like it much better if you could find a way to come and stay with me. I think you are the most completely lovable man I know, and on this grace-note I end.

Draft letter found in Chandler's files, obviously referring to a tax refund claim.

  ... The novel *The Lady in the Lake* was based on two novelettes called *Bay City Blues*, published in June 1938, and *The Lady in the Lake*, published January 1939. *The Big Sleep* was written in the spring of 1938 and was based on two novelettes called *Killer in the Rain*, published January 1935, and *The Curtain*, published September 1936. Included in this book also was a fairly long sequence taken from a novelette called *The Man Who Liked Dogs*, published March 1936. *Farewell, My Lovely* was based on two novelettes called *Try the Girl*, published January 1937, and *Mandarin's Jade*, published November 1937.
  In the early part of 1939, that is to say up to April 12, I seem except for fumbling around with plots to have been writing novelettes and short stories. There is evidence of about four of them, being written or partly written in that time. On April 12 I have an entry—'Page 10—*The Girl from Brunette's*' with a question mark after it. This is evidently *Farewell, My Lovely*, because

[1] *The Poodle Springs Story*, Chandler's provisional title for the novel on which he was working when he died.

almost immediately the title was changed to *The Girl from Florian's* on April 18, when I'd reached page 52. Florian's is the Negro dive on Central Avenue involved in the beginning of the book. There is on March 31 an entry called 'Page 14—*Law is Where You Buy It*'. That apparently died right there and frankly I'm not sure what it refers to, since later in the year in the diary there is some evidence that I switched the titles around and applied this particular title to more than one book, although the idea of the title evidently derives from the story *Bay City Blues*. That is a story which happens in a town so corrupt from the law enforcement point of view that the law is where you buy it and what you pay for it.

To resume, on April 23 I am at page 100 with the notation 'First lap—*The Girl from Florian's*'. On April 29 I am at page 127 and there is a reference to a girl named Anne Riordan who appears as a character in *Farewell, My Lovely*. This sort of thing goes on intermittently to May 22, when I'm at page 233, with a notation, 'This story is a flop. It smells to high heaven. Think I'll have to scrap it and try something new.' After that for several days I seem to have been toying with a story. I think this eventually developed into the short story called *I'll Be Waiting*. On May 29 there is a notation 'Tomorrow get out draft of *The Girl from Florian's*'. On May 30 I evidently did this because I am checking the draft up to page 87. But that's as far as it goes. I didn't like it. On June 1, 'Page 4—*Murder is a Nuisance*'. This in itself means nothing except there is a mention of a character named Adrian Fromsett who is a character in *The Lady in the Lake* book and nowhere else. Next day, June 2, I'm at page 10 and I'm calling it *The Lady in the Lake*. This apparently died on me, because on June 5 I wrote 18 pages of a novelette called *Goldfish*, but immediately dropped that for the time being. There are many notations that show that I didn't feel well. On June 12 I'm up to page 30; June 13, page 50; June 14, page 68; June 15 page 71; June 16, page 127; June 17, page 148; June 18, page 169; June 19, page 191, and the damned thing is now called *The Golden Anklet*.

Now this ties it clearly to *The Lady in the Lake* because one of the chapter headings of *The Lady in the Lake* novelette (inserted by the magazine editor, I never used chapter headings myself) was 'The Golden Anklet', and a gold anklet does figure in the story. June 20 I am at page 215 and I'm back to calling it *Law is Where You Buy It*, God knows why. June 23 I'm up to page 203, I'm now calling it *Deep and Dark Waters*. That title is self-explanatory. On June 28 I'm up to page 337. On June 29 there is this notation, 'Tragic realization that there is another dead cat under the house. More than three-quarters done and no good.' This certainly refers to the draft of *The Lady in the Lake* by whatever provisional title I might happen to have been calling it at the time. Now I write on half sheets of paper, turned endwise, and they figure out about six to a thousand words. Therefore 337 of these pages would make about 55,000 words of rough script, which is a very substantial hunk even though all done within a month. On July 1, however, having become disgusted with this project, I am back at *The Girl from Florian's*, according to the diary, page 234, and note that page 233 was exactly where I left it on May 22. From there on I proceed more or less steadily to September 15 and page 638 and the notation, 'Finished rough draft of *The Second Murderer*', which was apparently the title at that time. This title ties up with *Farewell, My Lovely*; I could quote from the book in support of it.

But if you think I was satisfied with this draft, you are much mistaken, because I rewrote the entire thing the next year in 1940 and finally finished it, although 1940 was a pretty hard year in which to concentrate in view of what was going on in Europe. I actually finished *Farewell, My Lovely*—I mean really finished it—on April 30, 1940.

From then on until the fall of France and Dunkirk I don't seem to have been able to accomplish anything. On June 5 I am writing at *The Brasher Doubloon*, afterwards published as *The High Window*. This went very slowly. It was not all I did during the rest of the year but it was most of what I worked at. But it was far from finished. We moved about a great deal. This job was finished on February 13, 1942. When you have a lot of plot material lying around and when one particular set-up has a tendency to go stale, you are perhaps too much inclined to drop it and start something else. Also during this period it was necessary for me to do a certain amount of magazine work from time to time. On August 14, 1940, for instance, I am working on a novelette which afterwards was known as *No Crime in the Mountains*, but on August 22 I have dumped this and gone back to *The*

Brasher Doubloon again. The year 1940, partly from reasons of health and still more from the state of the world, seems to have contained an abnormal amount of vacillation. By the end of November I had made less real progress than I sometimes would make in a week. I also puttered with at least three other stories, only one of which was ever finished. The end of the year finds me having written 157 pages of the novelette *No Crime in the Mountains*. I bring all these matters up just to show that I never worked on just one thing at a time for very long. *But* eventually somehow I would finish practically all these projects, no matter how long it took nor how many things I did in the meantime.

I do not during the entire year 1940 find a single specific reference to *The Lady in the Lake* by any title. I seem to have finished *The Brasher Doubloon* about September 9, 1941, because there is a reference to mailing manuscript. For the rest of that year it is difficult for me to tell exactly what I was working on. However on January 2, 1942, and on January 4, 1942, I am well along with *The Lady in the Lake*, page 205 on this last date; so I must have been working on it during the last part of 1941, intermittently at least. On January 3, however, I'm back on *The Brasher Doubloon*, so evidently I did not send the whole manuscript, only a part of it, in the previous year. I am also working on *The Lady in the Lake* up to January 8, as the page number shows page 281 on that date and then the following day, January 9, going back to *The Brasher Doubloon*, and for some unaccountable reason I actually finished it on March 1 and mailed the completed manuscript on March 3. Mostly, but not without interruption, I worked on *The Lady in the Lake* for the rest of that year, but not until April 4, 1943, is there any indication that I finished it.

From the foregoing it is clear that from 1939, specifically the month of June, to April 1943, I had this story in hand and worked on it intermittently, except possibly in 1940. It may be that I did no work on it in 1940. However, I certainly did do work on it in 1939, 1941, 1942, and 1943, and it seems almost certain that during the year 1940 I at least took it out and looked at it and thought about it. On the evidence of these entries and taking into account the method of work—a very bad method one must admit, although in my case it has proved successful—the job of writing the book *The Lady in the Lake* was definitely in hand from 1939 to 1943, that a very substantial amount of writing was done on it as early as 1939 (excluding the novelettes entirely).

The following extracts from letters all refer to The Poodle Springs Story.

Dec. 21, 1957
To: Helga Greene
. . . X has one of these very modern, very interior decorator, very showy houses, and I want to use it in my next Marlowe story which I am going to lay in Palm Springs. I am going to have him marry the eight million dollar girl from *The Long Good-Bye*, because Maurice[1] thinks he ought to be married, and if he marries a woman with a lot of money who wants to live a rather smart expensive life, after the dullness of her doctor husband, the contest between what she wants Marlowe to do and what he will insist on doing will make a good sub-plot. I don't know how it will turn out, but she'll never tame him. Perhaps the marriage won't last, or she might even learn to respect his integrity.

Feb. 10, 1958
To: Maurice Guinness
Your letter charmed me completely . . . Finally, I finished a book,[2] and mostly due to you I left Marlowe in a situation where he could be married. I hope I picked the right woman. It seems to me, from my point of view as a writer, that there would be nothing in his marrying just a nice girl. But if he married a woman whose ideas about how to live were completely antagonistic to his, even though in, shall we say, the boudoir, they met on very equal and satisfactory terms, there would be a struggle of personalities and ideas of life.

I plan my next Marlowe story with a background of Palm

[1] Maurice Guinness, author of crime fiction.
[2] *Playback*.

Springs. 'Poodle Springs', I call it, because every third elegant creature you see has at least one poodle. I have the very house in which Linda Loring might care to live.

Oct. 14, 1958
To: Roger Machell

... My next book is to be laid in Palm Springs with Marlowe having a rather tough time getting along with his wife's ideas of how to live. He loves her and they are beautifully matched in bed, but there is trouble looming. She won't like it that he insists on sticking to his own business and modest way of life, and she fills an overdecorated and rather chi-chi house with freeloaders, even if the damn house (of which I have a detailed description) is only rented for the winter season. I don't know whether the marriage will last or whether he will walk out on it or get bounded. Of course I have to have a murder and some violence and some trouble with the cops. Marlowe wouldn't be Marlowe, if he could really get along with policemen.

There is a lot to be worked out as I go along. I want a good opening first. Since I am on an alcohol-free diet, due to the hepatitis, my mind seems to lack a little or a lot of its exuberance. Very few writers can write on alcohol but I am one of the exceptions. I don't miss alcohol physically at all, but I do miss it mentally and spiritually.

Oct. 24, 1958
To: Helga Greene

... I have begun on *The Poodle Springs Story* and managed the rather difficult job of getting a fairly full description of the dreadful house (not dreadful in all ways but very overdone) in with some sly conversation.

Feb. 21, 1959
To: Maurice Guinness

I think I may have misunderstood your desire that Marlowe

should get married. I think I may have picked the wrong girl. But as a matter of fact, a fellow of Marlowe's type shouldn't get married, because he is a lonely man, a poor man, a dangerous man, and yet a sympathetic man, and somehow none of this goes with marriage. I think he will always have a fairly shabby office, a lonely house, a number of affairs, but no permanent connection. I think he will always be awakened at some inconvenient hour by some inconvenient person to do some inconvenient job. It seems to me that that is his destiny—possibly not the best destiny in the world, but it belongs to him. No one will ever beat him, because by his nature he is unbeatable. No one will ever make him rich, because he is destined to be poor. But somehow, I think he would not have it otherwise, and therefore I feel that your idea that he should be married, even to a very nice girl, is quite out of character. I see him always in a lonely street, in lonely rooms, puzzled but never quite defeated . . .

P.S. I am writing him married to a rich woman and swamped by money, but I don't think it will last.

THE POODLE SPRINGS STORY

The Poodle Springs Story

1

Linda stopped the Fleetwood convertible in front of the house without turning into the driveway. She leaned back and looked at the house and then looked at me.

'It's a new section of the Springs, darling. I rented the house for the season. It's a bit on the chi-chi side, but so is Poodle Springs.'

'The pool is too small,' I said. 'And no springboard.'

'I've permission from the owner to put one in. I hope you will like the house, darling. There are only two bedrooms, but the master bedroom has a Hollywood bed that looks as big as a tennis court.'

'That's nice. If we don't get on together, we can be distant.'

'The bathroom is out of this world—out of any world. The adjoining dressing room has ankle deep pink carpeting, wall to wall. It has every kind of cosmetic you ever heard of on three plate glass shelves. The toilet—if you'll excuse my being earthy —is all alone in an annex with a door and the toilet cover has a large rose on it in *relief*. And every room in the house looks out on a patio or the pool.'

'I can hardly wait to take three or four baths. And then go to bed.'

'It's only eleven o'clock in the morning,' she said demurely.

'I'll wait until eleven-thirty.'

'Darling, at Acapulco——'

'Acapulco was fine. But we only had the cosmetics you brought with you and the bed was just a bed, not a pasture, and other people were allowed to dunk in the swimming pool and the bathroom didn't have any carpet at all.'

'Darling, you *can* be a bastard. Let's go in. I'm paying twelve hundred dollars a month for this dive. I want you to like it.'

'I'll love it. Twelve hundred a month is more than I make being a detective. It'll be the first time I've been kept. Can I wear a sarong and paint my little toenails?'

'Damn you, Marlowe, it's not my fault that I'm rich. And if I have the damn money I'm going to spend it. And if you are around some of it is bound to rub off on you. You'll just have to put up with that.'

'Yes, darling.' I kissed her. 'I'll get a pet monkey and after awhile you won't be able to tell us apart.'

'You can't have a monkey in Poodle Springs. You have to have a poodle. I have a beauty coming. Black as coal and very talented. He's had piano lessons. Perhaps he can play the Hammond organ in the house.'

'We got a Hammond organ? Now that's something I've always dreamed of doing without.'

'Shut up! I'm beginning to think I should have married the Comte de Vaugirard. He was rather sweet, except that he used perfume.'

'Can I take the poodle to work? I could have a small electric organ, one of the babies you can play if you have an ear like a corn-beef sandwich. The poodle could play it while the clients lie to me. What's the poodle's name?'

'Inky.'

'A big brain worked on that one.'

'Don't be nasty or I won't—you know.'

'Oh, yes you will. You can hardly wait.'

She backed the Fleetwood and turned it into the driveway. 'Never mind the garage door. Augustino will put the car away, but you don't really have to in this dry desert climate.'

'Oh yeah, the house boy, butler, cook and comforter of sad hearts. Nice kid. I like him. But there's something wrong here. We can't get along on just one Fleetwood. I have to have one to drive to the office.'

'God damn you! I'll get my white whip out if you're not polite. It has steel inserts in the lash.'

'The typical American wife,' I said and went around the car to help her out. She fell into my arms. She smelled divine. I kissed her again. A man turning off a sprinkler in front of the next house grinned and waved.

'That's Mister Tomlinson,' she said between my teeth. 'He's a broker.'

'Broker, stoker, what do I care?' I went on kissing her.

We had been married just three weeks and four days.

2

It was a very handsome house except that it stank decorator. The front wall was plate glass with butterflies imprisoned in it. Linda said it came from Japan. The floor of the hall was carpeted with blue vinol with a geometric design in gold. There was a den off of this. It contained plenty of furniture, also four enormous brass candle holders and the finest inlaid desk I had ever seen. Off the den was a guest bath, which Linda called a lavatory. A year and a half in Europe had taught her to speak English. The guest bath had a shower and a dressing table and a four by three mirror over it. The hi-fi system had speakers in every room. Augustino had turned it on softly. He appeared in the door, smiling and bowing. He was a nice looking lad, part Hawaiian and part Japanese. Linda had picked him up when we made a short trip to Maui before going to Acapulco. It's wonderful what you can pick up if you have eight or ten million dollars.

There was an interior patio with a large palm tree and some tropical shrubs, and a number of rough stones picked up on the high desert for nothing, but $250 apiece to the customer. The bathroom which Linda had not overstated had a door to the patio and this had a door to the pool and to the interior patio and the outside patio. The living room carpet was pale grey, and the Hammond organ had been built out into a bar at the end opposite the keyboard. That nearly threw me. Also in the living room were couches matching the carpet and contrasting easy chairs and an enormous cowled indoor fireplace six feet away from the wall. There was a Chinese chest that looked very genuine and on the wall three embossed Chinese dragons. One wall was entirely of glass, the others of brick in colors to go with the carpet up to about five feet, and glass above that.

The bathroom had a sunken bath, and sliding door closets big enough to hold all the clothes twelve debutantes could want to buy.

Four people could have slept comfortably in the Hollywood bed in the main bedroom. It had a pale blue carpet and you could read yourself to sleep by the light of lamps mounted on Japanese statuettes.

We went on to the guest room. It had matching single, not twin, beds, an adjoining bath with the same enormous mirror over the dressing table, and the same four or five hundred dollars worth of cosmetic and perfumes and God knows what on the three plate-glass shelves.

That left the kitchen. It had a bar at its entrance, a wall closet with twenty kinds of cocktail, highball and wine glasses, beyond that a top burner stove without an oven or broiler, two electric ovens and an electric broiler against another wall, also an enormous refrigerator and a deep freeze. The breakfast table had a pebbled glass top and wide comfortable chairs on three sides and a built in couch on the fourth side. I turned on the cowl ventilator. It had a wide slow sweep that was almost silent.

'It's too rich for me,' I said. 'Let's get divorced.'

'You dog! It's nothing to what we'll have when we build a house. There are things here that are a bit too gaudy but you can't say the house is bare.'

'Where is the poodle going to sleep, in the guest bed or with us? And what color pajamas does he like?'

'Stop it!'

'I'm going to have to dust my office after this. I'd feel inferior if I didn't.'

'You're not going to have any office, stupid. What do you suppose I married you for?'

'Come into the bedroom again.'

'Blast you, we have to unpack.'

'I bet Tino is doing it right now. There's a boy who looks as if he could take hold. I must ask him if he minds my calling him Tino.'

'Maybe he can unpack. But he won't know where I want my things. I'm fussy.'

'Let's have a fight about the closets, who gets which. Then we could wrestle a bit, and then——'

'We could have a shower and a swim and an early lunch. I'm starving.'

'You have an early lunch. I'll go downtown and look for an office. There must be some business in Poodle Springs. There's a lot of money here and I might grab off an occasional nickel.'

'I hate you. I don't know why I married you. But you were so insistent.'

I grabbed her and held her close. I browsed on her eyebrows and her lashes, which were long and tickly. I passed on to her nose and cheeks, and then her mouth. At first it was just a mouth, then it was a darting tongue, then it was a long sigh, and two people as close as two people can get.

'I settled a million dollars on you to do with as you like,' she whispered.

'A nice kind gesture. But you know I wouldn't touch it.'

'What are we to do, Phil?'

'We have to ride it out. It's not always going to be easy. But I am not going to be Mr Loring.'

'I'll never change you, will I?'

'Do you really want to make a purring pussycat out of me?'

'No. I didn't marry you because I had a lot of money. And you had hardly any. I married you because I love you and one of the things I love you for is that you don't give a damn for anybody —sometimes not even for me. I don't want to make you cheap, darling. I just want to try to make you happy.'

'I want to make *you* happy. But I don't know how. I'm not holding enough cards. I'm a poor man married to a rich wife. I don't know how to behave. I'm only sure of one thing—shabby office or not, that's where I became what I am. That's where I will be what I will be.'

There was a slight murmur and Augustino appeared in the open doorway bowing, with a deprecating smile on his elegant puss.

'At what time would Madame prefer luncheon?'

'May I call you Tino,' I asked him. 'Only because it's easier.'

'But certainly, sir.'

'Thank you. And Mrs Marlowe is not madame. She is Mrs Marlowe.'

'I am very sorry, sir.'

'Nothing to be sorry about. Some ladies like it. But my wife bears my name. She would like her lunch. I have to go out on business.'

'Very good, sir. I'll prepare Mrs Marlowe's lunch at once.'

'Tino, there is one other thing. Mrs Marlowe and I are in love. That shows itself in various ways. None of the ways are to be noticed by you.'

'I know my position, sir.'

'Your position is that you are helping us to live comfortably. We are grateful to you for that. Maybe more grateful than you know. Technically you are a servant. Actually you are a friend. There seems to be a protocol about these things. I have to respect protocol just as you do. But underneath we are just a couple of guys.'

He smiled radiantly. 'I think I shall be very happy here, Mr Marlowe.'

You couldn't say how or when he disappeared. He just wasn't there. Linda rolled over on her back and lifted her toes and stared at them.

'What do I say now! I wish the hell I knew. Do you like my toes?'

'They are the most adorable set of toes I have ever seen. And there seems to be a full set of them.'

'Get away from me, you horror. My toes *are* adorable.'

'May I borrow the Fleetwood for a little while? Tomorrow I'll fly to L.A. and pick up my Olds.'

'Darling, does it have to be this way? It seems so unnecessary.'

'For me there isn't any other way,' I said.

3

The Fleetwood purred me down to the office of a man named Thorson whose window said he was a realtor and practically everything else except a rabbit fancier.

He was a pleasant-looking baldheaded man who didn't seem to have a care in the world except to keep his pipe lit.

'Offices are hard to find, Mr Marlowe. If you want one on Canyon Drive, as I assume you do, it will cost you.'

'I don't want one on Canyon Drive. I want one on some side street or on Sioux Avenue. I couldn't afford one on the main stem.'

I gave him my card and let him look at the photostat of my license.

'I don't know,' he said doubtfully. 'The police department may not be too happy. This is a resort town and the visitors have to be kept happy. If you handle divorce business, people are not going to like you too well.'

'I don't handle divorce business and people very seldom like me at all. As for the cops, I'll explain myself to them, and if they want to run me out of town, my wife won't like it. She has just rented a pretty fancy place in the section out near Romanoff's new place.'

He didn't fall out of his chair but he damn well had to steady himself. 'You mean Harlan Potter's daughter? I heard she had married some—well the hell with it, what do I mean? You're the man, I take it. I'm sure we can fix you up, Mr Marlowe. But why do you want it on a side street or on Sioux Avenue? Why not right in the best section?'

'I'm paying with my own money. I don't have a hell of a lot.'

'But your wife——'

'Listen good, Thorson. The most I make is a couple of thousand a month—gross. Some months nothing at all. I can't afford a showy layout.'

He lit his pipe for about the ninth time. Why the hell do they smoke them if they don't know how?

'Would your wife like that?'

'What my wife likes or dislikes doesn't enter into our business, Thorson. Have you got anything or haven't you? Don't con me. I've been worked on by the orchids of the trade. I can be had, but not by your line.'

'Well——'

A brisk looking young man pushed the door open and came in smiling. 'I represent the *Poodle Springs Gazette*, Mr Marlowe. I understand——'

'If you did, you wouldn't be here.' I stood up. 'Sorry, Mr Thorson, you have too many buttons under your desk. I'll look elsewhere.'

I pushed the reporter out of the way and goofed my way out of the open door. If anybody ever closes a door in Poodle Springs, it's a nervous reaction. On the way out I bumped into a big florid man who had four inches and thirty pounds on me.

'I'm Manny Lipshultz,' he said. 'You're Philip Marlowe. Let's talk.'

'I got here about two hours ago,' I said. 'I'm looking for an office. I don't know anybody named Lipshultz. Would you please let me by?'

'I got something for you maybe. Things get known in this burg. Harlan Potter's son-in-law, huh? That rings a lot of bells.'

'Blow.'

'Don't be like that. I'm in trouble. I need a good man.'

'When I get an office, Mr Lipshultz, come and see me. Right now I have deep affairs on my mind.'

'I may not be alive that long,' he said quietly. 'Ever hear of the Agony Club? I own it.'

I looked back into the office of Señor Thorson. The newshawk and he both had their ears out a foot.

'Not here,' I said. 'Call me after I talk to the law.' I gave him the number.

He gave me a tired smile and moved out of the way. I went back to the Fleetwood and tooled it gracefully to the cop house down the line a little way. I parked in an official slot and went in. A very pretty blonde in a policewoman's uniform was at the desk.

'Damn all,' I said. 'I thought policewomen were hard-faced. You're a doll.'

'We have all kinds,' she said sedately. 'You're Philip Marlowe, aren't you? I've seen your photo in the L.A. papers. What can we do for you, Mr Marlowe?'

'I'm checking in. Do I talk to you or to the duty sergeant? And which street could I walk down without being called by name?'

She smiled. Her teeth were even and as white as the snow on top of the mountain behind the Springs. I bet she used one of the nineteen kinds of toothpaste that are better and newer and larger than all the others.

'You'd better talk to Sergeant Whitestone.' She opened a swing gate and nodded me towards a closed door. I knocked and opened it and I was looking at a calm-looking man with red hair and the sort of eyes that every police sergeant gets in time. Eyes that have seen too much nastiness and heard too many liars.

'My name's Marlowe. I'm a private eye. I'm going to open up an office here if I can find one and if you let me.' I dumped another card on the desk and opened my wallet to let him look at my license.

'Divorce?'

'Never touch it, Sergeant.'

'Good. That helps. I can't say I'm enthusiastic, but we could get along, if you leave police business to the police.'

'I'd like to, but I've never been able to find out just where to stop.'

He scowled. Then he snapped his fingers. He yelled, 'Norman!'

The pretty blonde opened the door. 'Who is this character?' the sergeant wailed. 'Don't tell me. Let me guess.'

'I'm afraid so, Sergeant,' she said demurely.

'Hell! It's bad enough to have a private eye mousing around. But a private eye who's backed by a couple or three hundred million bucks—that's inhuman.'

'I'm not backed by any two hundred million, Sergeant. I'm on my own and I'm a relatively poor man.'

'Yeah? You and me both, but I forgot to marry the boss's daughter. Us cops are stupid.'

I sat down and lit a cigarette. The blonde went out and closed the door.

'It's no use, is it?' I said. 'I can't convince you that I'm just another guy trying to scratch a living. Do you know somebody named Lipshultz who owns a club?'

'Too well. His place is out in the desert, outside our jurisdiction. Every so often the Riverside D.A. has him raided. They say he permits gambling at his joint. I wouldn't know.'

He passed his horny hand over his face and made it look like the face of a man who wouldn't know.

'He braced me in front of the office of a real estate man named Thorson. Said he was in trouble.'

The sergeant stared at me expressionlessly. 'Being in trouble belongs with being a man named Lipshultz. Stay away from him. Some of that trouble might rub off on you.'

I stood up. 'Thanks, Sergeant. I just wanted to check with you.'

'You checked in. I'm looking forward to the day you check out.'

I went out and closed the door. The pretty policewoman gave me a nice smile. I stopped at the desk and stared at her for a moment without speaking.

'I guess no cop ever liked a private eye,' I said.

'You look all right to me, Mr Marlowe.'

'You look more than all right to me. My wife likes me part of the time too."

She leaned her elbows on the desk and clasped her hands under her chin. 'What does she do the rest of the time?'

'She wishes I had ten million dollars. Then we could afford a couple more Fleetwood Cadillacs.'

I grinned at her fascinatingly and went out of the cop house and climbed into our lonely Fleetwood. I struck out for the mansion.

4

At the end of the main drag the road swings to the left. To get to our place you keep straight on with nothing on the left but a hill and an occasional street on the right. A couple of tourist cars passed me going to see the palms in the State Park—as if they couldn't see all the palms they needed in Poodle Springs itself. A big Buick Roadmaster was behind me taking it easy. At a stretch of road that seemed empty it suddenly put on speed, flashed past and turned in ahead of me. I wondered what I had done wrong. Two men jumped out of the car, both were very sportsclothesy, and trotted back to where I had braked to a stop. A couple of guns flashed into their busy hands. I moved my hand on the indicator enough to shift the pointer to Low. I reached for the glove compartment, but there wasn't time. They were beside the Fleetwood.

'Lippy wants to talk to you,' a nasal voice snarled.

He looked like any cheap punk. I didn't bother taking an inventory of him. The other one was taller, thinner but no more delicious. But they held the guns in a casually competent manner.

'And who might Lippy be? And put the heaters away. I don't have one.'

'After he spoke to you, you went to the cops. Lippy don't like that.'

'Let me guess,' I said brightly. 'Lippy would be Mr Lipshultz who runs or owns the Agony Club, which is out of the territory of the Poodle Springs cops and the Agony Club is engaged in extralegal operations. Why does he want to see me so badly that he has to send a couple of shnooks after me?'

'On business, big stuff.'

'Naturally, I didn't think we were such close friends that he couldn't eat lunch without me.'

One of the boys, the taller one, moved around behind the Fleetwood and reached for the right hand door. It had to be now if it was going to be at all. I pushed down on the accelerator. A cheap car would have stalled, but not the Fleetwood. It shot forward and sent the taller hood reeling. It smashed hard into the rear end of the Roadmaster. I couldn't see what it did to the Fleetwood. There might be a small scratch or two on the front bumper. In the middle of the crash I yanked the glove compartment open and grabbed the .38 I had carried in Mexico, not that I had ever needed it. But when you are with Linda you don't take chances.

The smaller hood had started running. The other was still on his sitter. I hopped out of the Fleetwood and fired a shot over his head.

The other hood stopped dead, six feet away.

'Look, darlings,' I said, 'if Lippy wants to talk to me, he can't do it with me full of lead. And never show a gun unless you are prepared to use it. I am. You're not.'

The tall boy climbed to his feet and put his gun away sullenly. After an instant the other did the same. They went to look at their car. I backed the Fleetwood clear and swung it level with the Roadmaster.

'I'll go see Lippy,' I said. 'He needs some advice about his staff.'

'You got a pretty wife,' the little hood said nastily.

'And any punk that lays a hand on her is already half cremated. So long, putrid. See you in the boneyard.'

I gave the Fleetwood the gun and was out of sight. I turned into our street which like all the streets in that section was a dead end between high hills bordering the mountains. I pulled up in front of the house and looked at the front of the Fleetwood. It was bent a little—not much, but too much for a lady like Linda to drive it. I went into the house and found her in the bedroom staring at dresses.

'You've been loafing,' I said. 'You haven't rearranged the furniture yet.'

'Darling!' She threw herself at me like a medium fast pitch, high and inside. 'What have you been doing?'

'I bumped your car into the back of another one. You'd better telephone for a couple more Fleetwoods.'

'What on earth happened? You're not a sloppy driver.'

'I did it on purpose. A man named Lipshultz who runs the

Agony Club braced me às I came out of a realtor's office. Hé wanted to talk business, but I didn't have the time then. So on my way home he had à couple of morons with guns try to persuade me to do it now. I bashed them.'

'Of course you did, darling. Quite right, too. What is a realtor?'

'A real estate man with a carnation. You didn't ask me how badly damaged your car is.'

'Stop calling it my car. It's our car. And I don't suppose it's damaged enough to notice. Anyhow we need a sedan for evenings. Have you had lunch?'

'You take it awfully goddamned calmly that I might have been shot.'

'Well, I was really thinking about something else. I'm afraid Father will pop in soon and start buying up the town. You know how he is about publicity.'

'How right he is! I've been called by name by half a dozen people already—including an exquisitely pretty blonde policewoman.'

'She probably knows judo,' Linda said casually.

'Look, I don't get my women by violence.'

'Well, perhaps. But I seem to remember being forced into somebody's bedroom.'

'Force, my foot. You could hardly wait.'

'Ask Tino to give you some lunch. Any more of this conversation and I'll forget I'm arranging my dresses.'

Bibliography

By Chandler:

The Big Sleep. New York: Knopf, 1939; London: Hamish Hamilton, 1939.

Farewell, My Lovely. New York: Knopf, 1940; London: Hamish Hamilton, 1940.

The High Window. New York: Knopf, 1942; London: Hamish Hamilton, 1943.

The Lady in the Lake. New York: Knopf, 1943; London: Hamish Hamilton, 1944.

The Little Sister. London: Hamish Hamilton, 1949; New York: Knopf, 1949.

The Simple Art of Murder. Boston: Houghton Mifflin, 1950; London: Hamish Hamilton, 1950.

The Long Goodbye. London: Hamish Hamilton, 1953; Boston: Houghton Mifflin, 1954.

Playback. London: Hamish Hamilton, 1958; Boston: Houghton Mifflin, 1958.

Killer in the Rain, with an Introduction by Philip Durham. London: Hamish Hamilton, 1964; Boston, Houghton Mifflin, 1964.

Chandler Before Marlowe: Raymond Chandler's Early Prose and Poetry, 1908–1912, ed. by Matthew Bruccoli. Columbia: Univ. of South Carolina Press, 1973.

The Blue Dahlia, Original screenplay by Chandler. Paramount. ed. with an Afterword by Mathew Bruccoli. Carbondale: Southern Illinois Univ. Press, 1976.

Raymond Chandler's Unknown Thriller: The Screenplay of "Playback", ed. James Pepper. Introduction by Robert B. Parker. New York: The Mysterious Press, 1985.

Raymond Chandler, 2 vols., ed. Frank MacShane. Vol. I: *Stories and Early Novels*; Vol. II: *Later Novels and Other Writings.* New York: The Library of America, 1995.

General:

Bruccoli, Matthew J., and Richard Layman, eds. *Hardboiled Mystery Writers: Raymond Chandler, Dashiell Hammett, Ross Macdonald.* (Dictionary of Literary Biography Documentary Series, Vol. 6) Detroit: Gale, 1989. (Biographical documents)

Cawelti, John. *Adventure, Mystery, Romance: Formula Stories as Art and Popular Culture.* Chicago: Univ. of Chicago Press, 1976.

Fine, David, ed. *Los Angeles in Fiction*, Rev. ed. Albuquerque: Univ. of New Mexico Press, 1995.

Geherin, David. *The American Private Eye: The Image in Fiction.* New York, Ungar, 1985.

Hamilton, Cynthia S. *Western and Hard-boiled Detective Fiction in America: From High Noon to Midnight.* Iowa City: University of Iowa Press, 1987.

Knight, Stephen. *Form and Ideology in Crime Fiction.* Bloomington: Indiana Univ. Press, 1981.

Margolies, Edward. *Which Way Did He Go?: The Private Eye in Dashiell Hammett, Raymond Chandler, Chester Himes, and Ross Macdonald.* New York: Holmes and Meier, 1982.

Marling, William. *The American Roman Noir: Hammett, Cain, and Chandler.* Athens: Univ. of Georgia Press, 1995.

Ruehlmann, William. *Saint with a Gun: The Unlawful American Private Eye.* New York: New York Univ. Press, 1974.

Ruhm, Herbert, ed. *The Hard-Boiled Detective: Stories from Black Mask Magazine, 1920–1951.* New York: Vintage, 1977.

Parker, Robert B. *The Violent Hero, Wilderness Heritage and Urban Reality: A Study of the Private Eye in the Novels of Dashiell Hammett, Raymond Chandler and Ross Macdonald.* Dissertation. Boston Univ., 1970.

Porter, Dennis. *The Pursuit of Crime: Art and Ideology in Crime Fiction.* New Haven: Yale Univ. Press, 1981.

Skenazy, Paul. *The New Wild West: The Urban Mysteries of Dashiell Hammett and Raymond Chandler.* Boise: Boise State Univ. Western Writers Series, 1982.

On Chandler:

Chandler, Raymond. *Letters: Raymond Chandler and James M. Fox*, ed. by James Pepper. Santa Barbara: Neville/Yellin, 1978.

Chandler, Raymond. *The Notebooks of Raymond Chandler and English Summer: A Gothic Romance*, illus. by Edward Gorey, ed. by Frank MacShane. New York: Ecco Press, 1976.

Chandler, Raymond. *Selected Letters of Raymond Chandler*, ed. by Frank MacShane. New York: Columbia Univ. Press, 1981.

Gross, Miriam, ed. *The World of Raymond Chandler*. New York: A & W Publishers, 1978.

MacShane, Frank. *The Life of Raymond Chandler*. New York: Dutton, 1976.

Marling, William. *Raymond Chandler*. Boston: Twayne, 1986.

Speir, Jerry. *Raymond Chandler*. New York: Ungar, 1981.

Wolfe, Peter. *Something More Than Night: The Case of Raymond Chandler*. Bowling Green: Popular, 1985.

Index